Copyright 2014 © Lori L. Otto

All rights reserved. Except as permitted under the U.S. Copyright Act 1976, no part of this publication may be reproduced, distributed, or transmitted in any form or by any means, or stored in a database or retrieval system, without the prior written permission of the publisher.

Lori L. Otto Publications

Visit our website at: www.loriotto.com

First Edition: August 2014

The characters and events portrayed in this book are fictitious. Any similarity to real persons, living or dead, is coincidental and not intended by the author.

Printed in the United States of America

to second chances...

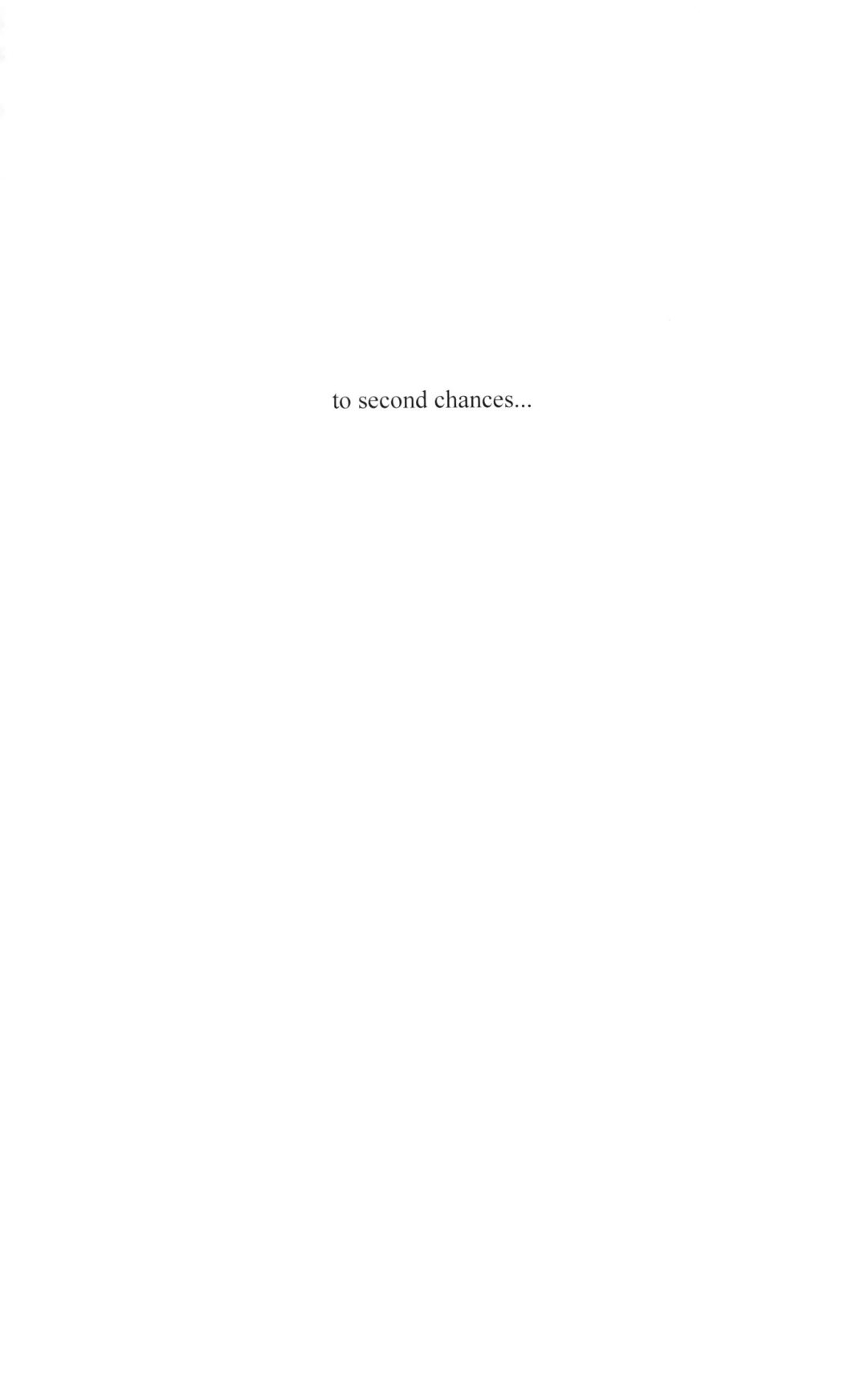

PROLOGUE - LIVVY'S GRADUATION

She needs me. Plain and simple, she needs me. How am I helping her by leaving her? I want her to be independent. I want her to be Livvy again, not half of Olivia and Jon. I can't leave and let her think that I don't want her. I want her more than anything, and if it means I stay to work this out, then that's what I do. My brothers have Mom and Aunt Patty. I'll go visit them for a few weeks, but maybe ten weeks *is* too much to ask of Olivia.

She's been lost for a year, and I've led her without showing her the way. I keep expecting her to find her own way, but clearly she's struggling. There are more options than staying and letting things continue in this unhealthy, codependent way or leaving her–alone–for the summer. I needed to focus on school these past two semesters. I can give her more attention over the summer. I won't lead her this time… I'll guide her to find herself again.

I listen to her voicemail once more as I make my way to the graduation ceremony.

"Jon, it's Olivia. I hope you're here, and I just can't see you. If you are, meet me by the magnolia tree in the west lot across from the auditorium after the ceremony. This is killing me."

I should have come for the whole thing. I shouldn't have wavered. Of course she wants me here, regardless of all the hurtful things that were said last night.

Across the street, I inspect the leaves to identify the tree she wanted to meet me under. A few people in front of me hold cameras, pointing at the space below the limbs. I glance beneath the thick magnolia blossoms, finally seeing Olivia with Finn as she knocks her cap off, then pulls away the bandage from her forehead. As her friend angles her head up, I feel sick in the pit of my stomach. The way he looks at her, and–

He's kissing her?!

Surely she'll pull away. Surely… she'll… I try to turn my attention elsewhere, but I can't. I watch her kiss him back. *This isn't right. This isn't happening.* Finally, she begins to pull away, but just as a sense of relief begins to surface, she holds his lip between her teeth, sucking gently.

This has to be what an earthquake feels like, as the world as I know it crumbles to my feet. My heart falls, obliterated into razor-edged shards that slam down on top of the residual pieces of my life. I can feel the blood draining, leaving me pale and weak. I stumble into a photographer, finally hearing the deafening roar of clicks and flashes. I think it seems loud because I know that all of these strangers are capturing an incredibly intimate moment in my girlfriend's life– and she's not sharing that moment with me.

And this moment will be news to everyone.

Finn?!

…

When I finally breathe, it's a gasp of air, audibly filling my lungs. I have to get out of here. I push through the growing crowd, taking one last glance. My eyes meet hers. She stops dead in her tracks as I move. I run. I run as fast as I can.

"Jon!" I hear her shout. And then, as if to betray me more–as if she could–she yells his name. "Finn!"

How dare she call after him!

"Finn, you have to stop him!"

"I'm trying, Liv!" he yells, his voice much closer than hers. I turn to see him gaining on me.

"Back off, Finn!"

"Or what?" he yells. *Damn, he's fast.*

"Or… I'm honestly not sure what I'll do."

"Let me explain!" His fingers brush against my arm, and I yank away violently. "Would you stop?"

I do. I stop fast and hard, and he rams into me. My feet planted, I barely move, and he falls to the ground away from me. Trying to catch my breath, I start to walk away.

"Jon!" Olivia yells again.

"What?" I have no desire to look at her.

Fingers close around my forearm, and when I realize it's Finn again, I turn quickly and swing. He ducks, missing my fist by only an inch or two. He pushes against my shoulders. He may be fast, but I'm much stronger than he is, and he knows it.

Olivia screams. Behind her, the crowd begins to catch up.

"We have an audience," I tell her. "Again."

"I don't care," she says.

"I do. I don't want any pictorial evidence of what I'd like to do to him." Even after saying this, after realizing the severity of my statement, my anger takes over and I push him back. He grabs a hold of my shirt and we start to wrestle, trying to knock each other off our feet.

"Stop it!"

"Why, Liv?!" I ask angrily. "Who's your dog in this fight, huh? Or don't you even know?" I stand still, firm, holding Finn's shoulders until he stops struggling with me.

"You, Jon," she says meekly. With one more shove, I push him lightly into her and walk away. There's nothing she could say that would make me stay now.

Frederick takes me to the airport after dropping off the last of my things at the storage place. I feel weird leaving my things at the place Jack had rented for his daughter's studio, but I don't have time to make other arrangements now. I always knew accepting help from the Hollands would come back to bite me somehow. Now it's created an incredibly awkward situation, knowing I'll have to see Jack or Emi–or God forbid, Livvy–when I return at the end of the summer to find a new place for all of my family's belongings.

I take a seat after passing through security, thinking of the conversation I'd had with Emi a few nights ago, the night of Livvy's graduation. She *apologized* to me. She asked if I was okay. She was empathetic, and I felt that she was feeling a fair amount of sadness at the strange turn of events. She didn't try to explain Livvy's choice. She didn't pass any messages to me, even though it was obvious Livvy had plenty to say. She's left messages, but I've deleted them all. Was she apologizing, or trying to end things on her terms? Do I really care?

I'm still numb, and for the first time in my life, I truly understand the lure of the alcohol my mother has had such a hard time giving up. Being hurt like this, accepting that the person I wanted to devote my life to doesn't feel the same, all I want to do is forget what happened. All I want to do is forget Livvy Holland.

I can't even begin to imagine what school will be like next year. I'll avoid art classes so I won't have to see her. I don't think I need them anymore. I've honed my craft enough, and I can continue to draw in my spare time. I won't give up my commitments to Nate's Art Room. If she wants to instruct, too, she'll have to find a different time. I won't hold classes with her anymore.

She's lost. Isn't this behavior of hers consistent with that? I've known she's been lost. A few days ago, I was committed to helping her. She's gone too far now, though, and I don't think I can ever forgive her for what she's done. I know I'll never forget it.

I know I'll never forget it–forget *Olivia*–because I have a constant reminder of her forever marked on my skin. I guess a part of me always knew it wouldn't work out between us. That day before Christmas a year and a half ago, I'd considered getting her name tattooed on my back, but at the last minute, I found a way to honor her with less of a personal commitment to her.

No future girlfriends would ever need to know the true significance of the phrase. I'll just tell them I like Shakespeare.

If it be thus to dream, still let me sleep.

But now, about the last thing I want to do is sleep. Despite the anger I feel for her during every waking minute of my days, she's still all I've been able to dream about at night.

In my dreams, she still loves me.

In my heart, I still love her.

DECLARATION

Mail from Manhattan.

I wonder who gave her my address. My mother? My aunt? I bet it was Will.

There's no return address, but there's no question in my mind who it's from. Even though the handwriting is shaky–even though the pen barely leaves an indentation on the white paper–I know Livvy wrote this letter.

I want so much to not care what's contained inside. Excuses? Empty promises? Does it matter? It's over. I want it to be over on my terms, and I'm deathly afraid that contained inside this envelope is a break up on *her* terms. That wouldn't be fair. She can't take that from me. She can't take it from me if I never open it.

Is there anything she could say? I try to envision the perfect letter that would change my mind.

Dear Jon,

I certainly don't want to see that line. I'm in no need of a *Dear John* letter. I don't think I can read this.

Setting it aside, I grab my borrowed design book and begin to thumb through the pages. I just need a distraction, one that keeps my mind engaged elsewhere. I'd looked online for design internships or drafting jobs, but there isn't much to choose from in the Middle of Nowhere, Utah. Does it matter if it's manual labor at this point? No. It's something to occupy my time.

Tomorrow morning, I'll shift gears on my job search and take whatever I can find. I don't even care if it pays well. I just don't want to spend any more time thinking of Livvy or the life that awaits me–or *doesn't*–back in Manhattan.

I glance at the postmark once more.

She's already out of my life by my choosing. I don't think she really needs me to tell her that to know I've broken up with her. I left her without saying goodbye, and surely she knows what she did was wrong–so wrong and so unforgivable.

My fingers are sliding under the lip of the envelope before my brain even realizes it. *Be numb. Detach yourself from this letter. It doesn't have to hold any meaning. Assign it none. She means nothing to me anymore.*

I brace myself for the overused greeting of a break-up letter. I close my eyes in denial, not wanting to see those words.

When I finally raise my lids and lower my head to the page, I see my name first. Seeing it in her penmanship energizes my heart, but it's false. How can I explain to my heart that she is not good for it anymore?

Jon.

But in front of *Jon* isn't *Dear.*

I love you, Jon.

My stomach takes the path my heart just took, startled by the intimacy in her first three words. *Why did they have to be those three words, Liv?*

When I sigh, I smell her. It's not perfume or shampoo. It's paint. A stripe of color at the bottom of the page briefly diverts my attention. The paint is red, and although it's a single stroke, there is so much depth in the color.

Paint. I still associate that smell with her even after she abandoned her hobby for nearly a year. Is she painting regularly already?

Whatever you're thinking right now, the most important thing for you to remember is that I love you. Do you remember the first time you told me that? The way you said it didn't feel certain. You said you <u>thought</u> you were in love with me. I never questioned it, though. I immediately returned a declaration of my love to you.

I was certain. Even though it happened very quickly for us, I knew it was love and I thought it would be forever. What you saw isn't what you think, Jon.

I'm not certain it could be anything else. I know what I saw. It was a kiss. It was betrayal. It was a serrated knife to the jugular.

I read on, wondering what her explanation is.

Go back to that day in the gallery, when you knelt before me and gave me a necklace that revealed your decision to select me to stand beside you. If not for life, at least for that moment. That glorious moment made me feel more special than the day I added Holland to my name. Remember how new everything was? Remember how we hadn't messed anything up yet?

As far as I'm concerned, I never messed *anything* up. That was all her doing.

We aren't finished.

I turn the page over, still wondering where the details of what actually happened between Finn and Livvy are confessed. The back is untouched. Confused, I look again at the letter to see what I've missed. This time, I only skim it, but nowhere is there an explanation. I deserve one, damn it! Why would she send me a letter without telling me what moved her to share such a private moment with her friend?

In the stripe of red paint is an etched message. It looks like she did it with a needle, the word barely pronounced amid the warm color.

Declaration

She didn't even sign her name!

I don't want to see it anyway.

WEAK

I have a newfound respect for men who work in construction. My second day on the site, I've never been more exhausted in my entire life.

After I'd switched gears about finding a job, the search was simple. I showed up for an interview on a construction location in a remote community outside of Provo, and based on my stature alone, they hired me. After the initial meeting, the foreman stuck around and talked to me about plans on the site. He was impressed with my understanding of the structure, and I even felt like I taught him a thing or two about design when he let me see the finished drafts of the home I'd be building over the next few weeks.

It's my dream home. Every element of the house and surrounding land has a purpose. What looks visually clean and simple is based on structural complexities that excite me about the plans in my own life.

I'd once thought about making a home with Livvy. I'd wondered where we would settle, when Manhattan was such an integral piece of both of us. Not being able to reconcile the two, I would always imagine we kept two homes. A place amid the bustling city we love, and another tucked away in a natural seaside environment where I would teach her about constellations at night, and where she could show me the predation habits of fish in the ocean during the day.

Her father had taken her diving when she was younger, and the way she would describe the colors of the fish fascinated me, made me curious to experience the things she had.

"Jon, you have mail." My aunt places the letter on my desk.

Seconds ago, I didn't think my body would move, but at those four words, I'm alert and invigorated. It's from her, I know it is.

Just as quick, I feel lifeless again. I wish I wasn't so excited to hear from her. The anger creeps back in as I walk to pick up the letter.

It looks and feels just like the last one. No return address, but postmarked from 10023. Still anxious to hear her reason that she cheated on me, I open the envelope.

I love you, Jon.

Same greeting. I huff at it, still disbelieving her words. The nostalgic smell titillates my senses again, and I wonder if she means to stir this reaction in me. I wonder if she has any idea that it does.

September 29th.

Recognizing it's June, I question the date. It's not our anniversary. That was a week later.

Our first kiss. It wasn't planned, but it wasn't spontaneous, either. You warned that you wanted to kiss me, and I gave you permission to do it. It was the first time in my life I knew what it was like to desire another person. I didn't know it would be so easy to teach my body the meaning of passion, of lust, but with one kiss, I learned quickly. Your desire transferred through me immediately as your lips touched mine, and I felt like I'd been marked for life. I was yours from then on.

From then on until June 2nd, though, right? Why, Livvy? Tell me about that date!

We were standing on the sidewalk that Thursday night. We weren't alone. People walked past us. I wasn't ashamed of what I was doing because it felt right.

I wonder if it felt right when she kissed Finn. I wonder if she's ashamed of that. *Answer that, Liv!*

Your desire toward me impaired your judgment, working against your need to show my father that you were good for me. Knowing others wouldn't approve, you took my first kiss and you made my heart soar. Dad wouldn't like it, but I didn't care. It felt right.

It felt like a turning point in my life. It was the start of something new and wonderful. That realization—and the fact that your kiss was sensual beyond the imagination of my then-fifteen-year-old mind—made me grasp on to you for support. I needed to be steadied, while I wanted to be putty in your hands. I would have done anything you asked, but you asked for nothing more.

That's not exactly true. You asked me to slow down.

You then walked me home and delivered me safely to my father.

Because I'm a good guy, Liv. I'm that guy your father would have wanted you to be with. I wonder, is he as disappointed in you as I am?

I would do anything for you.

She would do anything but apologize, apparently, or explain her actions! Does she think I'm just going to take her back? Doesn't she know what she's done to me? To us?

We aren't finished.

Etched in grey paint is another mysterious footnote.

Weak

And I *feel* weak. I feel physically weak from back-to-back 10-hour days carting around materials and clearing out the dead and dying brush around the site. I feel emotionally weak for letting myself feel the longing for her.

Of course I remember that first kiss. It was completely spontaneous, but my manners did intercede a little, moving me to tell her my intentions first. The thought hadn't even crossed my mind that I could attempt to kiss her, much less follow through, with all the studying I had done that day. But I needed a release from the building tension, and it was the only appropriate outlet I had. I was stressed about tests. I was nervous about our first official date. More than either of those feelings, though, in that moment, I was in love.

Her beauty gave me the courage to ask and the confidence to accept her first kiss. I didn't take it. She gave it willingly. Her inexperienced lips caught up quickly to mine, giving me the sensation I was desperate for, as well as the assurance that she wanted me just as badly as I wanted her.

I am weak.

IMPRESSIONS

My aunt has such good intentions. Since I arrived to her home in Utah just over a week ago, she's been talking about inviting people over to meet me. It's been important to engage my brothers in social outings and sports activities so they can find some sense of belonging in this place that's two thousand miles away from all they've ever known.

I don't need the stimulation. I'd rather be alone, do my work, read my books, and sleep, but I finally gave in to her gracious gesture. Last night, about eight families from her church came over for a cook out. Each of the families had a child around my age. There were six girls that spanned the ages of 17 to 20. The awkward introductions by my aunt made it blatantly obvious that she was trying to help me get over Livvy.

I smiled and charmed them all. I never let on that I was inwardly screaming to go inside and shut myself into the converted craft room that had become my home for the summer. The guys were friendly. We talked about sports, and I recalled the headlines I'd scanned that morning–and every morning–to keep up with the banter.

Most of the girls wore too much makeup. It was clear to me that they'd been prepped to hang out with me. A few mentioned that my aunt had told them I was "super smart," that I was going to Columbia on a full scholarship, and that I was interested in architecture and art. One of them–more brazen than the rest–made a comment that no one told her I would be so hot. She stated she would have dressed differently, had she known. I couldn't fathom what she would have worn instead. Already her tight shirt and ill-fitting skirt left little to the imagination. It was an instant turn-off.

There was one girl, Susan, who reminded me of my Livvy. *She's not mine anymore.* Still, when I spoke with her, I yearned to talk to Livvy. She was the youngest. She was Livvy's age, but she had the sweet naïveté that Liv had when she was a few years younger, when we started to date. Those were a few of the things that made me fall so hard, and last night, some of those feelings were stirred up again. It had occurred to me I was free to ask her out on a date. I'd be betraying no one. I was trying to find a good segue in our conversation about a movie we had both recently seen.

Then I thought about that movie. It was the movie I had seen with Livvy the night before her graduation. I didn't know the ending because we didn't stick around to see it. Instead, we fought, and that was the beginning of the end of us.

In thinking back on that night, I thought about all the nights we'd had. The sequence was like the fast-rewind function on a home movie. It ended with that day I'd caught up with her after art class, when she was sweet and naïve.

I pictured Susan instead of Livvy. My heart didn't let me even *pretend* that Susan and I could have the happy ending that Livvy and I will never have. I'm not sure I'll ever feel confident in myself enough to trust another girl with my affection.

Instead of asking Susan out, I told her I wasn't feeling well, and I retreated to the silence of my makeshift room, not even telling any of the other guests good night. I didn't get her number, nor would I ask my aunt for it. There was no happily-ever-after in my future. My happily-ever-after kissed another guy. My happily-ever-after obliterated my heart and my ability to love another woman.

"Jon?" Max says through the pine door.

"Yeah, buddy?" I roll over on my side to see him better when he comes in.

"Aunt Patty says dinner will be ready soon."

"Thanks. Did you help cook?"

"Mm-hmm!" he says proudly. "We're having *strawbanoff*. But it doesn't have any fruit in it."

I laugh a little. "Stroganoff."

"I said that! Strawbanoff."

I shake my head at him, wishing he could stay bright-eyed and happy forever.

"Oh, and you got a letter in the mail today." When I don't reach for it, he places it on the pillow in front of my face.

"How long until dinner?" I ask him.

"Ten minutes."

"I'll be there soon."

I love you, Jon.

She might as well start these letters with, "I'm lying, Jon." At least I'd believe her then.

I expect the smell before it hits my nose, so the surprise is significantly lessened. The longing for her is, too.

The rain nearly drowned you on the night you first spent time with my mother and father. I remember you telling me later that you almost lost the nerve to knock on our door that night, but that you didn't want their initial thoughts of you to be that you were a disappointment to me.

In the brief time you spent with my family at dinner, you went from kid-they'd-sponsored-at-Nate's Art Room to respectable-young-man in their eyes. In mine, you went from boy-I'd-kissed to person-I-could-spend-my-life-with.

I set the letter aside for a moment. I thought of her today, wishing she was still that person-I-could-spend-my-life-with. At the construction site, they brought in a large rock. It was about three feet high and five feet wide. From my vantage point, aside from its size, there was nothing spectacular about the stone.

A crane eased it down slowly, carefully, as the owner of the house gave instruction. Just before it touched the ground, I noticed that the earth appeared to be cleared in just that spot.

When the heavy machinery moved away, a woman joined the owner and they held one another while they looked at this rock. They kissed, took a picture of the lawn adornment, and then left in separate cars.

Later in the day, as I returned from a short lunch break, I first saw the words "I will" painted in red carefully toward the bottom. It took me a second to focus on an inscription above that. It was meticulously drilled into the stone in a flowing typeface: *Marry me.*

I felt silly, feeling sad as I stared at the sentiment, but it moved me.

"This is the exact spot Mr. Tyson proposed," the foreman said as he walked past. "They were regular hikers on the land, and they always rested on this spot to take in the view."

I turned around, giving myself a few seconds to look at the mountain that their home would overlook.

"Jon?" Max is back. "Dinner is on the table."

For my brothers' sakes, I love that we now eat together at a table, but I really want nothing more than to bring my plate into my room and eat alone.

"Start without me," I call out to him. "I'm finishing up something." I pick up the letter again and keep reading.

Your face lit up as you talked about your plans to go to Columbia, and then about your ideas of what you wanted to do with your life. Thinking back, it's very inspiring to me. I want to do something that matters, too. I know I've messed up, but I think I can still do good things with my life.

Remember what you said as you left that night? You told me not to worry about you.

Jon, I'm worried. I know I've already said it, but I love you.

And there she goes again with the empty words.

We aren't finished.

This time, I seek out the message in paint. The color is pink.

Impressions

If she keeps telling me she loves me, it will eventually remove all meaning from the words. It's actually a good thing, I think. It'll eventually make it easy to get over her, if I can take the emotions out of her words.

I realize I don't have to take the emotions out of them. She did that on her own. Feeling less broken-hearted all of a sudden, I decide to join my family at the dinner table.

An hour later, I find the signed CD Livvy had bought me at the Grizzly Bear concert last New Year's Eve. I'd avoided listening to our favorite band because there were so many memories attached to it, but I realize if I just start listening to it, over and over again, new memories will begin to mesh with the old ones, and dilute the nostalgia. It's not fair for her to get my favorite band in the break-up. I should be able to hold on to some element of my former life. I'll keep my music.

REVERE

When I get home from work, I check the mailbox on the way in. It's Saturday, and the last letter was on Wednesday. Looking at the pattern of her previous letters, it seems about time to receive another.

She doesn't disappoint tonight.

As soon as I think that, I realize she *will* disappoint me tonight, as soon as I read the first line. After setting the letter on my desk, I decide to take a shower before I open the envelope. My muscles sore, I let the hot water glide down my body as I try to figure out what this letter will say. Is she ever going to apologize? Wondering that makes me more tense, and I wish she was around to massage the pain from my muscles. I remember how she would kiss my right shoulder before she'd begin, every time. There's a pang in my chest at that recollection.

Missing her more than I want to admit, I leave the bathroom with only a towel around my body and go to my room, shutting and locking the door before grabbing the letter and sitting down on the bed.

I shiver as the water continues to drip down my back from my wet hair.

I love you, Jon.

I was once a virgin.

Heat overtakes my body at her statement. It's an odd way to start a letter, but it's a turn on, for sure. I can't keep my mind from drifting to the night when she left that virgin behind. I glance at the door as I try to remember what my aunt told me their plans were. I just wonder when they'll be home. Finding moments of solitude are admittedly difficult here. Being in a nice bed with sheets that don't belong to me makes what I want to do right now more taboo.

I should have taken care of this in the shower. The urge wasn't as bad then. I start the letter again.

I was once a virgin.

The night you found out I was a virgin was also the night I found out you were not. Your admission was a blow to my own confidence, and I was at first afraid you wouldn't want to be with someone who wasn't experienced, like you were.

I was disappointed in you. I felt betrayed—"

"Don't talk to *me* about betrayal!" I yell to myself, crumpling up the letter and throwing it on the carpet across the room. I'm so on edge, I feel like I might lose it tonight. I have to get rid of the tension. I decide to take advantage of my family's absence, even at the risk of them coming home. The door's locked, and I think this will be quick.

My go-to fantasy is my reality, my history. I return to Mykonos, where we washed away all the sins of our past and started our lives over again, together. I felt as pure as she actually was after we showered with each other. That was the first time she'd ever been fully naked in front of me. I'd seen most of her, taken a peek of nearly all of her, in our chaste moments of passion before that night, but altogether, she was her own work of art. The way her eyes widened as she first had a full glimpse of my body became the focal point of that gorgeous living, breathing artwork. Whoever her parents were, they had created perfection. Perfection looked up at me with a shy smile, and I was humbled that she had decided to be with me.

Impatient, I allow my thoughts to skip past the tentative moments, the gentle ones when I tried to put her mind and body at ease. Instead, I think of the seconds after she let go of my hand and moved her fingers to hold my body closer to hers.

As I suspected, it doesn't take long to alleviate the tension. What I don't anticipate are the tears that follow. It doesn't take long to wipe those away, either.

I miss her so much.

After cleaning up and putting on some clothes, I pick up the letter again and try to smooth the paper into a flat sheet.

I was disappointed in you. I felt betrayed by you, not considering what your life had been like in between the time you left the Art Room and the time we started dating. There were months that I didn't know anything about you. They were difficult months, following the death of a man you loved. I knew I had no right to feel betrayed. I had to understand, to forgive actions I never even needed to know about. Thank you for confiding in me, Jon. Thank you for telling me about your moments of need. I understand more now than I did before.

When I look back on that night, I look back in sheer admiration at the man I was getting to know. You quoted beautiful poetry to me. You took me to a special place where neither of us had gone before. You taught me things I didn't know. You showed me things I'd never seen. You didn't make me feel like the prettiest girl in the world—you made me feel like the <u>only</u> girl in the world.

You were the only boy in my world. You still are.

We aren't finished.

Anxious, I read the word scrawled in red paint.

Revere

My eyes lingering on the word, I catch the double meaning. The restaurant I took her to was One If By Land, Two If By Sea, which came from

Longfellow's "Paul Revere's Ride." In this letter, she also talks about her admiration for me.

 I gather the previous three letters in my desk drawer and look at the footnotes of each. *Declaration. Weak. Impressions. Revere.* She's summarizing the theme of each letter at the bottom of each page. Maybe she's giving me the opportunity to decide whether or not I want to read the letter by glancing at the bottom of the page first. *How simple. How kind of her.*

 I wonder when the *Why I Cheated* letter will come.

SECRETS

After my first week of work, the laborious tasks around the site are becoming easier. I can lift more, and I'm not as exhausted when I get home. For the first time in my life, I'm seeing actual definition in my muscles. It's a novelty I'd like to celebrate with a girlfriend, someone who could appreciate the newfound strength, but as with a lot of things in my life, the timing is off. Just like when Livvy kissed Finn. I wonder what would have happened had I made my presence known right away. Would they have ever shared that moment? Were true feelings exposed that day that they both had been hiding?

I may never know.

On my bed sits a book. I recognize the author, but I don't have any desire to read best-selling thrillers. Whoever bought this for me has good intentions, I'm sure, but this was a waste of their money. I pick it up to give it to Will, hoping that it might spark some interest in him. He needs to read more.

Hidden beneath the book is another letter. I leave it behind as I go to the room my brothers have been sharing.

"Will," I say from the doorway, his back to me as he plays a game on an old console and a small television. It's still a total luxury to anything I had growing up.

"Huh?" He doesn't look up.

"Pause it." He doesn't argue or question me. Had it been my mother, I know there would have been push-back, but he respects me.

"What's up?"

"Want this book? It's, like, a spy thing, I think."

"Nah."

"Let me ask again. Will you do me a favor and read this book? I thought it would be cool for us to do something together."

"Reading is a solitary thing, Jon," he says.

"But we can talk about it. You might learn something."

"How to be a spy? That's not really my ambition."

I laugh at his response. "What's your ambition?"

"I'm gonna be a professional gamer."

I stare at him blankly. I want to tell him the kids they hire for that have been playing since they were three. I feel the need to explain to him that the box he's playing on is five years old, and so far behind, technologically, that he wouldn't know what to do with today's games. I decide to let him dream, eventually smiling and nodding, trying not to look condescending.

"You might learn something about *women*," I explain. "Don't tell Mom, but I know there's a fair amount of sex in this guy's books." *There's not. He'll find that out after he's read it, though.*

He shrugs his shoulders, but reaches out for the book.

"Let me know when you want to talk about it."

"Cool," he says simply. "It's your week to cook," he adds.

"Yep. I'm making pizza tonight. Actually, I've hired someone to do it for me since I just got paid. It should be here in thirty minutes."

"Awesome!" It took some arm-twisting to get Aunt Patty to let me order in. I whole-heartedly agreed with her that it wasn't the best nutritional choice for my brothers, but I knew it was their favorite meal, and something we didn't have very often at home. The compromise was that I had to add lots of veggies to the pie. I didn't argue, knowing that my picky brothers would take off any toppings they didn't like. I ordered a large salad, too. Drowned in Ranch dressing, Max and Will will eat just about anything.

"Why don't you read until dinner?"

"Cool." Will moves to his bed and opens up the novel. I grab the letter before heading to the kitchen to set the table, wanting to get everything ready for dinner so I could have a few minutes to myself before the pizza arrives.

I didn't expect another letter from Livvy so soon. At what point do I not set aside time for her to read stories of our past? All I know is it's not today.

I love you, Jon.

I try to remember what her voice sounded like when she would say it to me. It always depended on the situation. On the phone, there was a slight whine to her tone since it was most often said when we were hanging up. In front of people, it was playful, no syllable repeating the same tone as her voice lilted with her sweet smile.

In bed together, it was an urgent whisper said with little breath. It was like an echo of my own voice every time, because she would repeat it anytime I said it to her. Was it out of obligation? Did she ever really feel it?

Does she really feel it now?

I made a mistake.

Finally.

When I look back now, I laugh.

Once again, I want to crumple up the letter and get it far, far away from me, but I keep reading, wondering how she can make what happened humorous.

I don't know why I thought it was a good idea to tell my parents about our discussion about sex after that first date. It was such an important fact I'd learned, and I was never one to keep things from my parents. As a good kid, I told them everything.

Upon seeing your reaction when you found out I'd told them, I realized I was venturing into a territory where I was no longer a kid. It was the first time I realized there was such a thing as a 'private life,' and you and I were about to embark on having one.

You asked me to keep our conversations between us, and it was in that moment that I chose to be loyal to you over my mother and father. No one had ever ranked higher than Mom and Dad, but you surpassed them that night. The power very often wavered between you, my mom and my dad, but when the matter was truly private, I kept those things between us, just like you'd asked. I know we didn't always agree on what should be kept private, but know that my heart was always in the right place.

I've kept one secret from you. I never thought it was important, but I realize if I ever hope to be with you again, it needs to come out.

I can see Finn's name without even reading on. I'm not sure I want to know whatever she's about to say. My eyes begin to water in anticipation.

Over Spring Break, Finn kissed me one time. I told you he'd tried. I didn't tell you he'd actually succeeded. The kiss we shared in Wyoming meant nothing to me. I felt nothing, and I told him so. It wasn't something that stuck with him, either. Telling you the half-truth seemed good enough at the time. I knew if you had all the information, you might hate Finn, and he's a permanent fixture in our family, so that wouldn't have worked.

And right there, she didn't just put her parents above me, she did that with this guy that she considered family. And *kissed*. The tabloid sites loved exploiting that relationship. I'd had to avoid the internet for a few days after her graduation just so I wouldn't be confronted with it.

How you feel about Finn doesn't matter to me anymore. I can handle the awkwardness of every future Spring Break, Easter, Thanksgiving, and Christmas as long as I know you're there, too.

He's my friend, though, and I have to be honest. I want to have him in my life as my friend.

That can't be a secret that I keep from you, either.

Who does she think she is, making conditions and telling me her non-negotiable terms? *Here's mine, Liv! I don't want him in my life.*

I don't want you, either.

Thinking that I don't want her makes my watery eyes unleash the tears they'd been holding back. *I don't want you, either.*

Would I ever have the strength to tell her that to her face?

We aren't finished.

Yes, we are.

In pale green, she adds her non-standard sign-off. I almost didn't notice it at all, it blended in so well with the paper.

Secrets

Hearing the doorbell ring, I tuck the note in my pocket and stand up quickly, composing myself. I clear the lump from my throat. I check my face in the TV's reflection, wiping away all evidence of my sadness. I wear a smile that hides the ruins of my heart and the crushing blow to my soul.

I keep my own secrets.

As I walk to the door with my wallet in hand, I realize that I'm not just hiding things from my family. My non-response to her letters keeps all my feelings from her a secret. That's its own sort of punishment.

As cruel as it is, she deserves it.

ENLIGHTENMENT

Enlightenment.

This time, the word is etched in dark purple paint and is the first thing that grabs my attention when I pull the letter out of the envelope. The word is so clear, so prominent. Why does it have to be so *vague*? I can't discern what the letter's going to be about from that.

I scan the letter quickly. *Intimate. Kiss.* Reading about either of those things makes me want her more. I'm trying to want her *less*. Why does she keep sending these?

I love you, Jon.

I love how you open my eyes to new things. Not many guys really care about their girlfriends' educations. Not like you do, anyway. Even though our study time wasn't always used for studying schoolwork, you made sure I had learned something in each session. I know that ignorance is something you won't tolerate, and I love that about you. I love how you always want to learn more. I love that you always want to share what you learn with me.

Not anymore, Liv.

You never just taught me what I needed to know, either. You went deeper into my lessons. You taught me how to learn better and how to think about things more thoroughly. Although I appreciate the emphasis you put on scholarly pursuits, I am personally more grateful for the patience you exhibited while I learned things of a more intimate nature.

I loved teaching her those things, too. I never had to tell her much. I could correct the mistakes that came from her inexperience simply by showing her in another moment. I never wanted to discourage her or embarrass her by pointing out what she was doing wrong– and it was never *wrong* when she touched me or kissed me. It was never wrong, by any means. I just knew some things were more pleasurable done differently.

When she first kissed my ear, she was clearly holding back. Her lips captured my lobe for a fraction of a second. It was sweet, but I knew it could be much more sensual. When I had the chance, I reminded her of how it should be done, moistening her lobe with my tongue and scraping it gently with my teeth, barely tugging before I let go. It drove her crazy. When she finally did it to me, I'd wished that I could show her more, kiss her other places. I'd wished *she* would kiss other places.

With patience, she eventually would, and with one of those places, I couldn't adequately show her in a reciprocal way. While her body felt familiar and beautiful to me, mine was foreign and awkward to her. Any man's would have been. At first, I had to direct her, to tell her what felt good when she did it. I had to pull her lips to mine when something *didn't* feel right, subtly correcting her without disturbing the intimacy. There was no way in hell I would do anything to make that experience unpleasant for her. Some men lived with wives who refused this act of pleasure, and after that first time, I couldn't imagine not being granted that indulgence from time to time.

Without spending the last year and a half with you, I wouldn't know how to show you I love you without having to say the words. Those were my favorite ways to tell you how I felt about you. If you were here–if you would see me–I would grasp your hand in mine. I would hold it tightly. I would hold you close to me while the fingers from my other hand caressed your smooth hair, massaged your scalp, rubbed your neck and pulled your lips to mine. I'd kiss you slowly. I'd kiss you hard. I'd kiss you however you wanted me to. I'd ask to learn more from you. You're the only teacher I want.

And I still had things to teach her. I still had things to learn *myself*. I'd always envisioned fumbling through them together. Such things, one only tries with people they fully trust and are okay to be completely vulnerable with. We were *there*. We were *that*. And now? How could I ever trust her again?

I know that what you taught me would only apply to you. You didn't teach me how to show someone else I love them. You taught me how to express my love to you alone. I want you to be the only person who benefits from what I now know.

My heart makes itself known, beating faster at her last statement. If I read between the lines, it's safe to assume she'd gone no further with Finn. But she'd already gone far enough, and in that, didn't he *already* benefit from what I'd taught her? She'd practiced on me to be the extraordinary kisser she'd become. She perfected the art in moments we'd shared–tender ones, loving ones, all-consuming ones that left our lips swollen and raw. It was always gratifying for me to send her back home with marks of our passion evident on her face.

I smile now, remembering how pretty she was with her lips naturally red and plump. They suited her face; offset her big, brown eyes.

Damn it, Livvy, why did you have to ruin everything we had?

We aren't finished.

Enlightenment

I'd love to enlighten her now; to teach her now. *Hey, Livvy, you can't kiss another guy and expect your boyfriend to look the other way. Maybe our lessons should have started with that.*

I just thought she had more common sense than that.

With memories flooding my mind of all the ways she had ever shown me her love, I decide to go to bed. I don't think I can be productive doing anything else this evening.

I can count on one hand the number of days she'd let me show her all of my love. It's surprising to me we'd only made love on five separate occasions. Our closeness made it seem like many, many more. She'd taken my heart at some point early on, and I let her have it for safe keeping. I held on to hers. We were entwined by that. It felt like we were one entity operating as two bodies, but we were always working toward one goal. We wanted to be together. It's safe to say we wanted to be together forever. I believed we had already started our forever. I never prepared myself for what she's done to me. I never prepared for her to take my forever. She's left me with never. She's left me with nothing. She won't even give me back my heart.

OLIVIA

The project has been moving along so quickly that we have been granted a day off. I'd gotten used to the long days and was actually disappointed when I found out last night. My family had already made plans to visit a few museums today, and they left before the sun came up, assuming I would be working today like I had to last Saturday. I should have informed them last night, but I wanted to be alone.

I'd expected the construction work to be physically demanding, but as I take on bigger projects at the site, I study the choices the architects made, looking for the reasons behind the materials or angles. It's mentally fulfilling, too. There were a few instances this past week that I realized I would have done something differently, and I've been sketching those plans all day. I have no intention of showing them to anyone, but maybe I'll take some of this new perspective back to my job in the fall. I feel reaffirmed in my interests, becoming more and more excited to return to the firm every day. They were bidding on a public works project in the city before I left. The outcome of that process should be announced mid-August, and I hope I will be able to work on it upon my return. I'd contributed to the plans. Some of the ideas presented were mine, and I was proud of my work.

I can pretend like Livvy hasn't been on my mind all day, but it's a lie. I fully expect a letter this afternoon, and with the blinds open, I've had my eye on the mailbox for the vast majority of the day. I'd even gone out to check it a few times when I had to leave my viewing post.

When the mail finally comes around five, I take the letters from the postman directly, not even letting him put them in the box. I avoid disappointment today, seeing Livvy's letter on top. I make a sandwich for myself, pouring a tall glass of milk to go with it and emptying the carton.

Looking through the refrigerator, I realize I'll need to walk down to the store after dinner. I look forward to the fresh air, to stretching my muscles a little.

After taking a bite, I open the envelope. The mustard on my sandwich masks the smell. I move the food away and hold the paper up to my nose, taking a whiff. When I pull it back, I see that she signed her name... sort of. It's this letter's footnote.

Olivia

Appropriately, her name is etched in black. Maybe she *does* recognize the dark cloud she's cast over me. And she doesn't say Livvy. No, she says Olivia, and the reference isn't lost on me.

I love you, Jon.

A week before our first Christmas together. Your apartment. On a blanket in front of a fire. All alone. You took your shirt off, and I had no idea what your action was leading up to. You turned around to reveal a quote disrupting the otherwise-unmarred flesh on your back. I'd never seen it plain before. Disrobed, in my eyes, the quote has always been there.

"If it be thus to dream, still let me sleep!"

If you were here, I'd ceremoniously kiss it like I did that night, and many other nights that followed.

Not only would you not do that, Liv, I wouldn't take my clothes off for you if I was there.

You were certain enough about me then to permanently mark your skin with a reminder of me. You were honoring me. You were honoring Olivia, the woman you wanted to be with, or so you told me.

I lost myself last year, Jon. I'm still struggling to find myself, and it's even harder without you here to help me. Who is Olivia? Who is Livvy? Who am I?

Does Olivia even exist without you? You brought her to life. You helped her flourish. I don't feel like her anymore. I don't feel like myself either. And that's part of the problem. Being Olivia to you and Livvy to everyone else made it feel like I was living separate lives. I couldn't continue to give all of myself to both of these people. I couldn't focus. I couldn't decide what was right for me.

Were you right for me? Were you good for me?

I suddenly feel like she's blaming me for this. As if giving her a pet name gave her split personalities. *Is this what caused your unfaithfulness, Liv? Is this my fault?*

If I could see her now, I'd make it easy for her. She's no longer Olivia. Olivia *was* the woman I loved, the woman I wanted to be with, but Livvy is the inconstant teenager who cheated on me with a kid she's known most of her life. Saying "I love you, Olivia" doesn't have the same tempo or tone. It doesn't roll off my tongue the way it once did. I'm not sure I could force the words out now if I tried.

It doesn't matter what you were to me once upon a time. Right or wrong, I love you now, and I want to find a way to prove to you that I am good for you. Maybe I wasn't over the past year as I struggled with myself. But I'm getting better, Jon.

I swear. I'm finally finding myself. I feel more like the girl you once loved than I ever did. I know you grew to feel differently for me as I changed. You probably accepted my changes as a progression of the woman I was becoming, but I wasn't growing into myself. I was becoming who I thought you wanted me to be when I was with you; and when you weren't around, I wanted to be the person everyone else wanted me to be.

I couldn't live up to everyones' expectations. I'm exhausted. I'm tired of being someone even I don't know. I have my own expectations of myself, and while you're away, I intend to live up to each and every one. When you return in a few months, I'll be a better version of myself.

I see things clearly now. I can be your Olivia and my parents' Livvy all at once. I've reconciled their differences and I've brought them together. Your Olivia and their Livvy just want me to be happy, and that's what I intend to be. I'll be ready for you. I'll be better for you. I promise.

I'll be happy for you. Will you be happy for me?

We aren't finished.

I don't buy it. My Olivia. Their Livvy. And who, exactly, is she to Finn? Who kissed him? Olivia? Livvy? A cheater. That's who kissed him. I didn't cause that. He didn't cause that. Only she could kiss him like that. She chose to do that.

She had a *concussion*.

Emi had told me that when I spoke with her before I left Manhattan. Again, she wasn't making excuses for her daughter. It was just a factual statement, something for me to think about. I've thought about it. Now, knowing more of the facts, a concussion seems to matter *less*. Finn kissed her over spring break. She kissed him after her graduation. They shared feelings. Those feelings didn't involve me. My feelings were not once considered.

Why do I keep replaying this over and over in my head? Every few days, she brings me back to a place I feel something for her. Anger. Love. Confusion. Desire. I am tired of feeling anything for her.

On the days when I'm working, I can go hours without thinking about her. Livvy. Olivia. The beautiful artist I admired from the first moment she spoke to me. The second I leave the work site, my mind drifts back to her, and I feel sorry for myself. The pity overwhelms me until I can go back to work. Or the pity becomes some emotion tied to her when I read her letters. Why am I letting her control me this much? It's pointless. It's unhealthy.

I am wasting precious time with my brothers. Once the summer is over, I'll only see them on breaks and holidays. This summer will probably be the last one I can be away from Manhattan for the entire three month period. I'll have courses next year, and hopefully the job at the architecture firm will be waiting for me, like my boss told me it would.

I have to stop holing up in my room every evening and every Sunday. My brothers are the reason I'm here in the first place. The sulking ends today.

I run my thumb over the paint stripe. Goodbye, Olivia. You've done all the damage you can do to this man.

And I believe it. I believe it all evening. I believe it as I listen to my brothers recap their day. I believe it as I help Max get ready for bed. I even believe it as I settle myself into the sheets for the night.

It's only when the dream of her awakens me that I doubt my conviction. The pain still carves away at me. There's more damage to be done, and I hate her for it.

PROMISES

"How's the book coming?" I ask my oldest brother as we do dishes together.

"I finished it yesterday," he says, then looks around to make sure we're alone. "And it was good, but I don't think there was any sex in it. They had *almost* sex."

"Almost sex," I repeat softly. "Like, foreplay?"

"Yeah, I guess. The spy took this lady's clothes off. He touched her *bosom*." He says the word more quietly than the rest, and I laugh a little. "That's what it said. Bosom."

"And then what?"

"Then it was the next day and they woke up in bed together."

"Ohhh," I say to him. "The fade to black."

"What's that mean?"

"Like in the movies... when something is alluded to, but you don't actually see it."

"So you think they had sex?"

"I didn't read the book," I tell him, "but–"

"You didn't read it?" he asks, nearly yelling at me.

"I was going to," I lie, remembering the deal I'd made with him. "But every time I wanted to read, you had the book."

"Oh," he says, accepting my explanation. "Well I'm done with it now."

"Good to know. But yes, if he took her clothes off and touched her *bosom*, and the author faded to black, it's safe to say they had sex."

"Is that what girls like you to call their boobs?"

It's an odd question, but I asked for it. "You know, Will, it depends on the woman. It's not really an everyday topic of conversation."

39

"But they like to be touched there?"

"Some of them, yes. But all preferences in sex are based on the individual. What one woman likes, another may not. You can't compartmentalize *women* as one entity. They're all different."

"I know," Will says. "I like the blonde ones."

"Hair color isn't all that matters in women."

"I like blonde ones with big *bosoms*," he adds, putting emphasis on the word even he thinks sounds silly. I wonder how old the author is, to use that terminology. It sounds old-fashioned. I'd expect it in poetry, not modern-day fiction.

"Let me be clear: looks are not all that matters in women."

"Then why'd you pick Livvy Holland? I'd take her, even though she's not a blonde. *Her* bosom—"

"We're not going to talk about her breasts," I tell my brother quickly. "We're not going to talk about her at all, in fact."

"Why'd she kiss that guy?" he says, drying a plate.

I stop what I'm doing and look down at my towel, pulling at the frayed edges. "I don't know, Will. I wish I knew."

"Are you broken up?"

"Yes."

"I thought you wanted to marry her, though."

"Things change." I shrug and pick up the silverware, drying each piece meticulously before putting it in the drawer. "People change. All I can do is accept her decision and move on."

"Does she like him better than you?"

"Does it matter?" I ask, because I think I can say with certainty that she doesn't. No matter what she did, how could she love him like she loved me?

"If she still likes you, you don't have to accept the fact that she kissed him. You could get her back. You could tell her to promise never to do it again."

"Promises are too easily broken," I say softly, thinking about the letter I'd left in my room. It's strange that we ended up on this topic. It makes me wonder if Will had gone through my mail.

40

Before dinner, I only took the time to check out the footnote before joining my family. I know my brother put away some laundry in my room after that.

"Did you read my letter, Will?"

"Huh?" he asks, and I can tell from his face that he did.

"Will, those letters are private, do you understand?"

"If they're so private, why do you leave them in your desk like that?"

"*In* my desk. Not *on* my desk. I put them *in* my desk to keep them out of sight. Stop going through my things."

"She says she loves you," he pleads with me.

"She says that all the time. They're just words strung into a sentence that no longer means anything to me. But don't change the subject! I respect your privacy. I expect you to–"

"Jonny?" my mom says, pouring herself a cup of coffee my aunt had made. "Stop yelling at your brother."

I bite my lip as I finish my part of the dishes. "Stay out of my room from now on," I tell him on my way out. "And where Livvy's involved, just stay out of my business."

"Jon!" my mother cries out to me, trying to summon me back. I can hear the pity in her voice, and I hate it. After quietly shutting my door, I find the letter placed neatly in its envelope in my desk drawer.

I love you, Jon.

Our first Christmas together was eventful, to say the least. The Holland family was going through its share of drama. You fueled that fire and got into a nice argument with my dad, too, and then I said some things that made my home life a little difficult for a few days. There were a lot of moments of passionate conversations, but there wasn't a whole lot of passionate talk between me and you.

There was sweet talk, though; when I opened up the small box that revealed the beautiful promise ring. You wanted me to have a constant reminder of how much I meant to you. It was a promise to be mine, forever.

Do you remember the promise you made?

Of course *I* remember it. I never forgot it. I'd hoped the ring would always remind her of my promises, but why didn't she think of me that day? Why didn't she consider all she'd be losing by kissing Finn?

I may never understand.

Would you ever honor it again?

Does she have any clue what she's done to us? Any clue at all? Honor? What does she know about honor?!

I'll make you any promise, Jon. Any promise in the world. You just have to give me a second chance.

We aren't finished.

Promises

I feel like I've already done that. Didn't we break up once before? Of course we did. I was mad at her and broke up with her, leaving her to consider the hurtful things she'd done to her father and the awkward position she'd put me in. She was acting like a child; acting like someone I didn't know.

Have we just come full circle? Again I find her acting like someone I don't know. She even admitted in my last letter that she'd become someone she didn't recognize. How could I possibly accept promises from someone who isn't even true to herself?

SECRETS II

"What's your temperature?" my mom asks from the doorway before she leaves for her waitressing job before lunchtime.

"It's 102.3," I tell her as I fight the urge to swallow because I remember how painful it was the last time. "The medication should kick in soon. That's what the nurse said anyway."

"Do me a favor, Jonny, and stay away from Max as much as you can tonight. If he gets sick, they won't let him in daycare, and I really can't take a day off since I just started working at Nan's."

"Tell me about it," I complain. "I didn't want to leave the site this morning, but I thought I would collapse after an hour. I wouldn't have been able to stay hydrated, anyway, with my throat swollen like this."

"I can pick up some ice cream later."

"I got some this morning. But thanks, Mom." I'm not used to her doing things for other people, and especially not for me. Sobriety is changing her.

"No problem. Just relax and get yourself better. Everyone gets sick from time to time. I'd come give you a hug, but I don't want to get sick."

"Thanks," I say. "The sentiment counts."

I can hear Will playing his video games for most of the afternoon, even as I weave in and out of restless sleep. I think it's nice that he doesn't have to watch Max every day. I'm sure my youngest brother has a lot of fun at daycare, and Will has some time to be a regular teenager. For a few days a week, he only has to be responsible for himself.

In the afternoon, he brings the mail into my room, surprising me with another letter from Livvy. Having all day to myself, I miss her more than I usually do. As much as I've tried to sleep or focus on other things, the medication is making it hard to actually think. The only thing I'm really able to do is feel. I feel bad. I feel bad physically. I feel bad emotionally, too.

"Want anything?" Will asks.

"I just want to feel better, and I don't want to get you sick. So get out," I joke with him.

"Hey, got anymore books to read?"

I raise my eyebrows, then quickly try to hide my astonishment. Pulling my arm out from under the covers, I point to the top drawer of my dresser. "Look in there. Read some of the jackets and see if anything looks good."

"I like this cover," he says, flashing *The Ultimate Hitchhiker's Guide to the Galaxy* for me to see, "but it's too thick."

"Oh, no," I argue. "There are five books there. Honestly, Will, I can't think of a better book for you to read. It's smart and funny. And I've read that one countless times. We could definitely talk about Arthur and Zaphod for hours. Please," I plead with him. "It'll be awesome."

"I can barely carry it," he whines.

"Then you need to work out more. It's a book, for Christ's sake. How wimpy are you gonna look to the fairer sex if you can't even carry an admittedly oversized book?"

"Wait, is there sex?" He looks very interested now.

"Sure is," I tell him convincingly.

"You said that last time and there wasn't."

"Well, then, I guess you'll just have to read to find out, won't you?"

"Whatever."

"But, hey, Will, there's so much more to life than sex. That seems to be on your mind a lot these days."

"You brought it up!"

I don't think I did, but I realize my mind isn't very clear. With the amount of time I've spent thinking about Livvy today, I very well may have brought it up. It's been on my mind.

I don't admit that to my brother, though. "Just go read, Will. And let me know if you want to chat about it. Come tell me when you realize you love the book, okay?"

"Challenge accepted," he says, nodding his head and leaving my room. He comes back moments later to shut the door.

Grabbing the letter, I struggle to decide whether or not it's good for me to read it. I already feel beat down and defeated today, thanks to the strep throat. I don't really need the added feelings of rejection that have accompanied every letter I've received from her. No matter what nice thing she says or what sweet memory she reflects upon, the lasting impression I have from each note is the image of her kissing Finn.

I'm too weak to say no today. I miss her too much. The footnote is a repeat of a previous one, which I find curious. I touch the paint surrounding the word to make sure it's textured. For a second, I thought she'd resorted to making copies of her pleading love notes.

I love you, Jon.

I wish I didn't love you, Livvy.

I remember your campaign to make my parents like you. You were always so conscientious of things you did and so concerned with how they saw you that your suggestion for Valentine's Day caught me off guard. My father would never have forgiven you, had he known, so it's safe to say Mom never told him.

The night before, I was scared. It wasn't just the fear of getting caught, though. I was afraid of your expectations of the day. I'd kept my plans a secret from you for one main reason. I wasn't sure what I'd be willing to give that day, and I was scared you'd be expecting me to give you everything. After all, in the four hours of alone time we'd had that week before Christmas, it went further than I'd planned.

She never told me that. Did I push her? Did I make her do something she wasn't ready to do, because that was never my plan with her. Not sexually, anyway.

So a full day with you—more than twelve hours—I knew the potential was there for things to spiral out of our control. I wanted you in ways I'd never wanted anyone, and you weren't afraid to tell me how you wanted me. Idle time, no chaperone, and two people in love were all the components required to make love—or to make a big mistake.

Making love to her was never a mistake. I hope she doesn't think that about any of the times we were together.

On the morning of Valentine's Day, I woke up with a nagging feeling that we would get caught, and the thought of my father catching us in the act made the act itself much less desirable in my mind that day. As I let the scenario play out in my head, I never could see you and him having another civil conversation, and I knew I didn't want that to happen. So before you could get your hopes up, I told you how I felt.

No, my hopes were definitely up that morning. I'd bought condoms. I'd showered twice that morning because I was so on-edge. Although we hadn't said we would have sex, I thought we would. I can't say I wasn't planning on it, because I was, but I hadn't plotted the steps to make it happen. I figured it would be something that came about organically. I figured our making out would naturally lead to it. I figured she would let me try things with her I never had–and on that point, she still did, even if it wasn't actual sex–and I thought her desire would build as her trust in me did.

But when she said she didn't want to go all the way that day, I didn't question her or pressure her. When we did make out, and when she did let me

46

go farther than we had gone before, I had to temper my own thoughts with non-erotic things, like science and stories I'd read. If I hadn't done that, I think I would have gotten carried away. I would have put her in the position to tell me *no*, and I didn't want to hear that word.

I never did that day, and I was proud of that fact.

Even though Mom did figure out where we were that day, I still consider our actions a secret that we kept between ourselves. It was a beautiful day with you, doing things we love on our own and together.

Let's keep more secrets between us, Jon.

We aren't finished.

Secrets II

There is no *us* anymore. Is this a secret I'm keeping from her? Because she certainly doesn't seem to realize that.

My swollen throat seems to get worse at the end of her letter. The throbbing headache won't be helped by crying over her again.

Rolling over on my side, I reach to get my *Science for Sustainable Development* text and open it up to the bookmark. Focus on science. Forget about Livvy.

EIGHTEEN

After work on Saturday, I feel like I could conquer the world. Over the past two days, I simply couldn't pull my weight. I was weak, and although the fever was gone, my throat still hurt and my head was pounding most of the time while I concentrated on my job. I didn't ask to leave early, and that option wasn't offered, either. The fact is, I've become someone they depend on at the site.

I like that.

"Will?" I ask my brother as I walk through the living room. "Do you want to go for a run with me? It's nice out. You look pale."

"Okay," he says, putting the large tome face down, bending the spine. I know that bothers some people, but I love to see books showing their wear. It's a sign of a good book that's been shared by a lot of people. This particular copy was my father's, and when it was given to me, it already had evidence of many, many readings by my father. Dogeared pages, coffee stains, even some notes in the column helped me feel more connected with my dad.

We both get changed quickly, passing my mom, aunt and littlest brother on the way out.

"Can I go?" Max asks.

"Buddy, I'll take you for a lap or two when I get back. Will and I have a lot of ground to cover, and with your short legs, I don't think you'll be able to keep up."

"I could ride my bike." He could, but I really wanted some time alone with Will.

"Max," Mom chimes in, "you said you'd help me make some cookies. Remember?"

Max still looks torn, and on the verge of tears. I check my watch. "We should be back just in time, then. You go help Mom, and then I'll swing by and we'll work off some cookie dough calories. Sound good?"

"I guess," he whines.

"Good."

Will takes off in a sprint, obviously racing me. I'm still taller than him, and stronger, so it's easy to catch up.

"What'd you do today?"

"We went shopping. For some clothes, and for groceries."

"Who?"

"Me and Max and Mom."

"How was it?"

"Okay, I guess. She bought us a lot of stuff. It was cool."

"Like clothes?"

"Clothes," he says, "shoes." I glance down and notice the new Nikes. "Pretty much anything we asked for. Ball caps, DVDs, some books. And then she bought a ton of groceries. So many that Aunt Patty was kind of mad."

"Mad?"

"She said she was spending too much money."

"I see. It does sound a little extravagant. I've never even owned a pair of Nikes."

"They're cool, right?"

"They're nice."

"Mom said it was payday, so she had a reason to celebrate."

"Sounds like she may have some lingering guilt, too."

"What do you mean?"

"You know she's an alcoholic."

"Yeah?"

"I think now that she's sober, she's able to see what she's been missing in your lives. I think she feels like she has a lot of making up to do."

"If I get new stuff out of it, that's fine with me."

"Don't go all materialistic on me, Will. They're just things. Things don't mean anything."

50

"Maybe not to you, but I'm tired of wearing worn shoes that don't fit me and make me look like I'm homeless. I'm sick of kids making fun of me for wearing your hand-me-downs. I want something of my own. Something nice. Something that makes me look normal."

Our run slows to a jog.

"Will, I know your life has been tough, but I've really tried my best to maintain some sense of normalcy with you and Max. I know I couldn't always buy you the nicest things, or even new things all the time, but I never sent you out looking homeless. I tried to do right by you. I did."

"I know, Jon," he says. "But that wasn't your job. It was hers."

"You're right. It was totally her job, but when she couldn't do it, someone had to step in."

"I'm glad you helped."

"Well, I'd do anything for my brothers." I shove him playfully. "What about you? Would you do anything for us?"

"Of course."

"Good. Because after this summer, Will, I probably won't be able to make any more trips like this. And I worry about Mom. I worry she'll fall back into her old habits, and I need to know that you can take care of yourself and Max, if it comes to that."

"How so?"

"You have Patty here, so even if Mom slips, you should be okay... but we don't know Patty very well, and I know it's tough to trust people you hardly know. I think you'd still feel on your own, even with our aunt here to help. Does that make sense?"

"How would I take care of Max?"

"The same way I've taken care of you. Make sure you have something decent to eat in the house. Play ball with him to keep him active. Give him books to read, and make sure he does his homework. If he has commitments, whether they're school related, or games, or parties, make sure he makes them. And if he needs to talk, lend him an ear. Try to give him good advice. If you can't think of any, then call me."

"That sounds easy." I think back to the past fifteen years. None of it was *ever* easy.

"Sometimes you won't want to do it," I tell him. "Sometimes you'll want to hang out with your friends, or a girl, but you have to promise me you'll keep an eye on him. Keep him out of trouble. Call me whenever you want if you need help, and feel free to go to Patty, too. She's a good person who's welcomed you into her home."

"Do you think we'll ever go back to Manhattan?"

"I hope so. When I graduate, I'll bring you back out if you want to come. Hopefully your grades will get you into any college you choose."

"What if I don't want to go to college?"

"Why wouldn't you want to go to college?"

"Because I don't want to cost anyone money."

"Nobody thinks of college as an expense that doesn't have significant dividends, Will. It's an investment. And I'll send you all of my test prep books so you can start studying now. You could get a free ride to college if you put your mind to it."

"You did it."

"I did. I did it to prove that you could, too."

"I'm not as smart as you."

"I disagree with that. You're just as smart as I was at fifteen." That might be a lie, but he really has no memory to compare himself to. He was just a kid with kid things on his mind. But I see no harm in letting him believe that. He could be as smart as me, if he applied himself more. That's what I need to convince him to do, and I think I've done a good job with the reading so far this summer. That's key. "Just study. Focus. Don't get too distracted by girls."

He grins at me. I fear that girls may be his downfall.

"You're allowed to get a little distracted. That's part of growing up."

"There's a girl from school that I like."

"Yeah?" I ask when we get to the front yard.

"Yeah. Maybe I'll call her tonight."

"You have her number?"

"She wrote it in my yearbook."

"That's a good sign," I tell him with a smile. "Can you do me a favor first?"

"What?"

"Put in some time with Max tonight. I need him to trust you like he does me. Can you take him for a run?"

"I don't know," he hedges.

"Come on. Please?"

"He'll be disappointed you aren't taking him."

"Initially, maybe, but once you start having fun with him, he'll forget all about me. Please?"

"Okay," he finally agrees.

"I'll send him out."

I'm winded, and finally feeling a little bit of exhaustion. I was wondering if the steroid shot had just kicked in late, but after the run, I'm finally starting to feel like I should feel after 8 hours of manual labor and a half-hour run.

"Max," I pant. "I think my strep is lingering a little. I'm worn out," I tell him. "Will said he wants to keep running, though. Go with him?"

"I wanted to go with you," he says.

"If I could, I would, buddy, but don't let Will down, okay? He wants to go with you."

"He does?" Max asks, looking surprised. I nod my head. He hops up, bounding to his room to put on his sneakers. "Cool! Bye!" In his excitement, he nearly runs into the glass door on the way out, setting him into a frenzy of giggles when he gets to the front yard.

Catching my breath, I see the pile of mail on an old secretary desk in the dining area. I hadn't received a letter since Wednesday. Finding nothing in the stack, I wonder if she finally gave up on me. A part of me thinks it's about time. Another part wishes she hadn't gotten over me so easily.

No sooner does the thought come that I notice an envelope on the floor. It's from her. I feel relief... and then I feel depressed. Quietly, I make my way to my room and shut the door, sliding out of my shoes before lying down on the bed.

I love you, Jon.

Happy birthday.

That was *months* ago. We celebrated together. I remember the present she gave me. She'd taken me downstairs to the media room in her house, and hanging over the oversized reclining chairs was an illustration of The Getty Center done by Richard Meier, one of my idols. At first, I was jealous, wondering why the Hollands would have something like that hanging in their basement, but realizing its value, I figured it was some sort of investment for Jack. I'd never told Livvy about my interest in Meier's work, so even though it was my birthday, the thought that it was my gift never crossed my mind.

But it was.

"It's the only one of its kind," Livvy had told me. "And it's signed."

And it was.

I'd seen his illustrations of the building before, but not from this angle and not with these colors. It was incredible. My heart was racing as I took in the details, eventually removing it from the wall to get a closer look.

"Do you like it?" she'd asked.

"How did you know?"

"I asked Fred for ideas," she said. "He listed some names, and I went on the hunt for something good." My roommate shared my fascination with Meier, and I couldn't wait to see his face when I hung the rendering on our dorm room wall.

"I don't know what you did to get this, Livvy, but this is the most incredible gift I've ever been given."

"Really? This? I've given you other things," she said softly, careful not to be overheard if anyone was listening from the foyer upstairs. "I've given you *better* things."

I set the framed artwork down and pulled her into me. "Aside from you... but I don't see you as a possession, Olivia," I told her. "And anything I've taken from you, I hope you feel I've given equally in return."

"I do," she'd said. "You have." I kissed her then, and I kept kissing her until her father came downstairs to wish me a happy birthday.

After that, she took me to a sushi place that the architect had once said was his favorite restaurant. The food was fresh and my company was perfect, but I'd greedily hoped that Livvy had found a way for us to be alone to celebrate after we ate.

"That'll have to wait until your 20th birthday," she said as I kissed her curbside in front of her home. "But I promise, I'll make it happen."

Another promise broken, I guess. Putting the memories behind me, I finally delve into the letter.

We celebrated a couple things that day: your eighteenth year of life, and your acceptance into Columbia.

So we've gone back a year, I guess. I wish we were talking about my 19th birthday, because I don't have a lot of great memories from my 18th. Some of it was my fault, for taking her with me to my uncle's bar, but her actions the following day were totally her responsibility. *She* was to blame for that aftermath.

Nothing I said or did that day or the next was meant to hurt you. I definitely spoke out of turn and gave you false hope when it wasn't mine to give. I just wanted all of your dreams to come true, because I knew how hard you'd worked for them. I just wanted you to be happy.

In the haze of tequila, I saw everything clearly. I saw our future together, and I was ready to leave my parents' side to make that happen, no matter who got hurt in the process—as long as it wasn't you.

But I ended up hurting you, too.

I never wanted that to become habit, or something you expected from me. I don't want you to think that since I've hurt you twice now, I'll keep doing it. I won't, Jon. I swear I won't.

No need to swear, Liv. You can't hurt me if I stop caring about you. And I swear, I will. Someday, I will.

> *I haven't forgotten my promise to you for your twentieth birthday, either. I hope you'll let me keep that promise.*
>
> *I want to spend the rest of your birthdays with you, and I want you there for mine. My eighteenth is coming up, and I'm hoping we will have worked through things by then—*

How can she be so positive that we're going to work things out!? I know if the tables were turned, and I'd sent her countless letters to which she never responded, I think I'd start to lose hope at some point. She obviously works differently, though. Maybe it's time to compose a letter to her. Maybe it's time to voice the words I haven't yet said, and really never wanted to have to say to her.

Why? Because it would hurt her? Why spare her feelings any longer?

> *I'm hoping we will have worked through things by then and that this mistake I made and this pain I caused you will be things of the past. I hope you will someday forgive me.*

We aren't finished.

Eighteen

I decide to text Fred, and find out if he'd done what I asked him to do on the day I moved out.

"*I couldn't throw that drawing away,*" he says in his message. "*It's priceless.*"

"*I understand,*" I respond, feeling relieved that he didn't follow through with my rash decision.

"*It's hanging back in my room,*" he admits, "*and I'll be happy to return it to its rightful owner when we move back on campus this fall.*"

"*Maybe I won't want it,*" I reply.

"*Maybe you will,*" he counters.

Maybe I will.

~~DEAR~~ LIVVY

LIVVY,

THIS HAS TO STOP. I'VE RECEIVED TEN LETTERS FROM YOU, AND NOT ONCE HAVE YOU APOLOGIZED TO ME FOR WHAT YOU DID. THAT SHOULD HAVE BEEN THE FIRST THING YOU WROTE, THE LAST THING, AND PRETTY MUCH EVERYTHING IN BETWEEN. INSTEAD, I GET BRIEF REMINISCENCES OF THE GOOD TIMES.

YOU KNOW WHAT? THERE ARE NO MORE GOOD TIMES. EVERY TIME YOU REFLECT BACK ON ONE, IT GOES SOUR FOR ME BECAUSE I CAN'T UN-SEE YOU KISSING FINN.

THE ONE TIME I'M NOT IMMEDIATELY THERE FOR YOU, YOU REACH FOR SOMEONE ELSE. I HAD EVERY RIGHT TO WAVER ON WHETHER OR NOT I'D COME TO YOUR GRADUATION. HURTFUL THINGS WERE SAID AND DONE THE NIGHT BEFORE, AND I DIDN'T APPRECIATE THE WAY YOU HANDLED YOURSELF. EVERY TIME I THOUGHT YOU WERE GAINING INDEPENDENCE AND GROWING INTO THE WOMAN I WANTED TO BE WITH, YOU'D DO SOMETHING STUPID, DESPERATE AND IMMATURE. THIS ONE OUTRANKS THEM ALL.

I THOUGHT YOU'D GET THE HINT THAT I WANTED THINGS TO END BY NOT RESPONDING TO YOUR LETTERS, BUT I GUESS INDIFFERENCE DOESN'T REALLY REGISTER TO YOU. YOU NEED EVERYTHING SPELLED OUT TO COMBAT YOUR IGNORANCE AND ARROGANCE.

WE ARE FINISHED. DOES THAT SOUND FAMILIAR? SORT OF? WELL, I'M TIRED OF YOU TELLING ME THAT

WE AREN'T. WE MOST CERTAINLY ARE, LIVVY. IT'S MY CHOICE TO MAKE, AND I'VE MADE IT.

"CHOISIE." NOT ANYMORE. I UN-CHOOSE YOU NOW, LIVVY HOLLAND. I CAN'T BE WITH SOMEONE WHO KISSES ANOTHER GUY AND THEN THINKS SHE CAN JUST SKATE PAST IT LIKE IT MEANT NOTHING. I MEAN, EVEN IF THAT KISS MEANT NOTHING TO YOU, IT SAID SO MUCH TO ME. IT TOLD ME I WASN'T GOOD ENOUGH FOR YOU. IT TOLD ME YOU HAD TO LOOK ELSEWHERE FOR HAPPINESS. IT TOLD ME YOU WERE IMPATIENT. IT TOLD ME YOU WERE HEARTLESS AND FAITHLESS. IT TOLD ME YOU WERE UNSTABLE. IT TOLD ME YOU WERE TOO NEEDY FOR WHAT I COULD GIVE YOU. I'D STARTED TO FIGURE THAT OUT LONG BEFORE YOU KISSED HIM.

WHEN I WENT TO MEET YOU UNDER THE TREE LIKE YOU ASKED, I WAS READY TO TELL YOU I WANTED TO HELP YOU. I WANTED TO POINT OUT THE FACT THAT YOU WEREN'T YOURSELF ANYMORE. I'D TRIED TO CONVINCE YOU OF THAT WITHOUT COMING OUT AND SAYING IT, BUT AGAIN—I UNDERSTAND YOU NEED TO HAVE THINGS CLARIFIED. I MADE ASSUMPTIONS THAT YOU KNEW YOURSELF, THAT YOU KNEW WHO YOU WERE, WHO YOU ARE, AND WHO YOU WERE BECOMING. YOU KNEW NONE OF THAT. FLAILING, YOU NEEDED HELP, AND YOU GRABBED HOLD OF FINN WHEN I WAS MINUTES AWAY.

TWO MINUTES, LIV! THAT'S IT! WAITING TWO MORE MINUTES, AND I'D STILL BE AT YOUR SIDE. GRANTED, I'D NEVER KNOW IF YOU AND FINN SHARED FEELINGS FOR ONE ANOTHER. DID YOU? DO YOU? I NEED TO KNOW IT ALL, LIV. I NEED TO KNOW EVERY ACT OF BETRAYAL, PHYSICAL OR EMOTIONAL... I NEED TO KNOW WHEN YOUR FEELINGS FOR ME CHANGED. WAS IT TRULY JUST IN THAT SECOND, FOR THAT SECOND? FROM YOUR LETTERS, I CAN INFER THAT'S WHAT YOU WANT ME TO BELIEVE.

BUT I DON'T KNOW WHAT TO BELIEVE.

ALL I KNOW IS THAT I NEVER ONCE FELT THE URGE TO KISS ANOTHER GIRL WHILE I WAS WITH YOU. TO ME, A

KISS IS AN EXPRESSION OF LOVE AND DESIRE. WHAT'S IT TO YOU? A DESPERATE ATTEMPT FOR ATTENTION? LIKE YOU DIDN'T HAVE ENOUGH OF THAT? YOU HAD TWO HOVERING PARENTS. YOU HAD COUNTLESS AUNTS AND UNCLES WHO WOULD DO ANYTHING FOR YOU. YOU HAD ME. AND YOU HAD LOYAL FRIENDS-SOME RELATIVES, SOME NOT-AND ONE FINN.

WHAT KIND OF ATTENTION DID YOU WANT THAT DAY? WHAT DID YOU WANT FROM HIM? AND DID HE GIVE IT TO YOU?

ARE YOU SORRY?

WE ARE FINISHED. I JUST FELT LIKE REITERATING THAT.

STOP WRITING TO ME.

JON

UNGRATEFUL

"Does God exist?" Will asks me after my shower Wednesday night. I'm a little taken aback by his question. Isn't he too young to ask questions like that?

I was thirteen. I think that's right. I'd discussed it with my father before he passed away. I guess it's time to ask existential questions, since he hasn't before. Not of me, anyway. I hate to think what the answers would be if he'd asked Mom, or his father.

"Why do you ask?"

"I read the part about the Babel fish, and it says God doesn't exist."

"First of all, in case you haven't figured it out yet, Will, *The Hitchhiker's Guide* is fiction."

"I know," he says. "I'm not stupid... but it got me wondering. I've wondered before, but I wasn't sure it was okay to wonder that."

"Of course it's okay to wonder things; to question things. Even things about God."

"Well? Is he real?"

I smile at him, trying to remember the things my dad told me. He was a smart man with good advice, even if I ultimately didn't share in his beliefs.

"It's not really cut and dry like that," I start. "It's kind of like if I asked you the meaning of life." He looks at his hands pensively. "I'm not asking you that, by the way. But, let's say I did ask you that, and I asked Mom that and I asked Max that. I'd probably get three different answers, wouldn't I?"

"But that's an open-ended question," he tells me brightly. I smile, proud that he sees a difference, even if it takes me off-topic. "I asked you a yes or no question."

"I can only give you an open-ended response, though. Ask me if *I* believe in a god."

"Do you?"

"I do."

He nods his head, contemplating my response. "Why?"

"Good question."

I first tell him about the conversation I had with my father. He'd met my dad before, but really had very little to do with him. Will has told me before that he thought my dad was cold, detached and hard to read. He was. But when we really got to talking about things he was passionate about, I felt closer to him.

My dad was very scholarly and well-educated. He believed in hard facts, and couldn't muster any faith in anything, really, but especially not in God. "Evolution doesn't lie," he'd told me, and when I was younger, I immediately saw where he was coming from.

"But the fact that you can see evolutionary details in our solar system and planet and species doesn't mean that there isn't a god," I explain to my brother. "In my mind, they can co-exist, and they do."

"So your dad didn't believe in God?"

"Nope," I tell him plainly. "From what I can tell, he never did."

"Is your dad in Hell?" Will asks, careful with his words.

"He certainly doesn't think so," I respond, "since he didn't believe in Heaven or Hell."

"But then he *is* in Hell, because he didn't believe, right?"

"If you believe that, then you must believe in God…"

"I just…" he begins, looking conflicted. "It's what we're taught."

"I know." I say I know, but I wonder where he was 'taught' this. Not in school. Not in our home. "Who's teaching you this?"

"My dad." I look away so he doesn't see the look of disgust on my face. *His* dad, the convicted felon, the man who knocked up my mother not once, but twice, and left her to raise their children on her own while he philandered and stole things and set a horrible example… *his* dad is the person teaching him about faith and God and Heaven and Hell.

I should have been talking to my brothers about this a long time ago. No wonder Will's confused. I finally look up at him and force a pleasant expression.

"So your dad," he starts again, "do *you* think he's in Hell?"

"No. I don't think so. I'm not sure *I* believe in Hell."

"But the Bible says that if you don't believe in God, you go to Hell."

"I understand that's what the Bible says. I understand that my response contradicts traditional Christian beliefs, or the beliefs of many religions. But faith in a god goes beyond religions, right?"

"You keep saying 'a' god. Do you believe in more than one?"

Another interesting question. "I... I don't know. I believe in a higher power, Will. I call it a god because I don't really know any other word for it. When it comes to faith, there aren't a whole lot of options in the minds of most people. You believe in God, or you don't. So I believe in a god, who may or may not be someone else's God."

My brother looks very confused.

"You're a Polytheist?"

"Whoa, little brother," I laugh. "Did your dad teach you that word?"

"No, I learned about it in a mythology book I found. So, you believe there are other gods?" Maybe I haven't given Will enough credit. Maybe he's applying himself more than I realize.

"I don't believe that my way of thinking is the only way of thinking, so I'm tolerant of others who do worship other gods, be it one or many. For me, though, if I had to give myself a name, I'd say I was a Deist. I believe in one higher power that created the world. I hope that there's some sort of happy afterlife, but I don't really know. No one in this life really knows."

"Unless you believe the Bible."

"Right," I say. "And it's perfectly fine if you do. I think the most important thing to take away from this conversation is that it's all about your own personal relationship with God. Or gods. Or not," I suggest, trying to let him understand that he has choices, but that he has to form his own beliefs. "I'll still love you, no matter what, as long as you live your life honorably and do your best to not hurt others."

He smiles, looking unburdened. "Do you pray?"

"Yes, I pray."

"Do you think your dad prayed, at the end?"

"No. I don't think he had a change of heart at all in those final moments. But I prayed. I don't believe that we were put on this planet to live solitary lives, and I firmly believe the actions of others play a part in peoples' destinies, on this planet and beyond. I believe other people are put here to help us, and to guide us in our paths. Honestly, Will, I didn't always believe in God. When I first had this conversation with my dad, I walked away thinking he was right. But then I really got to know another person in my life who showed me there was something more."

"It was Livvy, right?"

"It was you, Will. It was the friendship you showed me when my dad was sick. I had some really bad days. I'm sure you remember them. But I'd come home from the hospital, and you'd be here with a mitt, a ball, and a smile. After five minutes of playing catch, my spirits were lifted. I don't think I ever would have gotten through those months, or the months after he died, without your friendship. Someone put you on this planet to intervene in my life. It wasn't random. You reminded me that I had something to live for. And I always wanted to make sure you felt the same way."

"I'm glad you're my brother," he says.

"Me, too. Do you feel better about things?"

"I feel better about questioning things," Will answers.

"I never believed in blind faith," I admit. "I don't think that's in our DNA. But be your own man. You don't have to believe what I do, or what your father does. But it's important to believe in something. It's important to feel convictions about something. Don't spend your life in a fog. I don't think you'll be satisfied."

"I know what I believe right now," he says.

"What?" I ask, anxious for his personal philosophy.

"I believe I need to know what happens next with Zaphod and Arthur."

"Maybe you'll end up worshipping the Almighty Bob," I suggest in jest.

"Who's that?"

"Book five," I tell him. "Keep reading."

After he leaves, I finally settle in with Livvy's eleventh letter. Ungrateful, it says at the bottom. Once again, when I think I could just set the note aside without reading it, I'm intrigued enough by the footnote to keep going.

I love you, Jon.

I have never been made to feel so ungrateful as I did the day that you scolded me for the things I said to my father.

I've told her before, I can't *make* her feel things. It's in her power to feel however she wants, and if she felt ungrateful, that was her conscience stepping in and trying to talk some sense into her. Lord knows I couldn't.

The reality check was worse than a slap in the face would have been. Physical abuse would have been preferable than listening to you reprimand me for the horrible things I said to him. But I know you're above that, and I know, for me, getting over a face slap would have been much easier than facing what I'd done.

Getting over that day shouldn't have been easy for me, and it wasn't.

Because my father is a gracious and loving man, he easily forgave me. I was thankful for that, but it took weeks for me to forgive myself. There are still days that I look back and remember the look on his face. On those days, when I wish I could just forget those moments, I address them head on. I make myself suffer a bit, and then work on forgiveness once more. It's a never-ending process. I'm not allowed to forget, but I can forgive.

> *The process gives me perspective, though, and it makes me appreciate everything my family has done every time it happens.*
>
> *In kind, it makes me appreciate you, too. Thanks for being honest enough with me to tell me how you felt; to tell me the truth as you saw it, because I know you saw it more clearly than anyone did. You changed me that day, and every day since, I've strived to be someone my parents would be proud of. Maybe in the details of my actions, they would scrutinize me and even be disappointed, but in the larger picture, I think they'd be proud of the person I'm changing into every day.*

If her parents are proud of her betrayal to me, then I've underestimated them all.

> *Every day we're apart, every day you don't speak to me, you lose a little bit of me. I'm afraid by the time you decide to let me back into your life, you won't know me at all. It's a silly fear, isn't it?*

Silly because you don't think it's true, or silly because you don't think I'll ever let you into my life again? If it's the latter, it's not silly at all, Liv.

> *I've never taken you for granted, Jon. I never will.*
>
> *We aren't finished.*
>
> *Ungrateful*

Not wanting to dwell on her letter, I go back into my brother's room.

"Hey, about our conversation?"

"Yeah?" he asks, putting the book down.

"It's about your dad. I was thinking…"

"About what?"

"I know your dad hasn't done a whole lot for you to make you proud to have him as a father." Will shakes his head. "I don't have high opinions of him, and I know I've voiced that to you more often than I should have."

"It's true, though."

"Regardless. Harboring the negative energy toward him doesn't help," I explain. "It hinders you from believing he could change, and although we haven't seen it yet, it doesn't mean that it won't happen."

"It won't."

"Well, when did he start talking to you about God?"

"He's talked about God for as long as I can remember. I think he only uses Him for forgiveness, you know? Like, he thinks he can get away with these things because he prays to God and confesses his sins. I know it says that in the Bible, but that's one reason I don't really believe in that. It seems false."

My brother keeps surprising me with his insight. I'm so happy I get to spend this time with him and learn more about him.

"Yeah," I admit softly. "But look at Mom. She's been sober for a few months now. That's change. That's change that I never thought would come, either, but it has. And I have to support her and keep trying to encourage her to work for her sobriety. It'll always be a struggle, but I think it's important to accept that people can change, and to forgive them for what they've done in the past. It could still happen for your dad. It may not be something you can realistically hope for, but you know what? If you believe in prayer, it's definitely something you can pray for. I always do."

"Thanks, Jon," he says.

"No problem," I respond, giving him an encouraging grin as I start to leave the room.

"Can you forgive Livvy? Can she change?" he asks me, surprising me once again. I stop with my back to him, trying to formulate an answer for him.

"I don't know, Will. I don't know that I believe in *her* anymore." When he doesn't respond, I turn around to see if he heard me.

"I believe in her, Jon. I can pray for her."

"Don't waste your prayers on her," I murmur quickly, spitefully.

"I think she made a mistake, that's all," he says.

"Have you been talking to her?" I ask, starting to get angry.

"No!" he says defensively. "But she loves you, Jon. I don't know what I believe about a whole lot of things, but I *do* believe that."

"Blind faith," I mumble, dismissing his declaration.

"You don't believe in blind faith," he reminds me. "I've seen factual evidence. So have you. If you love her, you'll forgive her."

"Then by the process of deduction, I guess I don't love her, because I won't forgive a girl who won't even apologize for what she did wrong."

"If she's not apologizing in all those letters, what's she doing?"

"Manipulating me," I tell him. "Which is probably all she's ever done."

"That's not true," Will says.

"You don't know her," I argue.

He frowns at me, and I think I've won the argument. I turn to leave once more.

"If you think she doesn't love you, Jon, then *you* don't know her. And if you say you don't love her, then I'm not sure I really know you."

I glare at him hard, but he stares right back at me. "Go read your book."

"Go read your letters," he calls after me as I return to my room. "Harboring negative energy toward her doesn't help!" he says loudly, provoking me to slam my door.

How dare he throw my own advice back at me!

INTERVENTION

After three days, I'm sad to say that I'm elated to see a letter from Livvy in the mailbox when I get home from work. As much as I want to detach myself from her, these notes are somehow tethering me to her in an unhealthy way. I know this, and still, I can't wait to read tonight's submission.

I love you, Jon.

When you see this one, you won't have a corresponding memory. I experienced this without you, and I never told you about it. I never told anyone about it. In fact, I've lived the past 14 months denying that it ever happened.

But it did.

When you broke up with me, I thought my life was over.

So she *does* know I broke up. That's good to know.

Do you remember when you told me the world didn't revolve around me? And I returned that I did know that, and I tried to explain that my world revolved around you?

I didn't realize she was talking about the breakup last year. That telephone call was so difficult. I was so mad, and she seemed clueless to the reasons behind my anger. The conversation ended horribly. I asked if she was finished ranting, she said *sure*, and I said goodbye. For hours, I'd thought about calling her back to end it differently–*better*–but I realized there's no good way to end things.

She'd tried to call me many times after that. She left me messages, but I deleted them without listening to them. I needed some perspective, and I knew I wouldn't get it if I had to listen to her crying or pleading with me.

This sounds familiar. For 11 letters–now 12–she's pled her case with me. Not in any way I would have anticipated. Her case consists of compelling memories of when we were good together, but still… she has yet to apologize.

After the fourth message I left you went unreturned, I raided our medicine cabinet and I locked myself in the bathroom while my parents had taken my brother to the zoo. I was supposed to go with them, but I told them I wasn't feeling well.

What, she's telling me she tried to kill herself? This is manipulation at its worst. *Come on, Livvy. Let it rest.*

I sat on the floor and poured out the contents of seven medicine bottles next to me. I had Trey's allergy pills, three over-the-counter pain killers, Mom's migraine meds, Hydrocodone Dad had left over from a knee injury and some anti-nausea tablets. I started crying as I sorted the pills into patterns, and the colors began to blur into captivating shapes. Every time I shuffled them around, attempting to make them lose their order and beauty, they formed another shape that inspired me. At first, I was angry, until I saw the gift that was being presented to me.

Remember the paintings I did in that time period? How they were unlike anything I'd ever done before? That's why.

I took what I saw in the bathroom that day when I was at my lowest point, and I painted.

I'd taken seven pills: one of each.

A lump grows in my throat. Manipulation or not, imagining a world without her is more than I want to think about. It's one thing for us to be apart. It's another thing for her family to be without her, for the world to miss out on the amazing talents she has. I read on hurriedly.

After two manic hours of painting, I felt sick to my stomach. I was sweating and my heart felt like it was going to burst from my body. I forced myself to throw up. My parents came home and found me in the bathroom. All evidence of the pills had been hidden away in my bathroom drawer, so they just thought it was a bug. I couldn't walk to my bed, and I thought about telling my parents what I'd done. My dad carried me to my room, and when he saw the painting, he cried. He called it poignant. Painful. Hopeless. He didn't call it beautiful.

I knew I had painted something special that day. I knew I wanted to do it again, and if that meant hitting rock bottom again another day and taking another handful of pills, well... that day, it made sense to me.

God, Liv. That never makes sense. That's never the answer, baby. I have to set the letter aside for a moment. Thank God she's okay. I can't even imagine what the last year of my life would have been like without her. I don't allow myself to try, picking up a sketch I'd started last night and studying it intently.

It's a sketch of her. I did it from memory, and it looks just like her. She's painting in the picture. I'd tried to imagine her with a natural smile and glow on her skin that I used to see so often, but I couldn't envision it in most scenarios. The only way I could capture that vibrancy was to put her behind a canvas with a brush in her hand. She was always happiest when she was painting. It has been so long since I saw that particular glow. That happiness. That aura. I missed Livvy the artist, and wondered if she'd ever get back to the thing she was most passionate about. I had hopes that it would be easy for her, but after seeing her first painting after months of taking a break, I was scared for her. The 'muppet' painting lacked substance.

Something awakens in me. Somewhere along the way, painting came second to me. I was what she was most passionate about... and I think that shift must have changed her. I made her happy, yes, but I was never able to bring out in her the satisfaction that painting brought out in her. I sigh involuntarily, letting that sink in. Did I do this to her? Was she so weak in knowing herself that she allowed me to steal what was most important to her?

Shit.

It took me a week to get up the courage to take more pills. The second time, I only took five. I didn't want to end up vomiting again, because I knew I'd raise suspicions in my parents. Again, the painting came easily. What I produced was even better than the first. Even I could see the differences in my work. There was a depth and mood that I'd never been able to capture before. I sat in a stupor for an hour after I completed the second one. At least I think it was an hour. I really don't know, because my parents struggled to wake me hours later. I'd collapsed on the floor.

Shit, Liv! I am not worth it. No man is worth it. I feel awful.

I was scared that time. The first time, my body was rejecting the medicines. The second time, it just tried to absorb them. I'm confident I would have woken up on my own at some point, but I wasn't sure I would be so lucky the next time.

There wasn't a next time.

I take a few calming breaths. The fact that she's sending me these letters lets me know she's okay. Or what if she's not? What if she wrote these long ago, and is having someone mail them? How do I know for certain that she's alright this time?

Something had changed in me, and I thought it was an altered state caused by pills that weren't meant for me, but when I produced the third and fourth paintings, I did them under the influence of water and breakfast cereal. That was it. And they were even better than the previous two. I was grateful. Instead of crediting the drugs, I knew that it was my understanding of a wider range of emotions that guided me to complete that series. I was without you for that period of time, but Jon, I couldn't have created them without you. You showed me how to feel things I'd never felt before—when we were together and when we were apart.

You don't realize what you're doing to me now, Jon. Your absence is palpable. It's everywhere. Your absence is always present and it hurts like nothing ever has.

And I'm okay. I'm painting.

We aren't finished.

Intervention

I read over this letter a few times, trying to figure out if this one is a cry for help. She says she's okay. I don't think I believe her, though. I'm sure on those days when she'd self-medicated, if her parents had asked her how she was, she probably would have said that she was okay. It worries me.

I pick up my phone and stare at her number programmed in it. I can't believe how far down my Recents list it is. It's been nearly five weeks since her graduation. We've surpassed the span of time of the last breakup now. Last time, though, I had the chance to see her while we were apart. I sat at the cafe across the street from her school twice, and I walked by the art room one Thursday night, too. I knew she was coping. I knew she had the support of her friends and Donna. That gave me peace of mind.

I don't want to talk to her now, but I do want to know if she truly is okay, or if she's just saying that to mask her true desperation. I peek out of my bedroom and look into my aunt's, seeing her cell phone on her dresser. Sneaking into her room, I pick it up and dial Livvy's number. As soon as it starts to ring, I panic, trying to figure out what I'll do when she picks up.

"Hello?" A sense of relief comes over me at the gentle lilt in her voice.

"Uhhh," I disguise myself poorly, struggling to think of a person I should ask for. "Cameron?" It's the name of a new guy on the site who I'm responsible for training.

"There's no one here by that name."

"Who are they asking for?" I hear someone else say in the background.

"Shhh, Finn!" she says quietly, urgently.

"Sorry, wrong number," I say quickly, hanging up before I hear any more.

PRIDE

The shopping mall parking lot is packed when we pull in. This is the first time in my life that I can remember my mom having health insurance for us. I was covered under my dad's while he was alive, but my brothers have never been covered, and I can remember very few doctors' visits while they were growing up. When they absolutely had to go, we would eat light for awhile, and sometimes I knew Mom had to borrow money from neighbors or friends.

Max and Will have never had their eyes checked, and its been years since I've been. I've agreed to come now because Max was scared he'd have to get glasses and wanted me, of all people, to help him pick frames that didn't make him "look like a nerd." I told him I wasn't really a good choice for that. "I'm a nerd, and I rather like it," I had told him.

"You don't look like one, though," he'd assured me. It makes me wonder what he thinks a nerd looks like, and why he's afraid of glasses.

While Max is in with the doctor, Will tries on pair after pair of sunglasses with the assistance of a girl who's probably still in high school, working a summer job. If he's trying to flirt, he needs a lot more practice at it. It's painful watching him, so I stop.

"I'm going to walk around the mall," my mother tells me, "and see if there are any good sales on shoes."

"You just bought them shoes," I remind her.

"For me," she says. "The women at work say I'll get more tips if I wear heels."

I glare at her, shaking my head. I hate to think that's true. Things like that make me despise our society. Tips should be given on service that exceeds expectations, not on the look of the waitress who serves. After many years of alcohol abuse and lack of attention to herself, my mom has lost the beauty of her younger years.

"I'll be back in an hour or so," she says. "If you're finished before then, go take them to get some ice cream next door. Do you need some money?"

"I've got it, Mom."

"Okay, Jonny."

Once she's gone, I open up my messenger bag, reaching for the laptop Livvy's parents had given me a year and a half ago. I'd stopped feeling guilty about it some time ago, but every time I see it, I'm reminded of the Holland's and their generosity. Instead of taking out my computer, I reach for the three letters I'd brought with me.

After hearing Finn's voice, I wasn't really in any mood to hear what Livvy had to say to me. When the first letter arrived, I debated throwing it in the trash before I'd even opened it. Eventually, I'd decided against it. When the other two followed, I just filed them away in the drawer with the rest of them.

Bored and curious, I compare the postmarks looking for the earliest one. Two of them were sent on consecutive days. The third was postmarked five days later. I tuck the latter two in my lap and open the first one.

I love you, Jon.

My right thumb feels the texture of the paint in the corner. The feel of it is strangely comforting to me. The word *pride* is etched into the bright green pigment. I don't like the word very much, because my own pride created dissidence between us on more than one occasion. I'd even fought with her father over it, and almost requested we take a break after that incident. It wasn't my proudest moment, ironically.

When I left my house for the banquet at Nate's Art Room, having not seen you in a month, I was beaming with pride. I had made it weeks on my own, without you, and I had created paintings that had been highly praised by everyone who saw them. I couldn't wait for my students and their parents to see my newest creations, and when I found out you were going to be there, I knew that you were the only audience that mattered. I didn't paint them for you. I painted them for me, but it was the love you'd shown me that allowed me to do so.

Seeing you admiring them from across the room, I wished I had somehow implanted cameras into the canvases so I could see your expression. What if they disappointed you? What if you weren't impressed, like everyone else was? The fear of a negative reaction from you made me feel weak, but then you turned around, and I saw something in your eyes that put me immediately at ease.

You were proud of me.

I was incredibly proud of her, and even more so when I saw her. I wasn't surprised when I turned around, though. Her final painting told me I would see a more confident young woman than the one I'd left the month before. It didn't lie. Although meek and somewhat afraid to approach me, she carried her head higher.

I hadn't realized how much I'd missed her, but seeing her reminded me of all the reasons I'd loved her in the first place. I wonder what it would do to me now. I wonder, if she walked into this eyeglasses shop right now, if I would remember why I loved her, or why I left her.

Something happened, though, after the banquet began. I honestly didn't think I could feel higher than I did when I walked into the Art Room that night, but then my dad started talking about you.

Jack's introduction of me was incredible. If ever I thought the man really didn't understand me, I couldn't deny in that moment that he had me figured out. He somehow found a way to separate the Jon Scott that wanted to steal his daughter from the Jon Scott who wanted to change the world someday. I was embarrassed by the amount of compliments bestowed upon me that night, but I, too, had some pride in myself when my award was given to me.

I'd told you before that my world revolved around you, and I truly believed it had. But at that very second, I saw myself as you had seen me a month earlier. The world did revolve around Livvy Holland, and that was the only world I'd ever lived in.

I wanted to leave that world that night, and I think I did.

I never really knew what it meant to feel such pride for someone else, but I was absolutely moved by what you'd done, and how far you'd gone to get there. I wanted to be by your side from then on, cheering you on and doing whatever I had to do in order to support your dreams. I think I became a little less selfish that night. I know I'm not selfless. Someday maybe I'll find enough humility to be that, but I know I'm still not selfless. I think you are, though.

We aren't finished.

Pride

I'd never thought of myself that way because most of the things I do have been self-serving. I want to elevate myself and my family. I don't want to be victims of a society that doesn't care for those less fortunate, so I've never let myself feel that way. Isn't doing things for my family still selfish? I'm not sure. All I know is that most of the things I've accomplished were done because I wanted to be a better person.

I guess if other people profited from that, it's not as selfish as it once seemed to me.

"You're reading again?" Will asks as he browses the selection of sunglasses on the counter next to me. What he's really saying is, "you're reading *her letters* again?"

"Just one," I admit, looking up. The salesgirl smiles at me with a quick flush of her cheeks. "Hi."

"Hi," she says back. "Is this your brother?"

"He is. Is he bothering you?"

"Oh, no!" she exclaims. Will kicks my shin. "You both have the same eyes, that's all."

We don't, but I don't think she's really had a chance to study mine yet.

"Did you pick those out?" I ask her, pointing to the shades my brother wears.

"No," she laughs. "I picked these over here."

She nods her head, requesting me to follow her. I stand abruptly, dropping all three of Livvy's letters to the floor. I hurry to gather them up and stuff them back in my bag, carrying it with me to another case.

"I'm Audrey," she says once we're across the store.

"Jon." I hold out my hand and shake hers. She's wearing simple pink nail polish. "Speaking of eyes, yours are beautiful." I've never seen irises like that. The outer two-thirds are variations of dark and light turquoise, but the inner circle surrounding her pupil is brown. "I'm not coming on to you, I swear," I say with a laugh. "It's just a fact."

"Thank you." She hands me a pair of RayBans, showing me what she'd selected for my brother.

"You're giving Will way too much credit. He's not cool enough for these."

"Are you?"

"Absolutely not," I laugh harder. "And I don't think I'll be getting sunglasses today. I'm fairly certain I'm in for a rude awakening. I'm not seeing details of things far away anymore," I admit. "Leaves, grass… those types of things."

"I think glasses would look good on you," she tells me.

"Yeah?" I ask. "What would you recommend?" I hoist my bag up on my shoulder and follow her to another display. She stands opposite me, putting her hand on my chin and angling my face to hers. She squints, carefully studying my face.

"I've got it," she says as she quickly walks away and takes a pair of glasses out of a different case. We both start laughing when I see them.

"Alright, alright." I put the frames on, knowing she's kidding. "What do you think?"

"Close," she giggles. "Let me find some other ones."

We go through about ten pairs of insanely horrible glasses that make me wonder who's designing them before actually settling on a simple pair.

"Those look really nice," Audrey says. "It's like you were always meant to wear them."

"You think?"

She shrugs her shoulders, hesitates, but then says something that catches me off guard. "I'd date you."

My jaw hangs open slightly for a few seconds as I think of a way to thank her. "Would you? Next Saturday, maybe?" My heart is racing all of a sudden.

She bites her lip as a grin spreads across her mouth. One of her teeth is slightly off-kilter, but it's cute. "Yeah," she agrees with a nod.

"Great."

"Great!" she says, scrawling down her phone number in neat penmanship on the back of some receipt paper.

"Jon?" Max calls to me from behind, sounding sad.

"What is it, buddy?" I turn around, still wearing the frames.

"I have to wear glasses to read," he says with a frown.

"That's not a bad thing, right Audrey?" I ask my new friend.

"Who's this?" she asks.

"This is my other brother, Max."

"Well, Max," she begins, "don't you want to look as handsome as your big brother? I mean, look at him. He's had these on for three minutes, and already he has a date."

"What about Livvy?" he asks.

This might be the most awkward silence of my life.

I look at Audrey tentatively. "It's my ex-girlfriend," I tell her quietly. "She's back in New York. We don't talk anymore, but my brother hasn't really figured that out yet."

"You're from New York?"

"Couldn't you tell?" I ask, a little relieved that she's shifted the topic away from Livvy.

"You don't hide your accent well," she says.

"I don't try."

"It's cool," she says. "And I think it's your turn to see the doctor, Jon."

"Will, can you watch Max while I get my eyes checked?"

"Yeah," he says reluctantly, giving me a dirty look when I walk past him. He holds on to my arm for a second, and waits for the sales girl to walk a few more steps away from us. "I was gonna ask her out."

"Will, come on," I plead with him. "She's too old for you."

"Says who?"

I roll my eyes and follow Audrey into the small room as she instructs me to take a seat.

After settling in, she leans in front of me, looking me in the eyes. "Can I have the frames back?" she says with a slight giggle.

"Oh, oh!" I laugh. "Is that what you want from me?"

"Yeah," she says, taking them off of me and smiling. "I'll keep them up front. I'll give you this, though." She hands me the small slip of paper with her number on it.

"Thank you. I'll use it."

"The doctor will be in shortly. I'll keep an eye on your brothers."

"Thanks, Audrey."

As I wait for the optician, I take out the next letter. After going over one sentence three times and not getting its meaning, I put the note away. My mind's not on Livvy anymore. Not right now, anyway, and I don't want to send it back there when I can focus on better things, future things that I'm looking forward to.

I hear Audrey's voice echoing in my head. She said she'd keep an eye on my brothers, and all of a sudden, I panic. Will's pissed that I asked her out, for sure. I wonder what he'll tell her about Livvy.

Where is the doctor?!

After the exam confirms that I need glasses, I return to the sales floor, dreading what awaits me. One angry brother, one that was on the verge of tears when I left him, and a girl who was going to go out with me until she had a few minutes alone with Max and Will.

Please, Will. Don't mess this up.

"So," I say, returning to Audrey.

"So," she counters. "Livvy?" she asks.

"My brother is an idiot," I tell her quickly. "I'm sorry, but I'm not seeing her anymore and I would really like to take you out on a nice date to thank you for helping me out today. Please don't let anything Will said change your mind."

"It was Max," she whispers. "Will isn't speaking to me anymore."

"Oh," I say, cringing. "Sorry about that."

"It's okay. But really? You were dating Livvy Holland?"

"I was, yes," I admit. "She's just a girl. Just a girl I was dating, but I'm not anymore."

Audrey nods her head.

"You'll still go out with me?" I ask.

"It's a little intimidating," she says, "but yes."

"Don't be intimidated. Seriously."

"Okay," she agrees, settling into a rolling chair. "Now sit down so I can take your measurements."

"Gotcha." After I take a seat opposite her, we decide on a burger place that her brother-in-law owns. Before I could even voice my apprehension about meeting anyone in her family on our first date, she tells me he doesn't actually work there anymore. I like the idea of the casual joint, and really look forward to getting to know her better.

"So. I work until six on Saturday. You can pick up your glasses first, and then take me out. How does that sound?"

"Perfect," I tell her, genuinely looking forward to next weekend.

It's not for an hour after we all get home that I realize I haven't finished Livvy's other two letters from the past week. They don't seem as urgent to me right now.

PRINCESS

As my family settles in to a night in front of the television, I glance around the room and smile. Sometimes it feels like I'm stuck inside some 1950's family sitcom. I'm not used to life without dysfunction. I don't miss it, but I do like a *little* excitement. A *little* unpredictability. A little *edge* on things. I need it to remind myself that this may all be temporary. I don't expect my mother to stay sober. It's sad, but true.

"What are you reading, Jonny?" she asks. I glance down at the letter tucked inside a text I'd bought at the bookstore at the mall.

"The Pluto Files," I lie. I look over at Will who's next to me on the couch, and fully expect him to rat me out and confess that I'm reading her letters. He hadn't spoken to me since we left the eyeglasses shop. I assume he's still bitter about my interaction with Audrey. I never thought I'd be competing with my brother for a girl–not because he's not a worthy opponent. I never thought I'd be approaching any girl other than Livvy Holland… and while he had met her multiple times–even though she'd been to our apartment–he still sees her as some sort of celebrity, clearly out of his realm.

"Is it something I'd like?" Mom asks.

"It's about the celestial body Pluto, and how it got demoted to a dwarf planet."

"So, no, then?"

I grin at her. "Probably not."

"Can I read it when I'm finished with this?" Will asks, his finger holding his page in the large Douglas Adams book. He's more than halfway through the five-book set, and that makes me proud.

"Sure thing," I tell him. "The book, I mean," I say softly just to him, just in case he happened to be referring to the letter from Livvy that I know he's seen.

"I know," he whispers, opening his book back up and putting on some headphones to block out the noise of the show Max had wanted to watch. Not having the luxury of headphones for most of my youth, I learned how to tune out my surroundings, no extra tools needed.

I love you, Jon.

I've always been my dad's little princess.

His Contessa. From the first time I met him until the night of your prom.

I distinctly remember that you chose to remain his princess that night as well, Liv.

Dressing up in my gown and seeing you in a tux that most guys at my own prom couldn't afford made me feel like a queen. I became someone else that night, as if I was acting in a play or something. I felt myself stand taller. When we danced, I imagined us in a cavernous castle instead of the small ballroom we were actually in. When I remember back to that night, all of my memories are distorted and exaggerated. You couldn't convince me today that we didn't take a magical carriage to and from the prom. I'm certain we did.

You couldn't convince me today that you and I weren't the only people in the world that night. I'm certain we were.

Thank you for making me feel special.

We aren't finished.

Princess

To me, it's strange to see the letter end like that, as if she's signing her name as Princess. It's just her normal painted theme of the letter though… not a signature.

But still, she was never *my* princess, no matter how much she looked like one that night. I don't want to remember that night, but allowing my brain to linger for just two seconds on the way her hairstyle brought out the beautiful curve of her neck, there's no going back.

I close my eyes–part of my strategy for closing myself off from the room, the world–and remember every perfect detail of my perfect date on that perfect night.

No, it *didn't* end as I'd planned, but it was still perfect.

Her dress was floor-length–modest, and yet sexy at the same time. It was fitted around her torso, showing off her beautiful hourglass figure. Her ample breasts held the strapless gown easily, and with poise that mimicked her father's, she made it look easy to wear. Other girls who had on strapless dresses–not similar to Liv's, because there were none like hers among the girls of my high school–fidgeted with their outfits all night, hoisting their dresses up in a very unseemly manor, as if they didn't belong in their clothes.

Olivia didn't have that problem. It was as if her dress was made for her. I suspect it was.

While we were dancing, and colored spotlights raced around the room, her necklace sparkled and shone in such prismatic ways that I knew the stones she wore were real diamonds. It wasn't a flashy necklace, by any means–until we stepped out on the dance floor. If I trusted any of the guys I went to school with–and really, there were few–I became leery of everyone after that. Livvy would never understand desperation to the depths that poorer people do. While a diamond necklace might be standard attire at her private school's prom, I was sure few had ever graced the necks of any girls from my public school.

And of course, none could wear them like she could.

She also shimmered around her midsection, a tiny crystal belt highlighting her slender waist. My eyes danced back and forth from her neck to her waist to her feet, which were also adorned with rhinestones, and which I could see peek out from her dress every so often.

But then, there was the tiara placed neatly on her head, securing her long hair away from her face. *The chastity belt.* I laugh a little to myself, remembering. It was likely the main reason she wouldn't go back to the hotel with me that night. I should have been cursing that one beautiful adornment, that accessory, that gift from her father, but because I could tell it made her feel like the princess she was to him, I could do nothing but admire it. She radiated happiness, confidence, and love. Love that may have initially been for her father, but I had worked hard to earn her love, and it was obvious she loved me that night. Even though over the weeks leading up to prom, I'd had moments of clarity where I thought we had been rushing things, as she danced with her head on my chest, I accepted that I wanted to be the next one to buy her a sparkling jewel. I wanted her to wear something that said she was mine.

The promise ring wasn't enough. It was all I could do then, and it would have to do for the time being. Last summer, I started researching diamonds for her. It was not a long-lived pursuit, simply because I knew it would be awhile before I could buy something that suited her. She deserved an engagement ring befitting of her own beauty. I learned about color and clarity and knew exactly what grade to look for when the time came.

But one year ago seems like eons ago. I'm grateful I never bought her anything. She deserves nothing from me now. Someone else can have that burden of finding a ring large enough for her presumptuous ego...

...her beautifully stunning, I'll-never-find-anyone-quite-like-her, presumptuous ego.

I leave my family, telling them good night as I head to my room to read. Before I do that, though, I turn on my computer and look at one of the tabloid sites that had often featured pictures of Olivia. I'm saddened to see her on the home page. In one of the candids, the stress of the situation peeks through the hair she uses to shield her face from the photographers. She still is the most beautiful girl I've ever laid eyes on.

Damn it, Liv. Why did you do this to us?

WAITING

After thirty minutes of internet stalking, I've seen all I can stand of Olivia. Of course I stumbled across the video of her kiss with Finn. In high-definition, too. That was it. It was enough to make me shut down the computer, but with the image of her from my prom night still fresh in my mind, I decide to go ahead and read the other letter I received this week. A compulsion makes me read it. Saving them up for one night did allow my attention to focus elsewhere during the week. I think it was a good idea, and I'll try to do it again next week. I should have other things to focus on, too, with my date with Audrey coming up next weekend.

I peek at the subject at the bottom first.

Waiting...

If you're waiting for a response from me, it's not coming.

I couldn't mail the letter I'd already written to her. It was too honest, and I was too angry. I could anticipate her reaction, and it made my heart hurt. Remembering her 'Intervention' letter, I wasn't sure she'd be able to handle it. Until I can stand to own up to pain that I cause her–knowing she'll hurt because of something I said–I can't send that letter. She'll have to keep waiting for it. Maybe it'll never come. Maybe I'll move quickly from pain to indifference, and never have to worry about sending that letter or composing a new one.

I love you, Jon.

I can't stop thinking about prom. From the time I wrote my last letter, it's still the only thing on my mind.

I'm glad we waited, and didn't have sex on your prom night. Looking back, it was the perfect evening to me, and I wouldn't have wanted any one thing to mar the night. Maybe nothing would have happened to cause any negative feelings, but it's a chance I'm glad we didn't take.

I didn't need the extra time, though, to prepare myself for being with you. I think that—from the first time we said we loved each other—I knew that I wanted to be with you.

Maybe even earlier than that. I'd had a crush on you for awhile. I think, a few years earlier, I wanted us to be married. Sex really hadn't crossed my mind yet, but the end result was the same.

You and I would be together in some spiritual way that would bind us for life.

I put the letter aside for a second and think about that statement. I'm not sure she understands the concept of being bound to another person. Maybe she does, though, because I can see that there will always be a connection to Livvy Holland. No matter how much she's hurt me, there will always be something that draws me to her. I will spend my life deciding whether or not to go with it or to fight it. She's captivating. She's prepossessing. She's all-consuming sometimes.

I still have a choice to make. It's the same choice I'd already made, but I'm faced with the decision once more. I chose her to be my love, my life. I did that once. Could I do it a second time, knowing that her reciprocal choice may not be binding this time either?

She's bound to me. I'm bound to her already. The choice now would be to break those ties that bind us.

The decision to be with you wasn't really conscious, I don't think. It's not like I ever made a list that showed all the pros and cons of choosing you as my first. Maybe I should have.

Maybe I should now.

Pros: I love you. (That's a given.) You are respectful. You're incredibly smart. You have more ambition than the entire island of Manhattan. You're creative and inventive. You're patient. I'll never forget how you walked me home to ask my dad if you could go out on a date with me. You confessed you'd asked him a year earlier, and he told you no. You're persistent. You are literally the most attractive guy I've ever met... and I honestly think that even if you were physically unattractive to the rest of the world, I would still be so drawn to you that all of your traits would be the exact ones I was searching for.

Wow. She's good.

You're nice to just about everyone. And when you see others not doing that, you call them on it. You're brave. You defend me.

You were forgiving.

I catch the change in her verb tense. Past tense: *were*.

I'm not sure you are anymore, though. It's not fair for me to ask you to be, but it's what I want. It's what I need.

Forgiveness starts with an apology, Liv! Have you lost your mind?

You love me. Please tell me you still do. Or please tell me that you will again.

Cons: n/a

I feel uncomfortable now. She still holds me up on some pedestal. I am far from perfect. My flaws may not be as numerous as hers, but I have flaws.

Regardless, I'm thankful she's not listing them here. If she did, though, maybe it would make it easier for me to move on.

I gave you all any woman can give to the man she loves, Jon. While the decision wasn't conscious to me, my soul delivered me to you. It thought you were right for me—that you would be the one to give this woman all that a man can give to her.

It still believes that.

So do I.

We aren't finished.

Waiting...

Maybe we should have waited longer. After living through the past few months, I wonder if she *was* old enough to make the decision–conscious or not. She doesn't mention she regrets anything. I know I don't. But a year from now, after we've both moved on, will that change? Maybe she'll meet the *one* guy she can be faithful to, and wish she had saved herself for him.

Maybe the next woman I end up with will wish I hadn't been with–now–three other women. It's doubtful, but... it could happen. I just don't want to be that guy who was with ten or 20 other women before finding the one to commit his life to. Every girl I sleep with until I find her could be an entry on a list, a list of my history that grows every time I make a misstep, a list that I would be ashamed of bringing into the next relationship.

She was supposed to be *it* for me. I was okay with my short list of two girls. I can explain them away with grief, loneliness and curiosity.

Could I ever explain away Olivia Holland?

Can I?

INDEPENDENCE

The following Friday, I stare at the only letter that came this week. I'm disappointed there aren't more, and remaining determined to save all the ones I received to read at once–determined to only devote one evening to Livvy–I'd honestly wanted to read more from her. I'd wanted to give her more than the two minutes it would take to read the short note and the hour it would take me to digest the memory, think about how she's doing, and get over the lingering sadness.

My work week had flown by, though, anticipating my date with Audrey. I'm nervous. It's scary, looking ahead to spending time with someone I really don't know. I knew Olivia so well. She was comfortable and safe. There are so many unknowns about this new girl.

We'd talked on the phone twice during the week, so I'd learned a few things. She's a senior in high school. She's a self-proclaimed geek who apparently likes nerdy guys. She's been forthcoming with compliments, telling me she was immediately interested in me when I walked into her store with my messenger bag; more so when I sat down and began reading letters; and she had no doubts she had to do more than sell me glasses when she saw me in the pair we picked out together.

She was quick to explain that I didn't fit her typical nerdy guy expectation. "Your physique says jock," she had told me. "Your confidence says class president. The interaction with your brothers says boy next door."

I assured her that she was dead-on if her initial assessment of me was that I was nerdy. I went on to brag about my scholarships, about the books I've been reading this summer, and about my need to know something about everything.

Her favorite subject in school is history. Any type. She loves the past and thinks she was supposed to be born decades ago. "I should have been a flapper," she said. I could see it, too, when I remember what she looked like. Her shoulder-length hair fell in neat waves, framing her soft features and fair skin. She had been wearing apple red lipstick, but even still, nothing could take the attention away from her incredible eyes.

I decide to read Livvy's letter before calling Audrey to confirm our plans. Settling against firm pillows on my bed, I kick off my shoes and get comfortable.

I love you, Jon.

I got choked up when you addressed your fellow students as the valedictorian of your class. It was partly my mother's fault.

But–honestly–likely all *my* mother's fault.

You talked about finally being free of so many societal constraints. There was no more micromanaging. No more bells to warn you where you need to be at what time. No more parents to scold you for bad grades, or for coming home after curfew. You were now responsible for doing everything on your own, and that was exciting to you. That's what you said.

I remember that part of the speech, and I remember seeing my brothers and uncle and Livvy and Jack and Emi and Trey all seated together. There was also an empty seat next to Will. It had been empty for the entire ceremony. I'd been watching Livvy's mother, who had maintained eye contact with me and made it easier to address the swelling crowd in the hot gymnasium. After expressing my feelings of freedom, Emi looked down the aisle at that empty seat. She first squeezed Livvy's hand and looked into her daughter's eyes. Then she blinked and fixed her gaze back on mine. These pale green eyes were watering, but she smiled at me encouragingly. I saw her pity, though.

For three seconds, I forgot what was next in my speech and had to refer to the notecard I had crumpled in my left hand.

How could my mother not come to my graduation? To this day, she still hasn't apologized. I haven't yet taken the opportunity to address all of her shortcomings in my life. I know there's a step in her program that requires her to make amends. I think it's step nine… and I don't guess she's there yet.

At some point, my expectations of my mother lowered to such a point that she was rarely a disappointment. I think this lessened feelings of resentment. I realized that I didn't need her. I knew I was self-sufficient. That being said, I also knew how much my brothers *did* need her, *did* rely on her. Of all of her children, I think Will is the one she needs to make amends with first. He rarely speaks to her. He treats her disrespectfully.

Max is too young to know of her downfall and still thinks she's the best mom in the world.

I'm too old to need her motherly guidance anymore.

You took your own experience out of the equation for your speech, didn't you? You never needed bells to remind you to get to class. You knew the importance of school. You never had the watchful eye of a parent to make sure you were behaving like you should, studying like you should, staying out of trouble.

You've always been free of the societal constraints. You've always been independent. But now the rest of the world could accept those traits in you. Now the rest of the world was forced to accept that you were the adult your mom forced you to be years earlier.

My dad was forced to accept it, too, and I think he did. Begrudgingly, but he did. I'm not sure we ever had the opportunity to know the child in you, Jon. You were always too responsible, too careful, too smart. Maybe I shouldn't say "too much." You were just more than you ever should have had to be at your age.

When Mom looked at me as you stood on that stage, I realized all that you never had, and I started to cry. It wasn't just the material things, the ones that I took for granted. Your mom probably never stood at your door telling you to get out of bed after snoozing your alarm too many times. She never told you to pick up your things, and clean your room, did she? Did she ever sit with you and feed you soup when you were sick? Did she even take you to the doctor?

Damn it, Liv. My eyes swell with tears, something they should have done at my graduation, but I fought them with all the strength I had that day. I remained strong, wearing a mask I'd been forced to put on the first time my mother let us all down. I always tried to cover for her in front of Will and Max. I tried to make up for the things she didn't do. I tried to give my brothers what she couldn't.

Does it feel different to be free because you choose to be, and not because you have to be?

It absolutely does.

Because I hate being free because I have to be. I've never had to feel that until now.

I know she's talking about me. I never should have been a constraint to her anyway. I never wanted to be the thing that held her back. Does she not see that's what I'd become? Is she not even trying to find herself in this time I've given her?

And to be completely honest, I didn't choose this freedom right now. I feel just as forced into it as she does. *It's your fault, Livvy. You* did *choose this for us. I'm just upholding your wishes–the wishes that came out in your actions the day you graduated. The wishes that came out when you kissed someone other than me.*

We aren't finished.

Independence

Speaking of independence... I fold the letter back up and place it safely in the drawer where all her other letters reside.

I am free of her. I have options. I call Audrey, not allowing myself the time to dwell on the feelings of anger and resentment I now feel for the *two* women in my life who've let me down.

"Hello, Jon," she says warmly.

"Hi, Audrey. How was work tonight?"

"Fun. No one wants to buy glasses on Friday nights," she admits. "Drunk people tend to come in from the restaurant next door and take pictures of themselves in ugly frames. I become a part time photographer on Fridays."

"That does sound fun."

"How was your work?"

"Great," I tell her. "The weather was perfect. There was a nice breeze all day. I never realized how much of nature I was missing by being in Manhattan."

"I want to go to New York someday. That place seems as foreign to me as Utah must be to you."

"You should go. It's incredible. It's so diverse."

"So, what was your job today?" she asks.

"I installed a staircase today. Well, just the framework... and then some other odds and ends. Ceiling details.... stuff like that."

"It's so cool to think of you building a home for someone. Think of how many lives you'll affect with this one summer job."

"A handful," I say. "I hope to make much more of an impact in the future. I want to affect hundreds... *thousands* of people."

"Well, don't take this experience for granted. Focus on the mom and dad who will bring home their first baby and decorate the room you built with blue or pink. They'll appreciate the way the light streams through the window you installed."

"I think the architects are to be thanked for that."

"Well, I think what you're doing is romantic."

"I never thought of manual labor as romantic," I laugh. "Trust me, no one would want to be romantic with a man who just spent 10 hours putting up walls in a house."

"Do you always argue this much?" she teases me.

"Only when I'm right."

"So never."

"Is that how we're starting off?" I say in jest.

She huffs quietly into the phone. "I'm looking forward to tomorrow."

"I am, too. I've been so excited to get these glasses..."

"Well, that's just rude," she says.

"...so I can see you better," I add. "I bet you're even prettier with 20/20 vision."

"Well, that's just... *sweet*," she amends her earlier response. "I hope you're not disappointed."

"Trust me, I won't be. We're going to have a good time. I've enjoyed every minute of talking to you on the phone this week."

"Me, too. So... six, right? We'll have burgers and shakes... and fun."

"I am very much in need of all of that," I tell her. "I'll be there a little early for the glasses."

"Perfect. I'll see you tomorrow! Have a good day tomorrow."

"You, too, Audrey."

COMMENCEMENT

Killing time before heading off to the mall, I decide to read one of the two letters I got in the mail today. I check the postmarks to make sure I choose the earlier one, wanting to take in all that she writes in order.

I breeze past the first line, not wanting to read it. I don't want to hear how she feels about me hours before I spend the night on a date with a different girl.

Then why am I reading this at all?

"Knock knock," my mother says from outside my room.

"Hey, Mom."

"Would you like to see your handsome little brother?"

"Yeah," I say, putting my things aside and sitting up for a better view of Max with his new glasses. He's sucking on a milkshake, and the left lens already has a smear of chocolate ice cream on it. "Max, they look great. What do you think?"

"I'm smart," he says.

"He's only supposed to wear them to read," Mom reminds me. "He won't take them off."

"Buddy, that looks like a headache waiting to happen. Between the glasses and a brain freeze... come over here." He stands beside my bed, allowing me to remove his new frames. He blinks his eyes a few times as they adjust to his normal vision. I clean the dirty lens with a t-shirt and a bit of water from a cup on my table. "Did you get a case with these?"

My mother digs into her purse and produces a small case with a Superman logo on it.

"Clever," I laugh. "I bet Clark Kent had the same case." I put the glasses inside and secure it shut. "If you wear these all the time, you're gonna make yourself dizzy. Only wear them when you need them."

"But they make things look weird," he says. "It's funny."

"It'll be funny until you trip walking down some stairs or straight into a wall... and they aren't cheap, Max. You need to take good care of them. Okay?"

"Okay." He immediately takes them back out of the case and puts them back on.

"What did your brother just tell you?" Mom asks.

"I'm gonna go read!" he argues, grabbing the unopened letter and running out of my room.

"Is that from Livvy?" My mother looks away as she asks.

"Yeah," I say, getting up. I'm not afraid he'll read something he's not supposed to. He's not used to cursive writing, and most of Livvy's letters are written with such emotion that her penmanship seems rushed, and messy.

"I met Audrey," she adds, moving aside to let me out of my room.

"Yeah?" I don't really want to discuss any of the women in my life with her.

"I didn't realize you had a date tonight."

"I do."

"She was so good with Max. Really sweet. And so pretty."

"I'm glad you approve," I say, not really caring one way or another. I find my brother hidden on the side of his bed in the next room. The slurping of his milkshake gives him away. When I hold my palm out, he returns the letter to me unopened. "Glasses?"

He hands me those, as well, after putting them in the case. "Are you gonna kiss Audrey?"

"Max, come on." I turn around to see my mother sitting on Will's bed. I blush, embarrassed by his question. I'd been wondering that myself all day. "Some things aren't any of your business. Livvy's letter? None of your business. What I do tonight? None of your business."

"What are you doing tonight?" Will asks, joining us in the room but lingering in the doorway.

102

"Going out with Audrey from the glasses place. Remember?"

"You gonna have sex with her?"

"Will!" my mother tries to reprimand him, but he just rolls his eyes, ignoring her.

"You still mad at me for asking her out?" I challenge him.

"What's sex?" Max asks.

Mom takes that as her queue to leave, but urges my youngest brother to go with her. "He didn't say sex," she lies. "Will said Chex... like the cereal. 'You gonna have *Chex* with her?' That's what he said."

"You can't have Chex at night! It's for breakfast," he says before he's yanked from the room.

"Actually, you can have Chex any time of the day, Max!" I yell after them, happy that my mother may actually need to step in and teach my brother something. *It's about time.*

"Whatever!" she calls back to me. "I would hope that you would wait to have Chex with this girl!"

"Whatever," I whisper to myself, glaring at Will. "What was that about? If you have something to say to me, do it. Don't try to make things uncomfortable in front of Mom... don't think I don't know what you're doing when you take your long showers. I was your age once. I could point that out to her, if you really want to compete."

"Shut up." We both take a seat on opposite beds.

"You can't be mad at me for this. She's the one who made the suggestion to go out on a date, Will."

"You didn't have to ask her out."

"I'm interested in her. There's no reason why I shouldn't take her out..."

"I liked her."

"I promise you, Will, if she was some seventeen-year-old girl that you'd known for any reasonable amount of time, I would never have asked her out. Even though that's an incredibly unrealistic expectation for you to think some senior in high school is going to want to go out with you, I know there are some lines you don't cross. But face it, she showed you some sunglasses for five minutes."

"But she said I was cute!"

"Her job is to sell glasses, Will. She gets paid to make people feel better about themselves." I know by saying that, I'm not doing a lot of good for his self confidence. "The truth hurts," I add. "But I'm sure she wasn't lying... you favor me, and she's interested in me, so... of course she thinks you're cute."

"You didn't even let me have a chance."

"You want to come with us tonight? We'll fight it out. We'll make her pick. I mean, is that what you want?"

"I just don't want you to go with her."

"What... if you can't be happy, I shouldn't be happy, either? That's pretty selfish."

"She can't make you happy," he says. "You can't be happy without Livvy."

"Livvy is not my girlfriend anymore."

"But you're still holding her letter in your hand."

"That isn't relevant to this conversation, Will. I can't just *not read* what she writes to me. That would be rude..."

"Why do you care if it's rude, after what she did?"

"Because that's just who I am. I need closure, and I'm hoping one of these letters will give me that. It just hasn't come yet."

"Do you think Audrey can give you closure?"

"I'd be lying if I said that I hadn't hoped for her to provide something like that."

We sit for a minute or two, letting the tension settle. He picks up his book and lies back on his bed, opening it up to the dog-eared page. I start to go back to my room.

"Don't have Chex with her tonight, okay?"

I laugh to myself and turn around to answer sincerely. "That thought hadn't even crossed my mind–"

"Good–"

"Until you brought it up," I say, adding a mischievous grin. "Not a bad idea."

"Jon!" he whines.

"I'm not like that, Will, and I hope you know that by now. I hardly know her."

He nods, accepting of my response.

In my room, the other letter from Livvy sits where I left it on my bed. I skip the first line again.

> I think I was the happiest I'd ever been at the beginning of last summer. You were exhilarated to be out of school. You were enjoying your internship. I was loving to be homework-free for a few months. I couldn't wait to spend my free time creating some new pieces.
>
> But you consumed me. When we weren't together, we'd spend hours on the phone talking about hypotheticals. What would I do if you were always poor. (Stay by your side and give you anything you needed.) What would you do if I went blind? (Mix my paints and point me in the direction of my canvas.) We were invincible. It was bliss. I was high on you—on us—and I didn't think anyone could ever bring me down.
>
> And then Granna died.
>
> We only had a few weeks together before everything changed.

Even as it was all happening, I kept thinking it was too good to be true. I kept waiting for something to happen.

I didn't think Donna's death would have the effect on us that it did. In the end, it was this moment that turned Livvy's world upside down and sent her on a downward spiral of self-sabotage. She stopped painting. She put herself in difficult situations. She chose the wrong college. She kissed someone other than me–not once, but twice.

> *Now I go through my own hypotheticals. How would things have gone for us last year if Granna hadn't died?*
>
> *We'd made a physical commitment to each other, and it was wonderful. You loved me. I loved you.*
>
> *I would have kept painting, and that evens me out, Jon. It's my natural anti-depressant, but I didn't know that at the time. I didn't know it would be so easy to turn my mood around. I am whole when I paint. I'm a mere fraction of myself when I don't.*
>
> *I understand how I'd changed in your eyes. I couldn't see it then, but I do now.*
>
> *I am sorry, Jon.*

My heartbeat pauses for a second. There's the apology. I read over that sentence a few more times before allowing my eyes to wander back to the top of the page.

> *I love you, Jon.*

After staring at the period for a few seconds, I return to the letter, wondering what she's sorry for.

> *I am sorry for expecting you to treat me the same when I'd become someone else. After all, you hadn't made that commitment to me, for better or worse.*

I hate that she thinks I wouldn't have stood by her as she tried to get better just because we weren't married. She was all there was to me, and I was returning to her that day of her graduation with a compromise. I knew leaving her wasn't the answer. She drove me away.

She doesn't know this, though. She knows nothing about my willingness to cancel my plans this summer with my family and to sacrifice my time with my brothers for her. She'll never know that now.

But I don't want her to think I'm capricious like that. I never was. It wasn't her inability to be herself that made me leave. It was because she so easily and readily shared such an intimate moment with someone other than me.

It was bad, Jon, I know it. I'm feeling more like myself these days than I have in a long time. When I'm painting, it's as invigorating as any time I spent with you.

Reading between the lines, she's telling me she doesn't need me now.

As much as I want that for her, it's hard to accept.

Need. Want.

"What do you need?" I remember her asking me that night in the hotel. I'd answered her with loving actions, but few words.

"What do you want?" I'd asked her.

"I want you to take off your shirt," she'd answered softly, placing my fingers on the buttons of my shirt that she had asked to wear before we made love the first time that night. It was cool to the touch, moistened with the sweat of our bodies. She propped herself up, putting her weight on each arm as I removed the sleeves. Her breasts beckoned to be touched, fondled and kissed, but she told me she wanted me to kiss them anyway.

I'd wanted her to tell me in words what she wanted. I wanted her to be okay with her desires. This night was a breakthrough for us.

"*I want you to go down on me,*" she had said in a voice that was coated in need. It was the sexiest thing she'd ever said to me: the words, the voice, the panting breaths that lingered. "*I want you to make me come again.*"

"*Like that?*" I'd asked as I traced my tongue down her nude body.

"*Please,*" she begged me.

"*Then I need to come with you, baby,*" I'd told her. "*I need you to tell me when you're close, because I already am, and I need you, Olivia.*"

When I break free from the memory, I'm fanning myself with her letter. Had I finished reading it?

But I still want you.

I'm not surprised that those were the next words.

We aren't finished.

Commencement

Beginning? And here I thought we were at the end.

All I know is that I'm *very* worked up now, and ready to get *something* started. I look at the alarm clock on the desk. Five-thirty. Time to go pick up Audrey.

I tell Will goodbye on my way past his room, but get no response from him.

"Where are the keys, Mom?" I ask when I get to the kitchen. We've been sharing an old car of my aunt's this summer. Since the bus runs to her restaurant, she rarely needs it, but had been driving my brother around all day.

As she hands them to me, she says, "Look what you've started."

I look at Max, who's sitting at the dinner table eating a bowl of cereal.

"I was actually thinking Chex sounded pretty good tonight, too." I only glance briefly to see her expression, and she looks a little shocked. "With a little sugar. Don't wait up."

She doesn't respond.

I wear the glasses I'd picked up at Audrey's shop on our date. Everything looks sharper, clearer, more beautiful–including my companion. She, too, is wearing glasses tonight, and the lenses make her eyes appear even larger. Looking into them is like looking at a whole other species of human being. I've just never seen anything like them.

The restaurant is very casual with a rustic feel. The ceiling has exposed pipes, and an entire wall looks like a string of garage doors made of windows. Half of them are open to expose us to the warm, dry air. We sit down in a booth by the exposed area. I breathe in deeply, filling my lungs with unfamiliar smells of nature.

"What does New York City smell like?" Audrey asks.

"It depends," I tell her. "Car exhaust. The sweat of other cultures. Garbage on hot summer mornings. Beer-soaked partiers."

"None of that's going to get me to vacation there…"

"Hot dogs?" I continue, trying to be stereotypical before I get serious, thinking of the smells that I love about my city. "Hundreds of flowers lined up outside a local market. Italian food. Cuban food. Indian food. Every kind of food you ever imagined. Brisk winter, sometimes with the scent of burning wood mixed in. Rain. The smell of rain lingers, and there's something soothing, cleansing about it. A woman's perfume that produces nostalgia for memories you never even had."

She raises her eye lids. I stare impolitely, but I can't help it. "That was romantic."

"What?"

"…nostalgia for memories you never even had."

"I'm just describing what I've felt," I explain with a smile. "But I'll tell you, none of the burger joints smell as good as this one."

"Surrre…"

"It's, like, charred meat and fresh mountain air. It's safe to say I've never smelled anything like this before."

"I'm glad I could give you a new experience," she says. "I was worried… you seem so worldly already."

"I'm not. I may know a lot, yes, but I'd never left the east coast until last Thanksgiving when I came here to visit my family for the first time. This makes me want to travel."

"Well, good. Maybe you'll come back to visit us."

"Of course," I say, handing her one of the two menus on the table. She sets it back down immediately. "I guess you have your favorites here?"

"You have to get a milkshake." I remember my brother from earlier, and can't get Chex out of my head. "They serve adult milkshakes." She points to a special section on the menu.

"I doubt they will serve *us* adult milkshakes."

"No, but they make non-alcoholic versions. They'd go out of business if they didn't… Utah…"

109

Virgin.

I feel a pang in the pit of my stomach. I'm sure I'm blushing right now, just thinking back to that awkward conversation between Livvy and me on our first date. I know better than to segue into that topic. Lesson learned.

"Sounds great."

"We can each get a different flavor and share. I never can decide between the Orange Cream Pop one or the Chocolate Mint one."

"Then both it is."

After we place our orders, Audrey goes right into some questions for me.

"How did your family get separated from you?" she asks.

"My mother is a recovering alcoholic. She had to leave the city to escape her demons... and my aunt in Provo is the only relative she has. She kind of flunked out of rehab, but she's doing better now."

"And your dad?"

"He passed away a few years ago," I admit. "Cancer."

"I'm sorry to hear that."

"It's okay. Thank you." I hold her hand across the table. It looked lonely, sitting there. She smiles.

"That explains why you seemed so fatherly to your brothers at the store."

"Did I?" I ask.

"You care. Yes. Most nineteen-year-old guys I know care about two things: beer and getting laid. Granted, there isn't a whole lot to do around here."

"I guess that's probably pretty universal, wherever guys live... except if they have an alcoholic mom, and then the beer becomes less of a priority." I realize after the fact how suggestive my statement is.

She raises her eyelids again. I'm not sorry for that.

"Your brothers must miss having a father, but they're lucky they have you."

"They do, I'm sure, but that's because their father's in prison. They have the same dad... not the same as mine."

"That's sad."

"Some men don't deserve the title of 'father,' and he's one of them. Sperm donor's fine. But I don't mind being a good role model for Will and Max. They're both good kids."

"Sounds like they have you to thank for that." I'd never really thought of it that way, but I don't think that's an untrue statement.

I smile, proud. "Thanks."

A waiter interrupts, delivering our food and shakes together.

"When'd you get a job here?" Audrey asks the young boy.

"It's just for the summer," he says. "Mom and Dad told me I had to save to buy a car next year."

"We'll give you a good tip," she winks at him. "Jon, this is my cousin, Neil. Neil, this is… some random guy who picked me up at work."

"Pretty much," I say, holding my hand out to shake his. "Nice to meet you."

"Let me know if you need anything. I'll refill your shakes for free."

"Thanks," Audrey says.

Thanks to Livvy, I feel insecure meeting her cousin. "Are you and Neil close?"

"Nah," she answers. "We go to the same church and see each other on holidays."

I nod my head. "Any siblings?" I take a bite of my hamburger.

"I had a sister," she says simply. I swallow my food and look up at her, showing her my interest in hearing more.

"Had?" I prod her.

"She had a freak bike accident… broke her neck. She was ten. It's been five years this year," she adds.

"Still, I'm very sorry to hear that."

"Yeah. The hospital bills pretty much broke my family, financially… but I'm happy to say that my parents are still married. They say most parents divorce over money or after losing a child, but mine have beat the odds on both counts.

"So, needless to say, I'm no Livvy Holland."

I drop my french fry at the mention of her name. "I'm not sure I'm following…"

111

"I have no money… just in case you're looking for that. I mean, you have a good job and go to Columbia. I don't have money like that."

I wipe my hands on a napkin and hold my hand out to her across the table. "I'm Jon Scott." She shakes my hand. "We haven't met. I come from a rough neighborhood in Harlem, and spent the first 18 years of my life living in a cramped two bedroom apartment with no climate control and thrift store clothes. I met Livvy through a non-profit founded by her parents for poor kids. The scholarships for Columbia? They're full scholarships. I couldn't afford to go if I had to pay a dime on my own."

"So this burger place is okay for a first date?"

"Are you kidding? I feel at home here. No pretenses. It's nice. And I don't have to work overtime to pay for it." I tell her this for assurance, but I always felt like I belonged where Livvy was… she always made sure I felt welcomed. My own self-confidence didn't hurt in those situations, either.

"I was so worried."

"You shouldn't have been. It's perfect."

She grins widely and picks up both of the shakes, handing me one of them. "To thrift store clothes," she says, tugging on the collar of her shirt.

I don't bother to tell her I don't wear them anymore. I would, if I needed to. "To thrift store clothes. And to a date between two poor kids, being themselves." I feel a little disingenuous when I say it.

"Thanks, Jon."

ANTIO

Refreshing.

That's how I would describe my date, if anyone were to ask. It was easy, like I was just hanging out with a friend. I didn't feel on guard. I didn't feel like I had to be on my best behavior in case someone was watching us. I wasn't constantly looking around for photographers or other onlookers who might threaten my girlfriend.

I felt less responsible. I felt carefree.

I felt like it wasn't really a date at all, actually. Or is this what it's supposed to be like? It felt so unlike anything I've ever done with Livvy. There was no rapid heart rate before I picked her up, no self-conscious thoughts for things I said that didn't come out as intended, and there was no kiss to signify the end of the night.

I miss that. All of it.

Audrey's beautiful and sweet and humble and funny. All of those traits are ones that I like. Her background makes her very relatable to me, and she has ambitions to rise above her current situation, too. We have a lot in common.

I try to focus on the patterns in the ceiling, realizing seconds later that my new glasses may help with the cause. I grab them from the night stand and put them on, returning back to the warmth of my bed and gazing upwards, studying the space between the molded circles. They're just uneven enough to show that they were done by hand, and not some machine.

Staring too long, the lines start to converge, and I have to blink again to focus. I take my glasses off, giving my eyes a rest. I'd had a headache when I got home last night, which Audrey told me might happen as my vision adjusts. Returning my glasses to the table beside the bed, I open the drawer and pull out the second letter I received from Livvy yesterday. It never even occurred to me to read it last night when I got home.

I love you, Jon.

Goodbye to my childhood.

I'd had a good run. I was lucky enough to have two parents who loved me, a brother who looked up to me, and a plethora of family members who had no problem welcoming an outsider into their lives. I'd learned about love in all its facets. Love between friends, between family members, and thanks to my parents' excessive affection, I saw how it was supposed to be between lovers.

It's not something I like to think about, but I guess I'd rather that than the alternative. I'm happy Mom and Dad are so in love with one another. It's important, I think, that one of us could see a good example... otherwise, what were we aiming for?

I can't deny that I also admired what Emi and Jack shared between them. There was no doubt of their love for each other. You could *feel* their passion. It was something I had never actually seen in any other couple. She's right. Something like their love *was* the goal... with one exception: sometimes I felt Emi was too reliant on Jack.

If Livvy's trying to model after her parents, I can see why she turned to me so drastically over the last year. That's a huge dose of clarity… right there.

I sigh, returning to the letter. I glance at the bottom.

Αντίο.

It's Greek. *Literally*. I get up, adjusting my shorts before I leave my room to find my laptop. I stop by the bathroom first to avoid an awkward situation with my aunt, if she's home. It's quiet in the rest of the house.

The box of Chex is still on the kitchen table when I walk in. I laugh a little, grabbing the box and returning it to the pantry. The back door opens suddenly, startling me.

"You're up?" my mom asks.

"Yeah. What time is it?" I squint, looking at the clock across the room.

"Where are your glasses?"

"Eleven?" I ask, not really ignoring her question but proving that I don't need them as badly as she thinks I do. She nods. "Where's everyone else?"

"Patty and Will went to church."

"Really?"

"Yes. I would have gone, but Max has a fever."

"I'm surprised Will went with her."

"He told me this morning he's exploring his spirituality. He wants to know his *options*."

I grin at her.

"Remind you of anyone?"

"And I turned out okay…"

"You're better than okay."

"Is Max in bed? I think I'll go check on him."

"Jonny, he's fine," she says. "I was just with him."

"It's no problem–"

"Jonny!" she interrupts. "You can just be their brother this summer. You don't need to be their parent. I'm here now. One-hundred percent present."

I look at her and smile, hopeful.

"Have a seat," she suggests, sitting in one of the six chairs at the table.

Feeling strange in the setting, just in my boxers, I start to leave the kitchen. "I should put some clothes on–"

"You're my son, Jon. I changed your diapers when you were a baby. It's okay to be yourself around me. Please sit down. We haven't had the chance to talk."

115

I'd had a feeling this was coming. "Mom, I'm sorry about the sex talk last night. I didn't mean to raise Max's curiosity, and I didn't mean to make you worry about me."

"I don't worry about you," she says. "You're smarter than that... and I deserve a little bit of a hard time from you, I know. I spent years not worrying about anything."

"Nah, Mom. People make mistakes, I know that. I'm just happy this sobriety thing is working out. I'm happy you're working on your relationship with Will and Max. They need you."

Her eyes water. "I know you don't."

"I need you to be better for them. I need to know they're taken care of when they're so far from me... so I need you for that."

"Do you hate me?"

I tap my fingers on the table, trying to think of the right response. I shake my head before speaking. "I don't hate anyone, Mom. I hate *situations*. I hate that I couldn't really have friends for the last few years because you weren't there to make sure Will went to his games or Max got to school on time. I hate that Will is old enough to know about you, but not old enough to have empathy for you. That's going to make things difficult for both of you. I hate that you were incoherent the morning Max lost his first tooth, because he was so brave, and so proud. I hate that you didn't come to my graduation."

"It's one of the biggest regrets of my life, Jonny. I am so sorry I missed that. You should have had a mother in that audience, giving you the confidence to speak."

"I did," I tell her honestly. "She just wasn't *my* mom. There are always people to help pick up the slack... and yeah, I think I've done enough of that for you to last a lifetime."

"I know you have. That's why I want you to just have fun this summer. I don't know why you had to get a job, why you couldn't just relax with us..."

"Because I have a life in Manhattan to go back to, Mom. You know how expensive it is in the city. The scholarships pay for classes, and books, and the dorm, but there are other things I'm liable for... and I see what Dad left me slowly dwindling away, and I need to start saving. This is good money I'm making. And I'm learning things, too. It's beneficial in a lot of ways."

"But it occupies so much of your time."

"I need it right now, Mom. I need a distraction."

"From Livvy?"

I nod my head.

"Is it over?"

"Yeah." The sound barely escapes my lips.

"I'm sorry, Jonny. I know how much you cared for her."

"Cared, yes." Care. I still care for her. No one else needs to know that.

"Maybe you should take a break from her letters."

"Yes, my rational mind tells me that every second of the day, Mom. But they're magnetic. If I don't read them, I feel them pulling at me, wanting my attention. It consumes me sometimes. The letters are her. They're all that's left, and I'm hoping they bring me closure."

"Has she apologized?"

"She said she was sorry for the first time yesterday... and I'm still unsure what she was apologizing for. The notes are cryptic... they're like a puzzle I haven't pieced together yet. Which is probably why I can't stop reading them. You know I have to know... *everything*."

"Just like your father."

"Mom, I do *not* regret the role I've played in Will and Max's lives. Honestly, I wouldn't have it any other way. I'm proud of them."

"I'm proud of you for giving such good guidance when no one else in their lives could."

"It's because of them that I know I can do great things, Mom. They've taught me to be a leader. It's a lesson I may never have learned had we not gone through what we have. And I still want to be involved in their lives, even two thousand miles away."

"But I want you to be their brother."

"I am. That's what I am to them. It's all I could ever be."

"Well, I'll save you from the parental responsibilities as much as I can. I guess it's about time to have the sex talk with Will."

"No, Mom. We've had the talk."

She starts to cry quickly, looking ashamed.

"Shhhh, it's okay. First of all, fifteen's way too late for the talk. Maybe things have changed since you were that age… but he started asking hard questions when he was twelve."

"How can a sixteen-year-old give his brother good sex advice?"

"Books, the internet, and… well, and experience."

"I should have been there for you."

"I promise you, Mom, I wouldn't have wanted to talk to you… and I know Will wouldn't, either. They need a father for that. I'm lucky that Dad taught me the basics before he died. I figured the rest out… and learned about love with Livvy. That was one thing he knew nothing about."

"Well… Max is too young, right?"

"I think so… but you have to answer their questions honestly. That's how you'll earn their trust. It's not so bad when you stick to the facts and only provide responses to exactly what they ask. Details are not needed… until they hit about fourteen.

"And at that point, I'd just send Max my way. Or, hell, Will can probably help by then."

"You'll both be gone by the time Max is that age."

"I'll always be a phone call away. And maybe we'll live closer then… do you think you'll ever come back to the city?"

"When I feel well enough, I want to. It's all I know, and the pace here… I'm sure it's good for me, but I'm bored."

"As long as the things you do to kill your boredom are good for you, Mom."

"There you go, talking like a parent again."

"It's hard to see *you* as a parent, Mom. I don't know that I'll ever see you as that, in the traditional sense. I think you and I need to figure out where we fit into each others' lives. I'm never going to be coming to you for advice, or money, or emotional support. I've sought that from other people for too many years. Yeah, you lost my trust."

She cries again, but nods her head.

"But I still love you."

Sobs erupt now, and cause me to tear up, too. I move to the chair next to her and give her a hug. She holds me tightly, and I allow her to do that for as long as she needs to.

"Did you want me to make you some breakfast?" she asks.

"No, June Cleaver," I tease her. "It's my day to make lunch, remember?"

"Can I help?"

"I was going to make spaghetti and a salad. It'll be quick and easy; I've got it. I still need to shower and stuff."

"Let me help," she pleads, holding onto my arm.

"Sure, Mom." I kiss her on the cheek before getting up and grabbing my computer. "Give me a half hour."

Back in my room, I return to the letter, ready to translate.

Αντίο

Goodbye.

Shit.

I can't read anymore right now.

Will stayed in Mom's room all afternoon reading, clearly avoiding me because of my date and avoiding Max because of his illness. The house was too quiet for me, and I decided to go to a nearby state park and hike. One of my co-workers had recommended the trail to me when I had asked him for date ideas. It's hard to plan in a city that's completely foreign to me.

I hiked for five hours. Even though I know I'm in the best shape of my life, every muscle is aching when I arrive home. I know I overexerted myself. I needed to. I wanted to wear myself out so that sleep comes easily–and hopefully deep sleep, free from dreams of a girl whose words just don't coincide with recent actions. I wish I could trust her. If I could trust her again, I would probably love her again.

No, I would probably *commit to* her again. I can't *love* her again, because I haven't stopped loving her yet.

When I finally lie down for the night, I glance at my desk. Livvy's letter is out next to my phone, which suddenly lights up with a picture of Audrey.

I pick up the phone, my thumb primed to swipe the screen and answer the call, but I decline it instead. I set my alarm for 5AM and take off my glasses, physically exhausted. It doesn't help me sleep, though. My mind is still racing, wondering what the rest of the letter says. Maybe it's the last one I'll get. Should I hold on to it; savor it?

I'll never sleep if I don't find out what she's written. I skim through what I've already read and continue on.

> In the light of the moon, wrapped up in a blanket and the warmth of your arms, I said goodbye to my childhood on June 13th in a hotel room on the most beautiful island in the universe.
>
> You'd left yours behind long ago, and showed no fear or regrets. I never doubted the decision to take that step with you.
>
> Even when I fantasized about how it should happen, I never envisioned how perfect it all was. And the best part of it was that nothing was planned. What made it so perfect? You.
>
> I realize now that where or when didn't matter—but the where didn't hurt. Better than the scenery or the cool breeze was the fact that we were alone. Self-sufficient. Reliant only on each other. It was an incredible feeling.

I smile, remembering that I felt the exact same way that night. We took a car to a beachside restaurant. No one knew where we were, exactly. We stayed out late, strolling in the surf without checking in with anyone. I think she was stalling because she was nervous; I was taking my time, committing every second to memory. No one in Mykonos knew us. No one cared what we were up to. No one cared about us, and yet, I knew there would never be another woman in the world that *I* would care about as much as I cared about Olivia Holland.

I'd wondered if I would have to coax her or convince her, because I wanted to take advantage of this once in a lifetime opportunity with her. I didn't, though. Once we got back to the room, no words were needed to tell each other we were both ready. Desire radiated from her body. Love streamed from her eyes. She was timid and nervous, but still carried herself with the self-confidence only Livvy could pull off. She knew she was beautiful. She knew she was talented. She knew she was smart, and clever, and funny, and the desire of all men.

But I was the only man that mattered to her. Her shyness came only from the unfamiliarity of the situation. It had nothing to do with me. I loved her for who she was. She knew that, too. I assured her I always would.

I'm afraid I always will. I shake off the notion. Time heals all wounds, right?

Making love to her was like nothing I'd ever experienced. Sex with love is completely different from sex absent of love. I remember thinking that was just something cliché people said, but no. It was absolutely true... which was a relief to me. I wanted us to share something special. Only in that moment did I regret not waiting for her, but the regret was short-lived, because that night was not like those other nights, with those other girls.

I thought nothing of them while we were in Mykonos, and really hadn't given either of them much thought since then. I gave Livvy everything I had. In fact, I felt like a virgin myself that night. The strange excitement deep in my gut was the same feeling I felt the first time I kissed her. I imagine it's the same feeling you get when you step off a cliff into an unknown abyss. I had no idea what would come from that first kiss. I had no idea how our first night as lovers would change us. That was the great unknown.

I'm still not sure how it changed us, because what happened the next morning would change her in other ways.

I don't want to think about that right now. I want to return to that night, when the only certainty we needed was the constant love for each other.

The beach near the villas was quieter than I thought we'd find on an island known for its tourism. There were only a few restaurants and bars, spaced out, leaving a lot of sand and rocks for us to explore.

"What time is our flight back tomorrow?"

"Two o'clock," she said softly as she curled her toes in the sand, letting the clear water wash up on her bare feet. She looked across the expanse of the ocean at the white orb in the night sky. I kicked off my shoes, rolled up my slacks, and stood behind her. Wrapping my arms around her loosely, I kissed her cheek, then her neck, and she held my hands in hers.

"I can't wait to see this water in daylight. We could go for a swim in the morning."

"Maybe," she said. "If that's what you really want to do."

"You may be sick of me," I told her.

"Never."

"Maybe we should swim tonight, before we settle in," I'd suggested.

"You're crazy, right?"

"Some of us have never been in water like this," I reminded her. "This is nothing like the Atlantic."

"Jon, we can barely see what's in the water!"

"What water?" I asked, picking her up swiftly in my arms and wading further into the surf, toward the moon.

"Jon!" she shrieked. "You have no idea how deep it is!"

"Well, I know you can swim, so…" I kept walking, my pants now soaked to the knee. There were other swimmers wading nearby, so I didn't think we'd be in danger of finding ourselves in deep water. She put her arms around my neck and held on tight. I stopped walking to kiss her.

"There could be sharks," she whispered, her eyes sparkling in the light.

"Sharks here are harmless," I assured her. I took a few more steps, stopping just before she'd have any chance of getting water on her clothes.

"You're crazy. Definitely," she said.

"So no swimming tonight?"

"No," she laughed. "Even though you're halfway there."

"It's pretty cold. But that's the only reason I'm not dropping you in the ocean and stripping down to my boxers."

"Take me back to land, please. And remind me what the signs of hypothermia are… slurred speech, right? Poor decision making? See you've already got it," she teased me.

"Lethargy is a symptom," I told her, propping her up and turning back around. "And I am as alive and awake as I've ever been right now. I feel like I could swim out to the horizon and back."

"The horizon never ends, you know…" I stopped walking again and kissed her once more. Her kisses were slow and deep.

"I do know. I am so excited about tonight, Olivia… a shark attack couldn't stop me."

"Good, because there's a fin in the water."

I jerked, pretending like I was going to drop her as I took quick steps toward the shore, playing along. She screamed before laughing wildly, finally squirming out of my tight grasp when the water was at my ankles.

The flowing skirt she had worn skimmed the surf. I wrapped my arms around her as our lips met again. Her fingernails dug into my back through my shirts before she untucked them both and her palms met my skin. She massaged deeply. It felt so good. I caressed her face in my hands, holding her to me and kissing her until she needed a breath. We gasped for the same salty air, and as she tilted her head back, I kissed her neck again, then the top of her breast next to the necklace I'd given her. My final destination–at the time, there in the water, under the stars–was her ear. As soon as my tongue began to fondle her lobe in between kisses, she sighed my name, her hands moving to my hair.

"I love you." We'd said it at the same exact time. We both pulled away, smiling at each other.

"I'm wet," she said to me softly, blinking slowly, not taking her gaze from mine.

There was no mistaking what my interpretation of her statement was. Even though her dress had been dampened by the ocean water, I heard something else.

She knew what I was thinking. She didn't correct me. Instead, she took my hand and led me out of the ocean to our shoes.

We returned to the restaurant to call a car, and didn't have to wait long for our ride. I was not ashamed that foreplay started in the backseat of that car. She didn't stop me from putting my hand up her shirt, beneath her bra. I made sure my body was positioned between her and the rearview mirror, ensuring that her passion and beauty was visible to and adored by me and me alone. She couldn't contain audible sighs as we touched and kissed, though. I was jealous the driver could hear the sweet sounds she made. Wanting her to myself, I backed off and reduced our actions to kissing only. She followed my lead. She let me lead the rest of the night, and I never took that responsibility for granted.

When she came to bed with me, I was as turned on as I'd ever been. I kept hearing her tell me she was wet. I'd seen her body fully exposed in front of me, and had in fact touched and kissed her for longer than any guy could be expected to maintain sanity within the small confines of the steamy shower in which we bathed... especially with her touching me, too.

I get up and lock my door, permitting myself to get carried away in the memory.

In that bed in Mykonos, regardless of the images that were then permanently seared on my retinas (and I know I'll never forget for the rest of my life), I put on a perfectly patient facade. Rushing her wasn't an option, nor was it what I wanted. I felt pretty certain that night was going to be the highlight of my life. I wanted to make it last.

I'd nearly forgotten that her uncle had stopped by while Olivia was drying off and getting dressed.

"Can I give you a tip?" he'd said quietly from the hallway. I was only wearing a towel, and my hair was still dripping moisture down my chest, so I only cracked the door for him.

"I'm not sure... can you?" I'd joked with him. He smiled briefly, but then became very somber.

"Don't do anything you'll regret. Don't try to talk her into anything. If you have to convince her to do something, then it started out as a no... and you should take it as that."

It was good advice, but unnecessary to me. While I had never been so eloquent about it, that was how I'd always treated her.

I thanked her before we started, but it wasn't a conscious thought. I was that grateful. It's one thing for any girl to choose a guy as her first; it's another thing for that girl to be Olivia Holland, the crowned jewel of New York City, the most talented artist I'd ever met, the luckiest girl alive–chosen in so many ways–and the most beautiful sight my eyes had ever beheld.

I actually thought for a split second that it felt too good to be true. *Was it?*

The pacing of our night's events was perfect… it was constant, always moving toward the goal of making love, using just the right amount of restraint, and teasing just enough to make her plead with me, to ask for more. I loved hearing the need in her voice, and every time she requested more, I knew it was what she wanted. I never *had* to ask if things were okay–although I did a few times when I was certain she was experiencing something wholly new. She couldn't hide the tiny flashes of hesitancy from me. I knew and loved all of her expressions.

I kissed her everywhere, not ignoring any skin except the bottoms of her feet and the backs of her knees. Just dragging my fingers along either nearly got me a bloody nose. I had no idea she was so ticklish. She apologized profusely both times, and we both laughed about it.

Although my hands skimmed the edges of her panties, they didn't venture beneath the garment until she pulled one of my hands with hers. It was the signal I'd been waiting for. It wasn't the first time I'd touched her like that, but in all the past times, there were hard limits; we knew we weren't going all the way then. I was only trying to pleasure her those other times, and while that was also my intent in Mykonos, I knew I also needed to prepare her for what was to come.

I suggested a way for her to communicate with me if she needed me to slow down. She only used the hand gesture a few times, and it was mainly in this area of foreplay. I learned what she could tolerate, what she liked, and she also introduced me to a few more expressions. I felt like I had found a key to another world. Those moments were precious and surprising.

After bringing her to orgasm slowly, I removed her panties and slipped on a condom. She was still exhaling euphoric breaths with her eyes closed, but I felt it was the moment. I climbed onto her slackened body, careful to keep most of my weight off her. As I took her hand in mine, she opened her eyes. I watched her as I kissed her, maintaining eye contact as I slid into her in one quick but gentle thrust. Her grip on my hand only pulsed for a second, although her eyes closed tightly for a few seconds longer.

"Oh wow," she finally breathed. "That's... whoa." She shook her head.

"No?" I asked quickly for clarification.

"No, yes!" she corrected. "Just..." She looked perplexed.

"What does it feel like?" We carried on the soft conversation as I slowly moved out, then in, then out again.

"There are no words. How do you describe a color you've never seen before?"

"Leave it to you to bring art into this. And I describe a new color by comparing it to others."

"It feels very different than your finger, then," she said. I laughed, grateful. I'd be afraid if it felt the same. "It's... tight."

"Damn right it is," I agreed. I kissed her sweetly.

"It's... tension," she said, still trying to describe it. When she said it, her muscles tensed down there, and I almost lost it. I thrust a little harder than I'd intended, but stopped myself, breathing out quickly. "It kind of hurts?"

"Yeah?" I asked, easing up.

"But it's pain like I've never felt either... so don't stop. I don't feel like you're hurting me."

"Okay, good."

"It... *fits*," she said. The way she had said it was cute, like she was surprised by that. She pulled my head to hers to kiss me again. It started slow, but as her kisses became more needy, so did my desire for her. Things sped up naturally. When I would open my eyes, hers were still squeezed shut. I knew the first time may not be pleasurable for her... I just didn't want to hurt her. I wanted to make sure we had a second time, third, hundredth... but deep down I was hopeful she'd be moaning in ecstasy. I accepted that wasn't happening this time. When Livvy finally released my hand, I felt her right leg wrap around my back first, followed quickly by her left one. She was limber, and she held me tightly against her. We had a rhythm then, and I pressed my torso to hers. I put my arms beneath her shoulders and gripped the bedsheets as she hugged me into her with her arms.

As my muscles tensed and the stirring deep within me began, I shifted slightly, and as if she knew what I needed, she slid her hands down my back and further, pulling me into her. That was it. Restraint was no longer an option.

I continued until orgasm. I held my breath, extending the feeling, letting it fill every part of me. I was on fire. She scraped her nails up my back, adding kindling to the flame. It felt like an explosion. I was sure that the atoms that made up my body were scattered throughout the room. It took a few seconds for my eyes to see; for my ears to hear.

"Fuck," I grunted, breathing heavily. "Oh, god… fuck."

"What's wrong?" she said loudly. At least it *seemed* loud, but it was more likely that my ears were just insanely sensitive to sound. Everything was sensitive.

"No, nothing's wrong, baby," I said between breaths. "Was so good," I sighed. Exhausted, the remaining tensed muscles let go, and I hoped my weight wasn't too much for her. My lips next to her neck already, I placed gentle kisses where they could reach with little other exertion. I needed a minute to regroup. "I love you, Olivia."

She squirmed beneath me, faintly, but I stilled her with what little strength I had left. Not wanting to leave the comforting warmth of her body, I lifted my torso just slightly to give her some breathing room.

"Just a minute." I leaned down on one arm and moved the other hand to her thigh, holding her next to me. "You okay?"

"I'm fine," she said.

"This is where I belong, Liv."

She smiled, proud. I pulled out as I went in for more kisses. After a minute or two, I rolled over on my back, pulling her on top of me. She kissed my chest while I lay nearly comatose. It took an inordinate amount of energy to put my hands on her hips, squeezing just enough to get her attention.

She looked up at me, her hair obscuring one eye from me. She looked so sexy, climbing up to kiss my lips.

"Hey," I whispered. "I need to go take care of something… but when I come back, I want you, just like this." I nodded my head, making sure she was on board.

"I'll be waiting."

I open my eyes to find myself alone in a twin bed. Mykonos is a memory that's not as distant as it should be because I keep allowing myself to revisit that night… but Utah is where I find myself.

As in my memory, I make my way to the bathroom to clean up, happy to find the house dark and all bedroom doors closed.

Back in my room, I pick up her letter from the floor.

I regret nothing, Jon. A child flew into Mykonos, but a woman left there the next morning. I felt cherished and loved and... sexy... desired. I had no problem saying goodbye to that girl.

I felt honored to share that perfect night with you.

Never tell me you regret that. Even if you do, and that's the one thing you want to say to me, please never do.

Don't ruin my perfect night. I'm afraid I'll never have another, and I need to own that; to keep that.

We aren't finished.

Αντίο

A relieved sigh escapes when I realize she wasn't telling *me* goodbye. I'd worried about that. Maybe I'm not as ready for closure as I thought I was… because this letter brought back so much that I love about her.

LOSS

A mistake caused by a plumbing contractor creates extra work for us at the beginning of the week. I had to work until 8:30 Monday night, until we lost sunlight. We needed to work later, but couldn't get the industrial lights needed to assist us. Today, they got the lights, and at 10PM, we're finally caught back up and released from the site.

Mom needed the car, so I had secured a ride with another guy on site.

"We're gonna go grab some beers, kid. You in?" Zeke asks me.

"Yeah," I answer with no hesitation, knowing I'm at his mercy and don't have a choice anyway. I don't want to make a big deal out of it. On a regular day, I might try to walk home, but it's late and I am beyond exhausted.

Grabbing the backpack I bought with my first paycheck, I follow him to his pickup.

"This place is always swarming with BYU chicks." *Chicks*. Nice. "They don't all drink, but they're not prudes, either. I've taken a few home. I always bring a spare shirt with me and clean up in the bathroom a little."

I glance down at my work shirt, which is covered in dirt and sweat. I can't imagine why any girl would want to go home with me, looking like this.

"I got a few spares in the backseat. I got you covered."

"Thanks."

"College. Man," he says. "What a waste of time, right? We make good money. It's hard work, but we get a good workout and don't have to take orders from some idiot boss in the next cubicle. And Shane's not a bad foreman."

"No, he's great," I say, bypassing his comments about college. "He gives good direction… and really knows his stuff."

"Do a good job, and he'll hire you for his next job. This is my fourth."

129

"That's awesome… but I'm going back to New York at the end of the summer. I'm only in Utah to visit my younger brothers. They moved here with my mother last November."

"New York, huh? I thought you sounded like a Yank." I laugh a little. "You get lots of tail there in New York?"

I'm totally rethinking my decision to go with Zeke. We've talked for hours on the worksite, but looking back, it was mainly about work or his ex-wife. I'm hoping there are others there that I will be able to relate to a little more.

"I can't say that I do," I admit. "Not much luck with the ladies," I add, trying to be social.

"They must be picky bitches up there. You're not bad lookin'. I bet you won't be able to keep them off you tonight." I bite my tongue, hating when people refer to women as *bitches* in such a casual manner. I nod my head to answer him. "Unless you're a shy one. After a few beers, you'll loosen up."

"Probably." We pull up at the same time as five of our other coworkers. Zeke throws three folded t-shirts at me, telling me to pick one. One advertises Coors Light; the other two are concert shirts for country musicians. I almost think the filthy work shirt is better than these, but I decide on the beer shirt, knowing that if anyone asked me about either of the singers on the shirts, I wouldn't be able to sustain a conversation.

The shirt is a little snug around my biceps and chest, but I like my new physique and appreciate the fact that it helps to show off what I've worked to maintain. *Surely I won't be able to keep them off me tonight.* Oh, sarcasm. Save my sanity tonight.

As a group of us approaches the door, I see a sign that says "21 & up only." I hadn't really considered that I wouldn't be able to get in. I grab my wallet subtly, taking out my ID from the front pocket and tucking it into a hidden one. I'll just take my chances and tell them I lost my license.

I let the other guys go in before me. A girl stops me at the door, asking to see identification. "I would love to show you that, but I've lost it…"

"Leslie, he's with us," Zeke says.

"You twenty-one?" she asks.

"Twenty-three," I lie. She nods, letting me pass through and into the bar. I meet everyone at the three tables they've pushed together.

"First round's on me," I hear from behind me. Shane waves at the bartender on his way to our group.

"Shaaaane," the other men all call out in unison. I smile at my boss. He knows how old I am. He'd voiced concern about my age, saying that other nineteen-year-olds he'd hired weren't very reliable. I'd sworn to him that I was different. Aside from the day I went home with strep, I hadn't missed any work.

He pats me on the back and takes the seat next to me. "Hey, kid. Glad you came out with us."

"Yeah," I say, unable to keep eye contact. A waitress named Amy goes around the table, guessing what each man wants to drink. *I guess they come here often.* When she gets to me, she looks perplexed.

"You're new."

"I am."

"Am I to assume you want a Coors Light?" she asks, glancing down at my shirt.

"Uhhh, yeah," I answer, not knowing what else I'd order.

"I'm not letting you drink that," she says. "I'll bring you something better."

I nod, knowing that I won't have a taste for anything she brings me. The smell of beer brings back bad memories, and I never liked any of the ones I'd snuck from the fridge when I was younger and curious. When Mom asked where her beers were, she'd normally be so wasted that I could convince her she was the one who'd consumed them.

A few minutes later, Amy sets down eight shot glasses in the middle of our group. I grab one, following the lead of everyone else.

"Good job, guys," Shane says as he holds up his drink. "Don't get too crazy tonight. We're starting at six in the morning."

There's a collective groan at the table before everyone drinks. I follow suit, cringing as I feel the burn. It tastes *horrible*.

"Never had a snake bite before?" Cameron asks me.

"No. Yikes," I say, wishing I had some water to wash the taste out of my mouth.

"It's an acquired taste," Shane says. "Another round?" he asks.

"I'll pass. I'll be right back. I need to wash up," I say as I stand, grabbing my back pack and heading to the side of the bar where I saw a sign for the restrooms.

Immediately, I splash cold water on my face and run it through my hair. I repeat once the water is warmed up, still feeling grimy and disgusting. Maybe it would be better if I was in a different frame of mind.

Over our lunch break today, I'd taken my sandwich to a spot in the woods nearby the house. It was grassy, a natural clearing between the trees. I sat on the perimeter, next to a group of beautiful, full silver lindens. I'd never seen this type of tree before, but I'd decided that if I ever had a house outside of Manhattan, I'd like to plant some of them. I'd taken one of the unique leaves home a few weeks ago to identify the tree. The white underside of the leaf made it easy to find online.

As I sat alone, I'd taken out the letter I found on my desk when I got home last night. I was tired and in need of sleep, so I saved it for today. Wanting to know what I was getting myself into, I read the inscription at the bottom first.

Loss

Loss of innocence? Was it another letter about sex, because Sunday's letter had stuck with me. If I was talking to Livvy, I know she'd be happy to know that her *Goodbye* letter broke through. It affected me as I'm sure she hoped it would.

I looked up the page as two leaves flitted past my face in a swift breeze. I had seen the word Granna, and I knew it would be about a different kind of loss. One of permanence and sadness. I finished eating before I continued with her letter.

I love you, Jon.

I couldn't help but think how much I missed her.

I don't remember the day my mother died. I think God made it happen before memories form because he knew I wasn't ready to accept the death of someone close to me—and not just that, likely the only person I was close to.

I am not sure why God had to take Granna last year, though, because as I've proven, I still wasn't ready to accept death. It all happened so suddenly. I didn't have a chance to send her a get well card, or to make a special trip to church one Sunday to say a prayer for her. I never had the chance to cry with her, or to reminisce about the life she lead and the impact she had on mine.

I knew what she meant. I'd had the same feelings when she was taken from us. There was no time to mourn with her; only time to mourn after she was gone.

I wonder, though… is it better to know ahead of time, or worse? I wish I could ask you that, because you've known both. I know Granna was well admired by you. I know you felt the same loss I did. But you knew your dad was dying… was it better then?

I wasn't sure I could answer her question. I'd had no regrets about the weeks leading up to my father's death. I had plenty of time to come to terms with his illness, and I thought I was ready to let him go. The cancer had spread rapidly; it was declared terminal by the time they found it, so he refused treatment and was in a lot of pain. I didn't want to see him suffer anymore.

But once he was gone, I saw what I was left with, and it terrified me.

I knew my dad grew to care about me. When I was a baby, when my parents were still married, he had very little to do with me, but as I started growing up and asking questions–insightful ones, for my age–he saw himself in me, and he wanted to teach me things. Had I depended on words or emotions to see how much he cared, I never would have known, but his actions spoke volumes. He'd take me to the park, to museums, to exhibitions that were far too advanced for me to understand. But I tried to keep up, and asked him enough questions to create a strong foundation for learning later.

He was proud of me. He knew what inspired me. With him out of the picture, I had a mother who knew nothing about me, had nothing to teach me, and–based on her actions–didn't care about me. She told me she loved me, but it never felt like she did.

With the realization that she was the only parent left for me, I felt more immense loss than I'd felt in the time Dad suffered through his illness. It was a shock to my system, just as it was when we learned that Donna had died.

So I don't know what I would tell Livvy if she'd asked me that question in person. Loss is loss, whether you have time to prepare or not. I think of the Band-Aid analogy. It hurts less to rip them off suddenly. We all know and accept it.

But humans are not Band-Aids. No matter how they go–fast or slow– removing them still exposes a wound and requires extra time and care to heal. I'm still not healed from my father's death, because there are still things I need. There's one thing I still need. I need to feel loved. I need someone's actions to reflect that they care about me. It's so lacking in my life, that I feel hollow at times.

Spending the afternoon thinking back about all that my life is missing has enshrouded me in pity, and I can't shake the mood, even after a snake bite– whatever the hell that nasty thing was.

I hadn't finished reading the letter, and take it out of my bag before leaving the bathroom. I tuck it into my back pocket and return to the table where a bottle is waiting for me. *Magic Hat*. Why not?

The guys are mid-conversation with a few girls. These must be the BYU *chicks* Zeke was telling me about. One smiles at me, and I return the kindness as I take a drink. She keeps talking to Cameron and Zeke, but glances over at me every so often… catching me as I watch her. Thirstier than I realize, I finish the beer quickly.

"Let me get you another," she says from across the table, not waiting for a response before walking up to the bar. Would *her* actions show that she cares for me? Will anyone's?

"Hear the singer outside?" Shane asks me, bringing me out of a haze.

I hadn't, but I strain my ears over the bar noise and finally hear a guitar and a female voice singing a song that sounds familiar. "Yeah."

"The patio's nice. Let's go get some fresh air."

"Okay."

I follow my boss outside, taking a seat across from him at a picnic table. The song playing is mellow; thankfully not loud.

"You're not old enough to be in here, kid," he says. I look at him curiously. Sure, he knew that, but he also bought me a shot *and* a beer. "You know you don't belong here."

"I, uh… I came with Zeke. I didn't have a ride home."

"Zeke's your ride home? You're screwed, Jon. He's going home with a girl, not you."

"Great," I say with a laugh. I guess I should have figured that out. "Well, home's not too far from here. Two miles, maybe."

"There's a bus stop over there." He nods across the street. "Got money for the fare?"

"Yeah, of course. But why'd you buy me drinks if you don't want me here?"

"It's not that I don't want you here. It's that I don't want you gettin' yourself into trouble, and that girl who wants to buy you a beer comes with more baggage than a 747."

I laugh at his explanation. "Gotcha. Then thanks."

"Don't be thanking me. While you were in the bathroom, I let it slip that you were going back to New York in the fall for school. You didn't tell them you're in college?"

"I wanted to fit in," I tell him.

"Jon, come on. Be proud of who you are and where you come from… and what you're doing with your life. I wish some of these guys could see

135

there was more to life than work and women. Did you know Ralph is thirty-four and lives in his parents' basement?"

"No."

"Well, I told your secret to them. May as well give you some dirt on them. Zeke's wife left him after he went home with Little Miss 'Let Me Get You Another.'"

"Oh, wow. I didn't need to know that."

"Cameron's on parole for petty theft."

"Okay, too much," I interrupt Shane. "To me, they're just the guys who are helping me kill time over the summer, working hard to get this house built. I want to remember them like that."

"They're good guys. Missteps and all. And for the record…"

"Yeah?"

"I'm an Oregon State graduate. Civil engineering degree. You and I, Jon. We aren't so different. I married my high school sweetheart and we have three little boys… boys that I had to go kiss goodnight before I came to the bar this evening."

"That's great," I tell him.

"There are always temptations, but I know I can't do better than my beautiful wife. Just get to the heart of what you want… not tonight, not in a moment, but for your future… and go for it."

"Thanks." I smile, truly thankful for his advice.

"Now get home to your brothers," he says. "Don't think you can start setting a bad example for them because you're taking the summer off from school. They look up to you."

"I know. I wouldn't dream of it."

"Good. I'm gonna go have your beer so it doesn't go to waste. I'll see you in… six and a half hours?"

"I'll be there. Good night."

On the bus home, I finish reading the letter.

I was so hurt, the way she was taken from us. I was sad she was gone, but I felt awful that I had let her down… and as much as I wanted a little more time with her, I knew if I had it, I couldn't face her. That's why it was so hard to return to her painting.

After you left, I went back to the loft and found the painting I'd started of her. I stared at it for a few days before I primed the canvas again with a coat of light yellow paint and I started fresh. I didn't use the picture as my guide. I used my memories, allowing myself to reflect on them once again. I cried a little, but the tears were quickly replaced with joyous smiles and laughter.

Now her painting sits on an easel next to me while I work. She's a constant source of encouragement, just like she was when she was here. I feel her presence. She isn't totally gone. She lives on in lessons, in moments, in conversations I have with Mom and Dad. Her influence will be here for eternity, and I now know I never have to live without her.

I ask her daily what it is she wanted to tell me on the phone that night. It's selfish, but my biggest regret is not knowing that. It sounded important to her. I make sure she knows that what was important to her is important to me... but it doesn't make me gain the knowledge.

That's my punishment; my penance for not living up to my commitments to her before she died. A lifetime of not *knowing... I realize that the penance could be much worse, and I can live with this.*

I can now live with her loss... and it has started to prepare me for other losses that are sure to come in my life: losses that I don't even want to think about.

I don't feel like you're lost to me. I don't think I will until the day one of us dies, even if you never come back to me. It gives me peace to know that you're still on the same planet I'm on, doing things that you love, being with people you love.

It sounds like she's gaining perspective. It sounds like she's growing up. It sounds like the Livvy I loved is returning. *That* gives *me* peace.

We aren't finished.

Loss

When I get home, I check on my brothers before going to bed. Will's reading, using a book light so he doesn't disturb Max.

"Everything okay?" I ask him softly from the door.

"Yeah," he says. "We had homemade chicken tacos for dinner."

"That's good."

"I saved some for you. They're in the fridge."

As if on queue, my stomach growls. "Wow, thanks, Will. I haven't eaten, and that sounds perfect."

"Cool. Night, Jon."

"Night."

I smile on the way to the kitchen, feeling loved by one of the most important people in my life. I'm so lucky to have these brothers.

PARTNERS

Our hard work at the beginning of the week earns us an afternoon off on Thursday. Before I left the work site, I'd called Audrey, asking if she wanted to have dinner with me.

She beats me to the Chinese restaurant, and is already snacking on egg rolls by the time I make it to the table. She stands and hugs me before I sit down. It's nice.

"Sorry, I guess it took me a little longer to get ready than I thought it would."

"No, I was early," she says. I check my watch, and realize I'm right on time. "We had a busy day at work, and I had to skip my lunch."

"That's not good for you," I state the obvious. She rolls her eyes at me, and even though her unique blue eyes look nothing like Livvy's, the reaction is very much like something my ex-girlfriend did–often.

"Egg roll?" she asks.

"All yours," I tell her. "Never been a fan."

"What?" She looks very surprised. "I've never heard of someone not liking egg rolls."

"Well now you have. You've finally met someone who stands out, huh?" I ask, taking a sip of ice water.

"Man of my dreams… the one who doesn't like deep fried shrimpy goodness."

"God, you make it sound even worse," I say with a chuckle.

"You know, maybe you are the man of my dreams… because I will never have to share these."

I laugh at her. "Raise your standards a little, Audrey."

139

"My dream man won't make me share my General Tso's Chicken," she states.

"You had to say that... that's, like... my favorite."

"Really?"

"Love it. But hey. This doesn't have to be over," I state, motioning to both her and myself. "I can get my own plate. I'm famished, as well."

"Good. I didn't want it to end so soon... because you honestly do stand out," she admits shyly.

"Thank you. Hey," I say, changing the subject, "did you know General Tso never had this chicken?"

"I didn't know that... all I know is that he was a great military leader in China. I never thought to research his dish!"

"Well, I was curious one night... so even though the dish was created many years after his death, he wouldn't have eaten it had it been invented when he was alive."

"Chicken allergy?" she asks with a playful grin.

"Actually... it was considered a poor man's dish, and he was above this type of food."

"How appropriate that this poor man's food is our favorite!" she exclaims.

"Should we both be aiming higher?" I ask her teasingly. "I mean, they say to dress for the job you want, not the job you have. Maybe we should be eating like the social class we want to be in, and not the one we *are* in."

We both look at each other, considering the comment, when the waiter shows up.

"General Tso's Chicken," we both order at the same time. The waiter looks at us like we're crazy as we both start laughing together, then tells us he'll bring refills of our water momentarily.

"I like that I can be myself with you," Audrey tells me.

"It's nice," I respond.

Conversation is easy over dinner, but remains relatively impersonal, which I like. In fact, I kept steering it in that direction. I have a good time with Audrey; it just feels different. I'm not sure if it's good or bad.

Before we leave, Audrey asks me to an outdoor jazz concert next weekend. "We can bring a picnic lunch of poor man's food," she says. "Sandwiches, carrot sticks, you know… nothing fancy. I can't cook."

"I can cook," I tell her. "I'm not saying it won't be poor man's food, but I'll put something together that's a step up from sandwiches."

"Okay," she says with a blush. "Have fun with your brothers this weekend."

"I will."

"Maybe we can meet one night for dinner next week?" she asks tentatively. "I really like spending time with you, Jon." She knows the home is almost finished… and she also knows I go back to school in a few weeks. We've talked, and she recognizes that whatever this might be is only temporary. Neither of us wants a long distance relationship.

I still can't believe we had *that* conversation. That's what I get for calling her after a shot of whiskey and a beer on an empty stomach; but the next morning, I was glad it was all out in the open.

"It'll probably be impromptu, like this one. The schedule changes daily," I tell her.

"Well, I think I work Monday and Wednesday night," she tells me. "So keep that in the back of your mind. Next time, it's my treat."

"Perfect. I'll call you tomorrow," I tell her when we reach her car.

"Night," she says, leaning in for another hug. I open the door for her, and watch her as she drives away.

Not having the car again, I walk down the road to the bus stop and wait on the bench with a few other people. I know Audrey would have given me a ride home, but I'm not ready for her to know where we live.

I take my brothers out in the backyard and play catch and keep away for about an hour when I get home. Max is worn out; Will is anxious to get inside. Aunt Patty took him to a youth event at her church last night, and Will *says* he exchanged phone numbers with a girl. After I cautioned him that he didn't want to seem over-eager by calling right away, he said that the girl–Ellen–told him she'd call him at eight o'clock tonight.

An aggressive one. At this age, with Will, that's probably best. He needs a good boost of confidence, and a girl that knows what she likes will probably help with that. I'm happy for my brother.

> I love you, Jon.
>
> But we aren't soul mates.

Well, this is an intriguing start...

> My parents are. I know everyone has a different definition of the phrase. I'm not sure I can adequately define it, either, but with Mom and Dad... like, I don't think one could live without the other.
>
> Maybe that's my definition. A soul mate is half of an entity that can only survive as a whole.
>
> Okay, that sounds less romantic and much nerdier than I intended.

I laugh aloud, imagining her saying that. She'd probably crinkle her nose a little, and purse her lips as she smiled.

> So maybe I'll leave it undefined. I hope you understand my point, though.

I assumed we were soul mates, but she's right. *What is a soul mate? What's my definition?*

Definitely an intriguing letter.

> I know I can live without you. I will, if that's what I have to do. But getting over you will take some time. How much time? What do they say? Half the time of the relationship? So nine and a half months then. By the end of

the summer, I'll be one-third of the way there. And after my first year of college, I should be over you.

Right?

Can you put a timeline on something like that? Is there a magic formula? Will I be over her at the end of the school year? And what does that look like: "being *over* Livvy?" Will it take me that long to feel okay about going out with another girl?

I'll believe it when I see it. There are times when I cry so hard that my stomach cramps and spasms... but I know it's part of the process. It's lessening. I don't cry every day. The pity parties are much shorter now than they were at the beginning.

Healing has already begun. Healing feels good.

But there's something that no one took into account. So it takes half the time of the relationship to 'get over' someone. What if that person was your friend first? How long does it take to get over a lost friendship?

Or a partner? That's what we were, for so many years. Partners.

Using the same equation, it'll be five and a half years. Is that right?

Anyway. I'm not writing to talk about our time apart. I'm talking about the time we were together.

When we were partners. Two people working as individuals toward shared goals. I think that fairly defines us. If I've learned anything from this summer, it's that I know I can survive without you. Thrive, even. I've done so much over the past few months.

I don't need you.

She implied it in her last letter. Seeing the words on paper singes.

What do I want, though?

I grin, seeing the next line.

You. Always you. Only you.

The smile quickly fades. *Only* me? Where was that sentiment when she betrayed me?

I choose you. Choisie.

You don't complete me. I'm already whole. You add more to my life. You make me happier than I need to be. Maybe happier than I even deserve to be. Maybe it's selfish for me to want more, I don't know.

I can relate this to Christmas—well, Christmas at the Holland house. I know I'm going to sound spoiled... but I'll admit I am.

Some years, I'd open all the presents from my parents and be so grateful that I'd gotten everything I'd wanted or needed. I'd go to bed on Christmas Eve, smiling and content. And then Santa would bring one more thing... one more thing I hadn't asked for, or expected. The icing on the cake. The cherry on top.

You're the thing I never knew I wanted... until you first held my hand... and the want grew with the first kiss, the first time you said you loved me, and the first time you showed me.

But I'm grateful for the time you gave me when I thought I needed you. When I didn't feel self-sufficient. I'm just sorry I took so much.

I'm sorry I couldn't see that I was already blessed with everything a girl would ever need. I'm strong. I'm smart. I'm driven. I'm talented. I'm loved and am able to love. I am surviving on my own.

That actually does feel good.

And I know you don't need me. I know you'll get on just fine without me, too. After all, you don't need anything. You've made do with what you've had all your life.

But tell me you don't want me. Try.

I doubt you can.

I hope you can't.

She always gets what she wants.

There will always be moments of need. It's human nature. But it shouldn't be all the time. Not for people like us. Not for partners, like we were.

It always seems to go back to that want/need conversation. I remember it again, and chuckle to myself. It's fitting that I kept asking the girl who never needed anything what she *wanted*, and she kept asking the boy who wanted nothing what he *needed*.

She always wanted something from me. And it's safe to say I always needed things from her.

How does she always know exactly what to say? I don't want to read the next line, because it signifies the end of another letter.

We aren't finished.

Partners

She's really giving me things to think about, which is good... because I need to start figuring out what next year is going to look like. Going to school with her. I mean, it's a big campus, but I know she'll spend a fair amount of time at the School of the Arts and around the LeRoy Neiman Gallery. She'll have to take a lot of intro courses, sure, but I've seen some students get special attention if they truly are gifted. And Livvy is. I have no doubt she'll have her own studio space at Prentis Hall by her second semester, if not in her first. A lot of our critiques take place there.

I *will* see her. It's only a matter of time.

"Hey, Jon." I look up to see Will at the door, a huge smile on his face.

"I guess that phone call went well?"

"Yeah," he says simply.

"Details?"

"I don't know," he says, shrugging his shoulders. "We're gonna go out after class next Wednesday."

"A date?" I put Livvy's letter aside and sit up, anxious to hear more about this girl. "Where are you going?"

"I don't know. The mall's just down the street. Maybe we could have dessert somewhere."

"That sounds like a good plan. Suggest it to her."

He nods hurriedly. "Should I call her back now and ask if it's okay?"

"No, man. Call her this weekend... and don't ask her if it's okay. Maybe give her some options... go for a slice of cheesecake, or... or go to a movie. Then tell her she could pick the movie. But be assertive."

"What if she picks a girl movie?"

"If you truly like her, Will, it's not about the movie. It's about the time you get to spend with her, and her with you. I'll pick you both up, so no parents have to be involved."

"Got it. Cool."

"Cool. Got any other questions?"

"About girls? Nah," he says, waving me off. "But I was thinking... towels are incredibly important things. Would it be weird if I carried one with me all the time?"

"*Hitchhiker's* lore," I laugh. "I completely agree that they're one of the most useful inventions of... our time? That can't be right. But yeah. If you're looking to attract a bunch of nerdy friends–which isn't a bad thing–you go ahead and carry that towel with you. Next Wednesday, though? Leave it at home."

"She may like *Hitchhiker's Guide*!" he chuckles, sitting down on the floor of my room.

"Find that out first." I sit down across from him with my back against the bed. "Then get her a towel for the second date," I suggest, still joking with him. "Did you finish the book?"

"Yeah, last night. I loved it."

We spend the next three hours talking about Douglas Adams' masterpiece, taking a break once for a late night sandwich, even though I've already eaten. Will's growth spurt has kicked in full force, and he can't seem to get enough calories in a day.

It's the most fun we've had in as long as I can remember... and even though he's still disappointed that the books I've given him so far had no sex to speak of, he asks me to recommend another one.

I'll let him figure out *Lord of the Flies* doesn't either... but I don't think he'll even miss it. I hand him the worn paperback–another gift from my father–and decide to go check out a copy of *Nick and Norah's Infinite Playlist* for him next week. I remember it being entertaining and a little sexy, too, with a good overall message.

LIONS

After the exhausting week I had, I'm grateful to have a day off. Aunt Patty took Will and a friend to the movies while my mom went to work, leaving Max and me to fend for ourselves. Although an afternoon nap was on my agenda, my youngest brother has other plans.

"It's two, Jon," he whines. "I'm bored."

"Yeah, me, too," I tell him, yawning. "What do you want to do?"

"Go to the moon!" he suggests excitedly.

"We're not really dressed for that, buddy. Think of something else."

He laughs, sliding a Matchbox car on all the furniture surfaces as he runs around the living room. "The sun!"

"You got a death wish?" I ask him. "Do you have any idea how hot it is up there?"

"One hundred degrees?" he guesses.

"Try again."

"Two hundred?"

"It's one-hundred thousand times one-hundred degrees," I tell him. "And that's just on the surface."

"What's one-hundred thousand times one-hundred?"

"You tell me," I challenge him. "Go grab some paper and a pen." He hands me his red sports car while he goes to my room to get the supplies. Even though they put a bed in the craft room, it still houses all the scrapbooking and knitting projects that my aunt works on.

When he returns, he sets down a pad of flowery paper, hands me a Sharpie, and then sets a letter down on my knee.

"Where'd that come from?"

"I got the mail earlier."

149

"You did?"

"Yeah. When you were in the shower."

"Max? You don't go outside without an adult, okay?"

"Mommy lets me," he argues, furrowing his brow.

"Well, then on Mommy's watch, maybe it's fine. Not on mine, though... especially when I don't even know. Okay?"

"Okay," he says begrudgingly. "Show me how hot the sun is."

"You can do math. Come on." I hand him the marker and direct him to write out the two numbers we're multiplying, explaining to him what each zero represents. Even though he knows multiplication, the size of the number overwhelms him, so I give him the answer. "Ten million degrees, Max."

"Ten *million*?"

"Yep. Can you even imagine?"

"I'd be sweaty if I walked around on the sun."

"No, you'd be dead. What do you think the sun's made of?" I ask him.

"Lava?"

"Good guess, but no. Lava's only about two thousand degrees."

"The sun's hotter than *lava*?"

"Oh, yeah. It's hotter than fire. Hotter than anything we can imagine. The sun is made of gas, mainly hydrogen and helium. The gases become energy and create heat and light. So even if it wasn't hot on the sun, you couldn't walk on it."

"I'd fall into it?"

"I guess the gravitational pull would suck you in, yes... but if it wasn't hot, it would be something other than the sun, so..."

"I'm confused."

"Yeah," I tell him. "Too hypothetical for you."

"Hyper-what?"

"Never mind."

"Can I look at your space book?"

"The one with the pictures?" He nods. "Sure, it's still on the desk. You can go get it."

"Can I read in your room?"

"If you take your glasses, yes."

"Thanks, Jon!" He runs off, leaving me with his car, the flowery paper, the pen, and most importantly, Livvy's letter. I lie back down on the couch and open it up, taking my glasses off to read it.

I love you, Jon.

The moment I realize I'm smiling, I quickly correct my expression to one that's more stoic. Some days, as more time has passed, I forget that I'm angry with her. As soon as I think of Finn, though, I remember the feeling very well.

Do you know how strong you are?

If you could see me now, Liv. I shake off the nauseating bravado and read on.

I know. I'm just astonished at what one person can accomplish. Not just one person. One teenager. You have more mental strength and endurance than anyone I've ever met. You're clever and you find solutions to things. You always have the answer.

And it's almost always the right one.

School was never a struggle for me, but then again, life has never been a struggle for me. But yours pretty much always was. There was always a silence about you... but for other people who have lived a life similar to yours, there's sadness or there's anger, but there wasn't that with you.

Your outlook was always positive. You looked for the bright side of things. How does someone who's lived through so much darkness still have the ability to see so much light?

My brothers are my light. You were my light, Olivia. You kept me going. You kept me striving to be better.

There was no way this affluent girl who always had an aura of wonder and happiness would settle for someone who was depressed, or accepted the role as a victim. Whether it was her choice or her parents guiding her in that direction, she never hung around negative people. She came from the happiest of homes. Of course any home I'd want to make with her would have to keep her happy. I always knew Livvy felt relationships were more important than things. I was certain that came from Jack.

Had *things* been more important, Livvy Holland would have never been my aspiration… because even if I *earned* money or *found* money, I knew that I would never be frivolous with it. If I get the job I want and make the money I hope to someday, I intend to spend it on others who have needs like I have had. Needs I *still* have.

Would I still buy her that diamond that would catch in her brown eyes and make them sparkle even brighter? Sure. She wouldn't ask for it, nor would she expect it from me. And that's what I love about her. I would want to surprise her. Always.

Love.

I heard it. *Love.* I grin again, thinking of the smile it would bring her. I'd envisioned a proposal many times over the past few years. I allow the expression to linger naturally as I read on.

> I love your courage and your initiative. Your power. Your silence. Your brilliance. How you lead in school. How you lead your brothers. How you will always be a leader.
>
> When you started Columbia, I knew it was home for you. You didn't choose the college. I think the college chose you. I think it knew your power, strength, leadership, courage, and—most of all—your good and loyal heart would exemplify everything they wanted in a student at their college.
>
> We aren't finished.

Lions

Clever. I'd never really thought that our school mascot really represented me... but I can see it now. Symbolically, anyway, and maybe in nature, too. I remember seeing the lions at the zoo when I was little. Dad had taken me multiple times, but aside from hearing a roar or two from the beasts, they seemed to spend most of their time basking in the sun.

I remember walking away disappointed in them more often than not.

...your good and loyal heart...

That part jumps out at me from the page again.

She must be so disappointed in me now.

"Hey, Max!" I yell through the empty house.

"Yeah?"

"What are you doing in there?"

"Learning about black holes!" he says. *Learning* might be an exaggeration. The book I'd checked out from the library was a picture book, and one I'd hoped would pique my youngest brother's interest in astronomy. It sounds like it might be working.

"How about learning about something more *terrestrial*?" He's in the room within a few seconds, still wearing his glasses.

"Does that mean it's *extra* terrestrial?"

I laugh at his question, thinking it would be a cute joke if he'd meant it as one. "Well, kind of."

"I *want* to learn about aliens!"

"Terrestrial means it has to do with earth. Did you know that?"

"No," he says, squinting at me curiously.

"Glasses, buddy." He takes them off swiftly and sets them on the coffee table. "I was thinking we'd go learn about some creatures on earth."

"People?"

"No. How'd you like to go to the zoo?" His eyes light up and he starts to jump up and down.

"Really?"

"Yeah. We can catch the bus and go. I hear they have a nice, natural habitat for lions."

"Can we go now?" I love seeing him this happy. I love seeing *anyone* this happy.

I loved seeing Livvy this happy, and wonder if I'd ever be able to make her that happy again. As more time goes on, I realize it's not just about whether or not I can forgive her. By staying silent–by not responding to her letters–I know that I'm giving her more reason to be mad at me.

To distrust me.

To dislike me.

How much is too much? How much can she take?

Why am I testing her like this?

I'm not courageous. I'm a coward for not facing her. Even realizing that, I know I'm still not ready to.

But I'm not sure why.

EXPOSED

Audrey waves from the dirt road where she's parked her old car. She'd told me before she doesn't like driving it because she's certain its days are numbered, but it was the only way for her to get to my worksite in the middle of the day.

All the other guys working with me start making catcalls and teasing me as I walk toward her with my backpack in hand.

"Am I embarrassing you?" she asks when I reach her. I'd cleaned up as best as I could in the bathroom we finished earlier in the week, but if I was Audrey, I wouldn't want a hug from a guy looking like this.

"Are you kidding? A hot girl's visiting me at lunch. I'm the envy of every one of them, I guarantee that."

"Well, I wanted to see you before the weekend… thanks for making time for me. I hate the closing shift at work, but Maurice had a death in the family, and I'm the only one who can cover that late… but it certainly doesn't work well with your schedule."

"This is a nice change of pace," I assure her, holding her hand as I lead her through the trees to the opening I'd visited the other day. "I'm sorry we have to have a time limit, though. I only get an hour."

"I'll take what I can get." She squeezes my palm.

"What'd you bring for lunch?"

"We had some leftover pizza," she answers. "Only enough for one, though."

"I've got my lunch, too. You weren't responsible for me today… and remember, I'm bringing the picnic Saturday."

"I won't forget."

I clear some leaves from a patch of grass for us and take a seat. "What a view," she says with a smile. The sunlight does *amazing* things to her eyes. I look away, opening my backpack to get out my sandwich and some water.

"Wouldn't it be something to have a house up here? To get to see that mountain from your bedroom window? And breathe this air every day?"

"Probably not in the cards for us," she says.

"Oh, I don't know. I think it's fine to dream… and work toward it."

"I guess it could happen to *you*."

"Hey, we're not very different."

"Except…"

"What?"

"My ex isn't the child of a billionaire."

"Ah," I say with a slight chuckle. "Well… she's not an ex-*wife*, so I didn't get half of her things, you know? I never wanted her money. I want to make a living on my own. That was always a point of contention between us."

"But not the reason you broke up."

I look over at her curiously, chewing a bite of my sandwich, waiting for her to continue because I suspect she has something more to say.

"I've been thinking about finding a way to ask you what happened with Livvy Holland."

I swallow and shake my head. "I don't want to talk about it." Smiling politely, I divert my attention to the mountain in the distance.

"You don't have to. I looked it up."

Annoyed that people can find out such personal details about me simply because I was associated with her, I bite my tongue. It's so intrusive…

How have the Hollands lived with this all of their lives?

"It sounds like she had a really bad day."

"*She* did?" I ask her defensively. What could Audrey have learned about what happened, anyway?

"From her injury, to them calling her the wrong name at graduation–"

"Huh?"

"They called her by her birth name, apparently. I'd forgotten she was adopted. She apparently stormed off the stage, upset."

I can't believe she knows something more about Livvy's state of mind that day than I do.

"Right," I say, not wanting to let on that I didn't know.

"And then she cheated on you with her cousin?"

"Finn's not really her cousin. She's adopted, and they're only distant cousins by marriage. Really, he's her cousin's cousin. The tabloids blew that relationship out of proportion. And it wasn't *really* cheating… I mean, yeah, she kissed him, but she had a concussion, and…"

Audrey sits silently, surprised, waiting for me to continue my passionate rant. "And apparently a really bad day," I add simply.

My heart is pounding in my ears. The breaths come quickly to keep up. I never thought I'd hear myself defend her, or make excuses for her.

I can feel my cheeks turn red. I'm embarrassed by what I just said.

Livvy kissed another guy! What if it had been the other way around? What if I kissed another girl while I was with her? What if I kiss Audrey *now*?

I look up at her, trying to read her thoughts. She looks suddenly insecure. Her posture changes to a defeated slump. The corners of her lips turn into a faint frown. All the light that the sun had shone into her turquoise irises goes dim.

I feel awful, and feel the need to make assurances to her, but I don't feel confident enough to do that. I've never been more confused.

Maybe I should just kiss her. I *have* to. If I can't say what she needs to hear, my actions should reflect what she expects of me. If I don't do something, she'll think I'm not ready to move on. She'll think I'm not interested in her.

What am I doing?

"Audrey–"

"Don't," she says. "Just don't say anything. Don't ruin this, okay?" Her smile is earnest.

"Ruin what?"

"Our friendship," she says. "If you're not ready for anything more right now, I get it."

"I am," I try to convince her, setting my sandwich down to take her hand in mine. I lean in to kiss her, even though it feels like the absolute worst thing I could do. Livvy will be so hurt.

Livvy will *never know*. I am over her.

But I'm *not*.

Audrey looks down, away from me slowly, avoiding my kiss. I freeze, and sigh in acceptance. I press my lips to her cheek quickly and let go of her hand as I back away.

She picks a blade of grass and rubs it with the pad of her finger. I see the movements out of the corner of my eye as I focus on the mountain once more. Getting over Livvy is going to be a mountainous task. It will take time. And focus. And effort.

And it may not even be possible.

"Thank you," I tell Audrey. I'm so grateful she stopped me. Something I'd told Livvy at my prom echoes in my head. *I want all of my lasts to be with you.* One kiss would change so much between us. What am I thinking? One kiss already *has* changed so much between us… but one more might destroy us entirely.

Which means I still have hope. *Damn it.*

"I don't want you to regret your time with me… not a single moment we're together. Okay?"

I smile at her. "I don't."

"We already knew this wouldn't work," she reminds me. "I don't think either of us wants a fling."

I shake my head. "Not really my thing."

"Me neither, which is why I like you so much. But this isn't our time, Jon."

I laugh a little to myself. "I'm not sure whose time it is then."

"Just yours. And mine. Yours to heal and move on. Mine to get to know a new friend. Who knows? Maybe next summer when you come home again, it'll be our time."

"This will probably be the last opportunity I get to spend time out here. I've got a full curriculum for the rest of my college career."

"Really?"

"Yeah," I tell her. "I'm not sure when my next trip to Utah will be at all. I think my family's coming to visit me for Christmas, so…"

"Well, then," Audrey says simply as she starts to eat her lunch, which she hasn't even touched until now. "Let's enjoy our last few days, then. And you'll always have a friend back west that you can talk to."

"Sounds like a good plan."

"Maybe I'll even sneak back up here once the family moves in so you can see how much they love the home you've built for them."

"That'd be nice," I tell her.

After enduring an afternoon of teasing and tasteless jokes from the guys I work with, it's nice to be home in the silence of my room. I'm excited to get back to school, even if it means facing Livvy. I want to get back into my classes, and give my brain the challenges my body has endured all summer. I can't wait for the late-night conversations with Fred, talking about design and philosophy. I've never had a friend like him… someone who can keep up with me, mentally, and challenge my beliefs. I wonder what his summer has been like. At the end of the school year, he and his girlfriend had both made the decision to backpack through Europe together. Not only that, but she's transferring to Columbia for her second year. I've met her once, and she's just as smart as he is.

When she'd come to visit Fred last year, I wondered if she'd be someone that Livvy would be friends with. In the three hours I'd spent with her, I'd decided not to even attempt to find friends for my girlfriend. Fred's girl was going to be a physicist, and didn't have a creative bone in her body. I wasn't sure she and Livvy would have anything in common.

It was one of the first nights I'd wondered if Livvy and I could make things work. I'd begun feeling the strain of her dependence on me. I liked how Fred's girlfriend was so strong-willed. She spoke her mind, and didn't care that Fred didn't share her opinion on things. They embraced their differences.

Olivia and I have such different pasts, but we really are very similar. I open the blinds to the west-facing window of the craft room and sit on the floor next to it, getting ready to watch the sun set. I wonder if Livvy watched the sun set tonight, too–if her focus was to the west, facing me. It seems her attention is on me often, with the letters.

I wonder if she can feel me in the mornings when the sun rises… because I'm always watching, looking back east, thinking about her. At the beginning of the summer, the orange and red hues mimicked my anger, but as the weeks have gone on, the colors have softened. As I work in the mornings, I take in the full view–the deep blue of the night sky as it morphs into daylight, the rays of light that remind me that everyday is a new day, full of new opportunities. Each day, I think of starting over. Somedays, forgiveness is top of mind.

Watching as the sun begins its descent behind the house next door, I wonder if it's time to stop carrying around the resentment and pity. I open the envelope I've had in my hand for the last half hour, waiting for this moment to read her next letter.

I love you, Jon.

When you took the picture of me in the loft, I felt desired.

I loved that you wanted to keep that moment with you forever.

I still wish that was a moment that could have stayed ours. The picture was so lovely. Her happiness came easily that day. She was relaxed and comfortable with me. I'm still angry that my roommate violated my privacy like he did. He tainted the sweet innocence of that picture. There was nothing dirty about it. Nothing illicit, but once the rest of the world saw it, Livvy Holland's image was forever changed.

When the photo showed up in text messages on Camille's phone, I didn't know what to think. My first thought was that you shared it with her. Once she said someone else had sent it to her, I knew you weren't behind it. When people started pointing and laughing at me at school, I felt ashamed.

I want you to know, though, I was not ashamed that day in the loft. It's horrible that the media can take what was a private, loving moment between two people and twist it into any story they like.

Exactly.

The day that photo came out, our secrets were finally exposed. In the end, I didn't care what the rest of the world thought... but addressing my parents that day was one of the scariest things I've done.

I'm sure it took a lot of guts to admit what she did that day, but I don't think she could have been half as scared as I was in the office with her dad. I'd stood up to the man before, but this was different.

He'd asked me about being tested for STDs... I'd never told anyone I had. I'd gone to a public clinic, and I had to fill out a questionnaire to assess my risk of diseases. I remember back to that day, and how my hand was shaking as I answered the questions.

How many people had I slept with? [Two.]

Within the past three months, how many people had I slept with? [None.]

Had I participated in anal, oral or vaginal sex? [No. Yes. Yes.] *Did I always wear a condom?* [Yes.] I now know I couldn't answer that question the same.

Was I ever paid for sex? [No.] *Was I ever high or drunk when I was having sex?* [No.]

Had I ever had sex with someone with one of these diseases? The list was scary. [Not sure.] I never wanted to answer that way again, and was disappointed that I couldn't answer it definitively at the time.

Have I ever had a tattoo? [Yes.] I got tested about a week after I got it, because of what happened the night I showed Livvy. We'd gone farther than we ever had before.

I never thought I was at risk of an STD, but when I left the clinic that day, I felt dirty. I'd decided I wouldn't go any further with Livvy until I knew for certain that I was *clean*.

The day the picture went viral, after I'd assured Jack that I had no diseases, the intensity of the conversation escalated. I was angry he was prying, and he was mad I'd taken his daughter's innocence.

I'd threatened him. I told him I'd go behind his back to be with her. I'd hoped he hadn't heard my voice crack, because it did so more than once. There were a few times I actually ran out of breath. My throat was so dry I wasn't sure how long I'd be able to continue talking.

At the height of our argument, he'd conceded.

He said I was *right*. I'd felt unsteady through most of our conversation, but when he said that, I had to grip onto the chair I'd been standing behind–the only barrier keeping him from throwing me against a wall like I'd seen him do once before with his nephew. I knew what I did to Livvy was symbolically so much worse to Jack than what Brandon had done, but in the bigger scheme of things, I knew he could see the difference. I knew he could see my good intentions with his princess.

Even then, though, I wasn't ashamed of what we'd done, and I didn't feel the need to apologize to anyone—not for us being together, anyway.

Jon, I am so ashamed of what I did with Finn. I am so sorry it happened. I am so sorry that you're not here for me to tell you this in person—that you haven't been here every day to hear me tell you, because I say it every day as I paint. I pour my remorse into each droplet of pigment, and I coat every bit of each canvas with my regret. Every brush stroke is penitence. There have been thousands, Jon. Tens of thousands. Before this is said and done, there may be hundreds of thousands.

I feel cleansed at the end of a painting, and then I write you. I have tried to write you with a clear conscience, not wanting to dwell on the few seconds that could represent the biggest mistake of my life. I haven't wanted to remind you of that, in case there was any way you could get it out of your mind. I know how much that must have hurt you. I hate that I hurt you in that way.

I am so, so, so sorry.

This summer, I have felt more exposed than I felt the day that photo was leaked.

Because the exposure was an act of betrayal? And the whole world knew it? I don't want to feel sorry for her, but I do. It had to be so much worse for her, being the notable person she is in New York. Had it been any other seventeen-year-old kissing a friend, it would have been overlooked by others.

Still, the loyal boyfriend would hurt just as much as I am hurting.

I pour my emotions and thoughts and memories onto these soft, linen pages, and I hear nothing from you. I wish you would either confront me or comfort me. I would take either one. I deserve the former; I prefer the latter. But hearing nothing makes me feel naked and scared. I feel like I'm standing here, with you peering at me though a telephoto lens from far away. You see me—all of me—but I have no idea what you actually see. Or if you are getting a glimpse of anything at all.

Are you reading my letters?

Does she think I'm not? What if I hadn't? What if I just threw the first one away, and every one that followed? How would I feel about her today?

If you are, should I have been apologizing all this time? I am that sorry. I am more sorry than that. I will never love anyone again like I've loved you, Jon. I will never hurt anyone again like I've hurt you. I promise you, I will be honest and loving and loyal.

I can't explain what happened that day, in that moment. I know that's probably what you're waiting on. I was confused. I was upset.

What guarantee can you have that it won't happen again? I'm sure that's what's going through your mind.

She's exactly right.

I wasn't myself, Jon.

I am myself again now. I see the difference. I know what I have to do to be myself now. I know what I have to continue to do, and I vow to you, I will keep doing it.

I'll keep painting. It keeps me level. It makes me happy. It's an outlet for my emotions and a spigot that feeds me energy and life and confidence, all at once. I drink it in.

I'm sorry for being someone you think you don't want anymore... but please don't throw me to the side. Don't throw away the years we've had.

We aren't finished.

Exposed

I stare out at what remains of the sunset, and it's a beautiful sight. Low-lying, pink, wavy clouds overtake streams of yellow, but above all that is a blue sky already prickled with glistening stars. Livvy would love to see this.

I snap a picture with my phone and save it, wondering if I might take the opportunity to show her some day.

YOUTH

I'd told my brother I'd wait in the car while he and his date, Ellen, went to the cheesecake restaurant in the mall, but it's too hot without the car running, and it's wasteful to leave the car on just for that.

Plus, I kind of want to see how he's doing.

Mom had given him thirty dollars before she dropped him off at his religion class, but before he said goodbye to me, I slipped him another twenty, just to make sure he had plenty.

Ellen talked non-stop once she got in the car. I wondered if she was just nervous, or if that's what she was normally like. Her voice was still very childlike, and I was glad the car ride was only three minutes long.

Regardless, I will say nothing to my brother about how annoying she seems to me. I'll support his choice in girls, provided they're good for him… and she seems harmless.

I wait for Will and his date to be seated before I pass the restaurant, heading up to the shop where I got my glasses. Audrey smiles from behind the counter as she helps a customer. I wave at her, taking a seat in the chair I sat in when I first saw her.

She really *is* charming–with the people she's with, with my brothers, and with me. She's been one of the highlights of my summer, even though I've only known her a few weeks. There's just something so… *unburdened*… about her. She's weightless. She's effervescent. With her, she's exactly as she seems. She's uncomplicated.

I realize immediately that's why we'll never be anything more than friends. I *like* complicated. I like being challenged. I like having someone who pushes me farther.

167

Livvy always did that for me. Her view of the world is different than mine, and in art, and design and theories, she always made me examine things from her point of view... and it was always fascinating what–together–we could see, and create.

"Hi," Audrey says, sitting down in the leather chair next to me. "I'm surprised to see you here."

"Will is on a date at Cheesecakes, Etc. I'm the chauffeur, and I thought I'd stop by and make sure we're still on for our picnic Saturday."

"Why wouldn't we be?" she asks.

"I don't know," I tell her. "Yesterday was just... a little weird, I know. I'm sorry."

"You were fine," she says.

"Okay." I smile at her, happy that things aren't strained between us. "I'll pick you up at five... that's when you get off, right?"

"Yep!" she says, getting up and nodding at another awaiting customer.

"Any food allergies?"

"Nope!"

"Any food dislikes?"

"Oysters. And olives," she says, walking toward her customer.

"So all aphrodisiacs are out," I mumble to myself.

"Huh?"

"Nothing," I say with a grin. "Have a good night at work. I'll see you Saturday."

"Bye!" she says with an eager wave.

I stop by the bookstore before going back to the restaurant, picking up a fresh copy of *Nick and Nora's Infinite Playlist* for Will and a book about Mars for Max. At the cheesecake place, I ask to be seated at a table across the way from my brother and his date.

I pull the letter out of my backpack that I'd found in the mailbox just before I left the house.

I love you, Jon.

I know she does. Emotions stir deep within my body, awakening me to her sentence. I know she loves me, still.

"Can I take your order?" a waiter interrupts, killing my buzz.

"A soda and… just a regular slice of cheesecake. No, make it strawberry. To go."

"The soda, too?"

"The soda's for here." He nods and walks away, leaving me to my letter in the tiny, two-person booth in which I was seated. I imagine Livvy sitting across from me. *My Olivia.*

On my seventeenth birthday, you were allowed into our private family dinner to celebrate with me. It took about five years for me to convince my parents to let Camille come. They trusted no outsiders… but they were finally starting to trust you.

I don't really think that's true. Maybe Emi trusted me. I always felt like Emi was on my side, but not Jack. I got glares and snide comments for what felt like a year after the night in Mykonos. I know he knew we were lying to him. Maybe Matty told him, I don't know… but I don't think he trusted me after that.

He'd coached me before we went inside. I wasn't allowed to discuss anything personal with any waiters or to let my phone out of my sight. He also reminded me that people are always watching, no matter how private the party may seem.

I didn't need to know any of that. I knew it all already. He'd acted like it was the first time I'd been around his family, but that wasn't the case. Because of this conversation, I was a little stand-offish to him all night, causing Livvy to have her defenses up a little, too, although she didn't know why. She just seemed to feed off my prevailing emotions that night. She was already becoming too attached at that point. I felt it then, but at the time, I wanted it, because that meant she was choosing me over her father.

Do you remember my dad's toast to me?

I really don't, either, but I'd wished I had been listening. You were distracting me, though, as your fingers dragged slowly up my thighs. You were cautious in your movements, careful not to give your actions away, but I could tell Dad knew something was up at that one part of his toast. Everyone sighed and ahhhed-and I didn't know what he'd said. I didn't react the way he'd expected me to, and I saw his disappointment.

I acted like I heard him, though, and he had my attention for the last part of his speech.

"Don't be in such a hurry to escape your youth, Contessa. Mark my words, you'll wish you had it back once it's gone. Knowledge and experience will steal it from you without you even realizing it's happening... and then you're simply left with a silly wish for the rest of your life. And-God-willing-it'll be a long life. There's plenty of time to grow up. No need to rush into it."

He'd then wished me a happy birthday, and I cried, feeling like I'd already grown up... like I'd ignored his advice and gone against him. I didn't need to tell you that's why I cried. You knew. After I hugged my dad, I returned to you, and you tried to dry my tears with your shirt sleeve... but when they wouldn't stop, you gave me my present-a nice pair of sunglasses- that hid my emotions from everyone else. Then *you kissed me so sweetly... and my decision to "escape my youth" with you didn't seem like such a horrible decision.*

Sex isn't synonymous with adulthood, though. They say that's when a girl becomes a woman, but I don't believe it. It's my dad's definition, but it isn't mine. I think mine will be when I leave their home and stop being fully dependent on them anymore. It has nothing to do with sex. It has nothing to do with a boyfriend. It has everything to do with me. Me, supporting myself. Me, making all the decisions. Me, taking risks. Accepting new challenges. Doing things no one expects me to do.

I hope to surprise a lot of people at college next year. I'll become the adult they assume I am now. I'm ready to start this new life... and I know it will be different than anything I've known, with or without you.

We aren't finished.

Youth

"Sir? Did you need anything else?"

I look up at the waiter, and then at the table. Water droplets of condensation drip from the glass. The cheesecake sits in a bag next to it. I have no idea when he brought them.

"No, just the check," I say, checking my watch. I glance across the restaurant. Will and Ellen are gone. After paying, I rush out to the car, expecting to cross paths with my brother on the way. Checking my phone, I see a text message from him.

It's going great. We're going to walk around the mall. Another half-hour.

That's my brother. I grin proudly, getting into the car and cracking the windows.

I tuck Livvy's letter safely in my bag, and remember back to her birthday. I was listening to Jack intently.

He was reminiscing about the time when Livvy, at the age of three, before she was officially adopted, had asked Jack if she '*had*' to call him Daddy then. She had just moved into their house for the state-mandated supervisory period that they had to endure before the courts would make the adoption official.

Jack said the question moved him to tears–not because she wasn't ready, but in anticipation of the day that she would be ready... the day she would *choose* to call him Daddy.

Emi had told her she could wait until they'd done a good job at parenting first... but reiterated their desire to be her mother and father.

Since her adoption was finalized on her fourth birthday–something that Jack, Emi and Donna had begged the courts to accommodate–he had said that he wasn't celebrating Livvy's 17th birthday that night.

He said, for him, it was the 13th anniversary of being a daddy to the most precious little girl he could ever even hope to meet. Then he told her he'd hoped he and Emi had done a good job of parenting.

Livvy didn't have to stop my hands from creeping up her skirt anymore. I felt guilty at that, feeling suddenly that my parents must have done a horrible job for me to be so sexually aggressive at the dinner table with her family. And why? To prove to Jack that I didn't need to be coached to be a part of their family? That his daughter was mine?

I spent the rest of her birthday trying to encourage her to interact with her family more. Without her parents, I'd never have had the chance to know her. Without their good parenting, she wouldn't have turned out to be the girl I loved.

As much as I didn't want Jack Holland to be an influence in her life or in her decisions, I was suddenly grateful he had been. I respected the man for how he raised his *princess*.

"Knock, knock!" my brother announces before banging on the back door of the car, startling me.

"Well, get in," I tell him after unlocking the door. "Wait!" I say, stopping when I see him climbing into the car before Ellen. I get out to show him how it's done. I have to nod at Will to get him to get back out of the car. "Ladies first," I tell Ellen, watching my brothers skin turn a dark shade of pink.

"Thank you, Jon," she says. Will stands there, as if waiting for her to scoot over. I shut the door.

"Go around to the other side, man," I tell him, knocking him gently upside the head.

"Oh, okay." He rushes to the other side, getting in and closing the door gently.

"Where to?" I ask, starting the car.

"I live in the Nottingham neighborhood," Ellen says. "It's not far from your place, right?"

"I believe that's on the way home... just tell me where to turn when I get close."

"'kay," she says, and the back of the car becomes more silent than I expect. She'd been so chatty before. I look in the review mirror cautiously.

"What are you doing?!" I yell, stopping the car abruptly in the parking lot. I turn around, staring at the white sticks hanging out of each of their mouths.

"They're candy cigarettes," Will says.

"They still make those nasty things?" I ask.

"They make us look older," Ellen says, taking the stick between her fingers as if she was smoking a joint, and not just a cigarette. She blows out air between her lips, looking utterly ridiculous.

"Mmhmm," I say simply, judgmentally, putting the car back into gear. Before I put my foot on the gas, I glare in the backseat at my brother, causing them both to start laughing. "Someone once told me, '*Don't be in such a hurry to escape your youth. You'll wish you had it back once it's gone.*'"

"Sounds like an old man," Will says. I shake my head, beginning to drive toward the freeway that will take us home. It *does* sound like something an old man would say, but no one actually gave *me* that warning when I was younger. In fact, my youth disappeared one night when I wasn't watching... one night when Max was a baby, sick with colic. When I went to take him to my mother to stop his crying, I was met with a locked bedroom door. Mom said something to me that was entirely unintelligible... just before a man started grunting, repeatedly. I wasn't positive what it was, although I'd heard it before and had my suspicions. I'd asked if my mother was okay. She'd said, *'Go away, Jonny. Mama's fine.'*

Unable to get in touch with my dad, I had gone next door with Max and Will, and we had stayed with a neighbor that night. She taught me how to feed Max properly. I'd been feeding him too much, and wasn't holding the bottle right. She showed me how to soothe him, too.

And that was the night I stopped being dependent on my parents. That was the night I became an adult, a parent to my brothers. I was *eleven*.

RESISTANCE

"Max, seriously," I plead with my youngest brother as he jumps on his bed, "please stop acting like the little monkey you are and go to sleep."

"Will isn't even home yet!"

"Will is at the movies. Remember? We took him there."

"With a girrrl…" he says.

"Yes, with a girrrl." After work, I'd rushed home to pick up both of my brothers and headed to the mall. Ellen met Will there to watch a double feature of some movie based on books she'd read. Max and I stayed for an animated picture he'd already seen once with my mom.

It was actually pretty good, but I'm regretting buying my youngest brother a slushie on our way out. *Too much sugar, for sure.*

"Max," my mother says. "Stop giving Jonny a hard time. He's had a long day. What if you read me a book?"

"The book Jon got me?"

"If that's what you want." He finally stops jumping and steps off the bed to grab the thin hardback with Mars on the cover. "Jonny, take the rest of the night off. I'll go pick up Will and his girlfriend. And Aunt Patty can keep an eye on our monkey, if this book doesn't settle him down."

"You're sure?" I ask my mother.

She reaches up and ruffles my hair, something I'm not sure she's ever done before. "Go."

"Thanks."

I'd seen Livvy's letter before we left earlier, and I've had a hard time keeping my mind off of it all night. She'd drawn a little heart next to my name. The second I saw it, *my* heart fluttered. Some reactions, I can't control.

I'm starting to worry that one of these letters will be the last one… but I hope there is some sort of warning in one of them to signify the end. So far, I don't get the impression she'll stop writing anytime soon. I'm not sure what my reaction would be if she'd decided to end her communications with me. I think I'd probably reach out to her. I don't think I'd be able to stop myself.

Another reaction I wouldn't be able to control.

I trace over her sketch a few times before turning the letter over to open it.

I love you, Jon.

I love you, Olivia. What a relief, to allow myself to say what my heart has been screaming for months. *Years.*

I wonder what happened in your life to give you such confidence to stand up to people like you do. I wish I had the guts to say some of the things you've said to my dad. I know I should have been the one to say many of the things you talked about.

But I wasn't brave enough to take such a stance. I still don't think I am, but I'm seeing that as an option. As a way to respond to him. I'm figuring out that I don't always have to do what he asks, or obey every rule. That, too, must be a component of becoming an adult. I still want to make my parents happy. I still want to impress them. I want them to think they raised a good daughter.

And that's where I stop myself… using that logic, that would mean your parents didn't raise you right, and I—of course—don't think you're a bad person. I think you're one of the best people I've met.

I wasn't raised by my parents, though. That's one thing she's forgetting. But I disagree with her assessment of what makes her good or bad. It has nothing to do with standing up for herself. I may have been raised poorly–possibly by myself and *definitely* by my lack of formal parenting–but being able to speak my mind is something that makes me think I'm a good person. I don't feel like I've ever used my conviction or voice to defend anything bad or negative. I stand up for myself. I stood up for her. For us. Because I believed in us that much, that passionately.

You've been so resistant to the rules my father has set forth. He's been so resistant to me growing up. All the fights were driven by how much you both care about me. My dad tells me he loves me every day.

Still.

And he says it even when we fight. I never doubt how much he cares.

...

The letter ends there, or so I think, but I *do* see writing on the backside through the paper. She leaves a third of the front page blank, though, making her point loud and clear. It hurts that she doubts my feelings, but what else *should* she feel? It's what I've wanted her to feel since I received the first piece of mail from her. Since I walked away from her in Manhattan. I wanted her to think I don't care anymore.

But do I really still want that? No... and in that same thought–that same moment–I don't want her to know how much I *do* care, either. It can't be like it was. I don't want her to expect me to welcome her back with open arms as soon as I land in the city. There has to be a discussion. Many conversations. I need to trust that she's grown up. I need to see it with my own eyes before getting more involved–*too* involved.

I want distance, still. The distance of acquaintances. The process of becoming friends again. Would this changed Livvy still even want the man I've become? Will I want her?

The only way I can see this happening is to keep my guard up. No assumptions of friendship, and especially no assumptions of anything more. I don't think either of us could make that commitment at this point anyway.

I flip over the letter and see her continuation.

> I am beyond sorry, Jon, but I've forgiven myself for the lapse in judgment. Yes, I was angry. Yes, I was upset. Yes, I was confused. No, I never, ever meant to hurt you. It was not vengeful. It was not done to make you regret our fight, or not coming to my graduation. I wasn't even thinking about you... and I know that sounds bad, but be objective, please.
>
> I was absorbed in myself, feeling immense sorrow for myself. I needed someone to comfort me, and no... I didn't want comfort from just anyone. At the time, there was not a thought of the source of my comfort. It was a basic need for compassion... like people need shelter, or water, or air. That's the best way I can describe it. I felt like I would crumple and collapse within myself. It was a melt down. It was a subconscious reflexive response.
>
> Finn kissed me, but yes, I then kissed him back. I'm not trying to deflect blame or change the facts.
>
> Do you know how, when you cuddle under a blanket on a cold night, your body curls up, and you gather all the folds of

the blanket to create a warm barrier around yourself? You're not thinking, "I want more blankets." Your body just knows what it needs, and does what it has to.

I felt acceptance. I felt friendship. I felt support. I felt love. I needed more. I didn't want more. I needed it. I took it.

I wish it had been you to comfort me... to provide me with that support when I had felt the world around me falling away. I wish it had not been Finn, because I know he took things farther than any other friend, family member, or stranger would have done... but I don't think he was being mean or malicious, either. He was comforting me the only way he knew how to, in the moment. It was impulsive and unplanned.

And we both regret it.

I've replayed that moment a million times since it happened. I know I wouldn't do the same thing if it happened again, because I know where I stand. I know that all the things that lead up to the turmoil of that day are small things that should not have rocked my foundation like I let them.

But I felt like I had no foundation at the time. I was lost, Jon.

I'm found now. I won't stray from my path again. I promise you that.

What do I need to do to provoke a response in you?

Is she kidding? I hang on to her every word... my *heart* responds to it all. Everything she writes, I take it all in. I haven't let go yet. Every memory. Every promise of love. Every word of devotion. Every apology. Every explanation. Everything. It's all contained within this one man that has no idea how to proceed.

What would I say to her? How should I respond? I don't even know where to begin.

DEAR LIVVY,

I CANNOT RESIST YOU. I WANT YOU LIKE I ALWAYS HAVE; LIKE I WILL NEVER WANT ANOTHER PERSON. I DON'T KNOW WHY, THOUGH. I DON'T KNOW HOW TO RECONCILE THESE FEELINGS OF MINE THAT WON'T DIE; THAT WON'T STOP TELLING ME I'M BEING STUBBORN AND MAKING THE WORST DECISION OF MY LIFE. I SHOULDN'T WANT YOU LIKE THIS. I SHOULDN'T TRUST YOU. NO, I DON'T TRUST YOU. I'M NOT SURE I KNOW YOU. I KNOW THE CHILD YOU WERE WHEN WE MET. I KNOW THE TEENAGER YOU WERE WHEN WE STARTED DATING. I KNOW THE LOST GIRL THAT I BROKE UP WITH AT THE BEGINNING OF THE SUMMER.

I DON'T KNOW THE WOMAN YOU'VE OBVIOUSLY BECOME OVER THE PAST FEW MONTHS WITHOUT ME. YOU DIDN'T KNOW YOURSELF IN JUNE. I DON'T KNOW YOU NOW.

I don't know what else I'd say to her... because I have this urge to make plans with her to figure it out. I can't just take her back, I won't.

Even if it's all my heart wants.

Please let me prove my unfaltering devotion to you. Please. That tiny window of time spoke nothing about how I really feel, Jon. All the other minutes of my life—that's what

I want you to see, and hear, and feel. Please don't let one stolen moment keep you away from me.

I know you love me like I love you. I don't need a response from you to know that, because I've seen all the minutes of your life when you were devoted to me.

What we share isn't fleeting.

We both know this.

We aren't finished.

Resistance

I love reading her confident declarations. She knows me like no one can, or will.

I loved the girl I walked away from with all of my heart. How will I feel about her when I see her? Will the sight of her bring back the feelings from all the time we were happy together, or the pain I felt in those twenty seconds of watching her with Finn from afar.

I'll only know when I see her. I know I can plan all I want, but everything hinges on the moment we reunite. Only then will I know if I can forgive her and move on to meet this new person she's become.

HEART

"You have a plethora of salads to choose from," I tell Audrey as we unpack the cooler. "Dill and shrimp tortellini, mixed greens with vinaigrette dressing, and a fruit salad with strawberries, oranges, melons… frankly, anything I could find."

"Perfect," she says as she settles into the blanket she'd brought with her. We'd chosen a spot far enough from the stage that would allow us to talk to each other without having to scream over the music or the people around us. "What's this?"

"Ice cream. To beat the heat, of course." I pick up both pints to show her the varieties I'd chosen.

"Mint chocolate chip and orange swirl. You remembered my favorite shake flavors…"

"I figured if you hated the salads, you'd at least enjoy dessert."

"Let's eat," she suggests as a jazz singer takes the stage with the band that was already assembled. I prepare plates for both of us as Audrey pours soda into two cups. "To our last date," she says, holding up her drink.

It's bittersweet. I've enjoyed her company, but I know it will be the last time I see her. I'm pretty sure she knows that, too. "To the memories," I counter as we tap the rims of our cups together.

"What will you do when you get back to New York?"

"Move back into my dorm," I answer. "And I have to find a new storage place for my family's things. They've been in a temporary gallery space all summer."

"Like an art gallery?"

"Yeah. Livvy's a painter."

"I didn't know that," she says. "You did say you met her at an art school or something, didn't you?"

"Yeah."

"She has your stuff?"

"Her *building* has my stuff," I say. "Her parents offered it to me before we broke up. I didn't have time to make other arrangements before I left for Utah, so…"

"So you'll have to see her?"

"Not for that, but I will eventually. She's going to Columbia, so I'm sure our paths will cross."

"How do you feel about that?" she asks.

"I didn't want her to go to school with me," I admit. "Even while we were together, but Livvy does what Livvy wants," I say with a laugh.

"Why didn't you want her to go to your college?"

"Because she's not *just* a painter. She's probably the most accomplished artist to come out of New York in years. She needs the best art school, the best professors, the best mentors… and she needs new experiences. I thought it would be good for her to go away. I thought getting out of Manhattan for a bit would be good for her."

"But that wasn't your choice to make."

"No, it wasn't," I say with a wistful smile. "But her reasoning for going to Columbia was all wrong. She was going to be with me."

"So were you planning on breaking up with her… anyway?"

I put down my food for a minute and think about the best way to handle this conversation. "Never," I tell her honestly. "Did we need a little time apart? Yeah, but I never wanted things to end."

"But now that she kissed that guy… how do you feel?"

"I think it was a chaotic mess of unfortunate situations," I say. "If one element had been different in the twenty things that happened that morning, she wouldn't have kissed him. She doesn't love him."

"Are you sure?"

"I know how I love her." I swallow and clear my throat, maintaining eye contact with her. "I know she loves me the same way."

Audrey smiles sweetly, surprising me. I thought she might be hurt or offended that I was discussing my feelings for my ex-girlfriend with her.

She lies down on her side, propping herself up on one elbow, still eating her salads. "What do you mean?" she asks. "How do you love her?"

"Ummm…" I start, a little hesitant. "Really?"

"Yeah," she says. "Jon, I could tell you weren't over her when I asked you about the break up. The way you defended her… but I really want to know *how* you love her."

"She is alive, and present," I tell her. "She's clever and funny. She's open-minded, worldly, and willing to try anything. When she was younger, she traveled all over the place with her parents. She's gracious and giving. You'd think she was materialistic, being able to afford anything, but she's not. She has nice things, but she doesn't have a lot of anything. The Hollands aren't wasteful. She respects people from all walks of life…"

Audrey nods her head. "Obviously," I add. "Old or young, rich or poor, she never really distinguished between them. Her parents have always been philanthropic. They taught her well. Integrating her in Nate's Art Room was probably the best thing they did for her–and me.

"I remember one Monday a long time ago, we had an art class after school. It was the day after Easter, and she'd brought a basket of candy with her to the Art Room. I guess she was probably about eight years old, and when she set her stuff on her desk, she asked me what the Easter Bunny brought me as she unwrapped a chocolate duck.

"I told her nothing, and she whispered to me that she knew the Easter Bunny wasn't real, and then proceeded to ask what my parents had bought for me. 'Nothing,' I'd answered again.

"I'll never forget the look on her face. 'Because you're poor?' she'd asked. I can remember feeling so ashamed that I didn't answer her, and instead just started to draw."

I chuckle a little, remembering that day and how amazing I thought she was in that moment.

"'What kind of candy is your favorite?' she asked me softly. I told her I liked jelly beans… and she plucked every last one out of her basket and put them on a sheet of paper next to my drawing. Then she went around the room and gave out the rest of her candy and little toys to all the other students. She even gave the basket away to the youngest girl in our class, who had told Livvy the green paint on the wicker was her favorite color."

"That's sweet," Audrey comments.

"She always wants to learn things," I continue. "And she often came to me with questions. When she was in middle school, she would bring a list with her of things to ask me... just things she'd been curious about over the week leading up to our art classes.

"When she'd ask philosophical questions, we'd spend time discussing things while we painted. Sometimes, she'd ask me questions about history or science, and if I didn't know the answer then, I'd go to the library and find out, armed with the answers for the next class. I never wanted to be the reason she didn't know something.

"She is beautiful beyond comparison. She was always pretty, but I loved her most when she'd come to class in the fall after spending the afternoon in the park. Her hair would be wild from the wind, and she didn't care. Donna would try to brush it out with her fingers, but Livvy would wriggle away, sometimes messing it up even more. 'Granna, I'm here to work,' she would say. And as she'd work, I'd steal glances at her, wondering if she'd let *me* move strands of hair that were blocking her face from me. I never tried."

"Wow," says Audrey. "You've always loved her."

I nod my head. "Pretty much." So many times when I was younger, I'd wondered if what I felt was love. I always knew she was different. I knew she affected me like no one else ever had.

"What else?" Audrey asks.

"I love how she is with her brother... very much like I am with mine. Playful but honest. She'd do anything for him. And the same goes for her parents and cousins and aunts and uncles. They're all so close. I love her family–with the exception of one opportunistic guy who took advantage of her that day. I still don't really care for him," I admit with a sigh. "But I care more about Olivia than I could ever dislike him.

"You sure you want to hear all this?" I ask my friend, feeling mildly awkward but enjoying the time I'm spending recollecting on old memories.

"Yeah," she says. "Because I want someone to love me like this someday. I want a guy to talk about me like you talk about her. I want him to look as smitten as you do at the mention of *my* name."

"Smitten, huh?" I ask.

"Totally. It's adorable. Go on…"

"Adorable," I laugh. "Know what's adorable? The way Livvy curls her toes. Only eight of them do–not the two smallest on her right foot," I remember. "She broke her leg when she was younger, and after the bone was set and the cast was removed, her foot muscles didn't quite heal like they should have." I think back to the first time I noticed this, which was the first night we'd made love in Mykonos. I was treasuring every moment and every inch of her body. I kissed a scar on her ankle and tickled her foot. I watched the reflexive action and noticed the two toes that just didn't cooperate. I kissed each one separately, making sure she could still feel them. She could, and I was glad, because I wanted every part of her to know how much every part of me loved her.

I look up, realizing my silence once the band stops playing their song. I could go on about her all night, but too many moments and memories are private, and things I want to keep just between Livvy and me.

"And she was happy," I add finally. "She was always happy before Donna died… when we were together, she would be smiling or laughing or perfectly content. For most of my life, I'd been at her side as she painted. When we were in art classes, I saw her work and create, and that is when she's happiest… when she's herself… I couldn't help but become enamored with her. I was lucky I shared a desk with her and spent so much time getting to know her. I think I knew her in a way no one else did. I understood her process, because mine was similar. She could focus as if in another state of consciousness. I do that, too."

"I'm guessing she changed because this woman passed away?" Audrey asks.

"She changed because she stopped painting. She couldn't get in touch with herself anymore, and she became disconnected. She stopped being able to make herself happy, and she looked to me to do that. It put a strain on our relationship–on all her relationships, really.

"I'm not the one to make her happy." I remember Livvy's letter about soul mates. She's absolutely right. "She's the only person who can do that for herself."

"Hence the reason you simply wanted a break."

"I thought she needed some time for introspection."

"And now she's had it, huh?"

"I guess. I wish it hadn't been forced on her."

"But maybe if it had been an amicable split, she still would have been overly reliant on you. There's a reason for everything."

"It's quite possible."

"She writes you letters?" Audrey asks. I look at her, wondering how she knows that. "Your brothers told me the day we met... that's what you were reading when you were in the waiting room."

"Yeah," I admit.

"What does she say?"

She tells me she loves me. She tells me she's sorry. She tells me she was lost. She tells me she's found. She tells me she's painting. She tells me she's happy. She tells me she doesn't need me anymore. She tells me she will always want me.

"Nothing really," I lie, not allowing her into that part of my life. It's one thing for me to tell Audrey how I feel about my ex-girlfriend. It's another thing to tell this girl I've only recently met about Livvy's deepest emotions. I won't do that to her. I *will* protect her privacy–*our* privacy.

"I see," Audrey says. "I totally understand."

"Thank you," I say with a smile, finishing off the last of my salad. We talk for another hour. Most of that time is spent giving her advice on ways to get assistance with money for college.

"Ready for dessert?" I ask, reaching into the cooler now filled with mainly cold water and a few chunks of ice.

"Sure," Audrey answers, sitting up and taking one of the pints out as I grab the other one.

"This isn't good," I say, squeezing the container. "They're a little melted, huh?"

"Perfect," she says, putting the orange ice cream up to her lips and sipping off some of the liquid. "It's so good," she laughs. "Go ahead!"

I open the chocolate mint pint and take a drink, getting ice cream on my upper lip. Audrey hands me a napkin and takes the container from me.

"Where are the spoons?" she asks. I realize I never packed any.

"Yeah, ummm… I guess we're supposed to enjoy them as shakes," I respond, admitting to my unpreparedness.

"Can we share?" she asks.

"Of course," I answer, picking up the orange swirl pint and tasting it, encouraging her to do the same with the other flavor. She holds up the mint container and gestures for another toast.

"To you, getting what you want… whatever it is," she says.

"And the same to you," I respond.

At around ten, Audrey and I have had enough of both the music and the heat. The drive to her house is quiet, and I struggle to find words to say to her. She picks at her pink fingernails, only looking up periodically to tell me where to go.

When we reach her parents' home, I get out of the car to get the blanket out of the trunk.

"Today was fun," I tell her.

"Thanks. I had a great time, too. And I think that's how I'll eat ice cream from now on." We both chuckle a little, leaning on the back of the car.

"Audrey, I think you're pretty incredible."

She blushes in the light of the street lamp. "I've never met anyone like you," she says back to me. "But I hope to meet someone like you again someday."

"You're going to make some guy very happy. Make sure he loves you like you love him."

"I hope he loves me like you love Livvy. And I really hope things work out for you."

"Yeah, I'm not sure what that looks like at this point, but I hope we can work something out. Thank you for listening… and for your empathy, and friendship."

"You, too."

"And, you know, I have been working on Will, so… if you like younger guys," I tease her, nudging her in the side with my elbow, "he loves blonde girls."

"As tempting as that is, I think I'll branch out… maybe meet a nice college guy," she says with a smile. "If you're ever in town again, though, I'd love to meet for some poor man's food."

"If I make it back, General Tso's Chicken is on me. And if you ever come to New York, I'll take you to the best hot dog cart in the city."

"Perfect." She faces me, arms stretched out for a hug. I put her blanket on the car and pull her into me tightly. "Thank you, Jon."

"Thank you, Audrey. I'll never forget you."

"Ditto," she says, patting my back twice before letting go. Her eyes glisten as she looks up at me. I lean in to kiss her cheek.

"Take care," I whisper.

"I will." She grabs the blanket and walks up to her front door, turning back once before going in to wave goodbye.

I love you, Jon.

I kick off my tennis shoes and push them into the closet before turning off the overhead light and lying down on my bed. The lamp on the desk illuminates just enough of the room for me to keep reading.

Valentine's Day 2.0. Remember?

Livvy had been grounded on the romantic holiday after we had fallen asleep together in her bed, so we celebrated two days later. We renamed the day to commemorate that, as well as to signify it was our second Valentine's Day together.

It worked out in our favor. It was much easier to get reservations to a decent restaurant, and it allowed us a full day to celebrate instead of just meeting together on a school night. It was insufferably cold that day, too, which kept a lot of people at home on a Saturday.

Not us, though.

I met her at her house around noon, where she greeted me with a thermos of hot chocolate. She was bundled up and ready to leave, dressed in a quilted black coat, a flared black skirt, black tights and black knee-high boots laced up with a black bow that tied mid-calf in the back. Around her neck was a dyed scarf with reds, oranges and pinks. Her lipstick matched it, as did two tiny barrettes that kept her hair off her face.

"Do you think you'll be warm enough?" I had asked her, glancing down her body and stopping at her knee, where I could see the hint of a dark freckle through her leggings.

"Don't worry about me," she said, then pointed at different articles of clothing. "Quilted and layered," she said, "wool and leather."

I kissed her even though her parents sat in the adjoining living room watching us. "Your legs are going to be cold," I whispered.

"We'll run." And after walking for three blocks on the way to MoMA, we did run the rest of the way, even though there were plenty of cabs to take us to the exhibit we'd both wanted to see. She was happy to be ungrounded, feeling totally free.

I had so much fun with you, recreating the romantic works of art that were on display that weekend. 'Couples in Love' was the perfect collection for us, because I felt so in love that day.

The museum was featuring works of art that celebrated romantic love between two people. It was a brilliant marketing effort, and I'd heard that, on Valentine's Day, they had offered candlelight dinners in various parts of the museum to elite members.

It was perfect that most people didn't want to fight the bitter cold, because it gave us time to enjoy ourselves in public, privately. The only pictures snapped of us were taken with our cameras: selfies of us kissing, or silly pictures of us as we posed in front of outrageous works of art.

I printed out the one of you by the bronze sculpture, where you were whispering in the ear of the girl statue, talking her out of accepting the obvious proposal of the boy statue on one knee.

"He's emotionless," you'd told her, "and cold hearted."

I smile, remembering what came next. "Let me show you how it's done," I'd said, then gestured for Olivia to join me by the sculpture. She posed next to it, mimicking the girl's surprised expression. I kneeled down in front of her, and snapped a picture of her, wanting to remember what she'd look like when it came time to propose someday. I took her hand in mine as she propped up her oversized purse.

"Olivia?"

"Yes?" she'd said, grinning from ear to ear.

"Will you… give me another sip of hot chocolate? Please?" I'd begged. She laughed, handing me her bag. After glancing around to make sure we were alone, I got out the thermos and took a drink of the still-warm beverage. When I stood up, she had taken off her coat, and was wearing a beautiful flowered top that had the same colors of her scarf with black stripes. It was form fitting, and after she handed me her coat to carry, I admired her perfect figure momentarily before setting everything I'd been holding on the floor and pulling her into my body. I kissed her as I imagined the couple in the statue would have kissed after the girl said yes to her suitor.

"A chocolate kiss," Livvy whispered as she pulled away, licking her lips. "Can I have another?"

"Gladly," I had said with my lips already pressed against hers. We'd kissed deeply until we heard voices approaching.

I can't help but wonder if that's what's happened to you. Have I caused you to shy away from your emotions? Did my actions harden your heart? Is that why you won't write me back?

If you don't love me anymore, Jon, please tell me so. I admittedly want your love. After what I did, though, I could accept your hatred. What I can't deal with is your indifference to this situation. Do you feel nothing for me? Nothing at all?

Her question is aptly placed, because I remember the conversation we'd had at the restaurant that night, two days after Valentine's Day. After I'd told her where we were going for dinner earlier in the week, she had made further arrangements to make sure we had a private area. One had been set up on the second floor, where there was only room for a table for two on the side of the staircase. The area was hidden from the rest of the room by a stained glass wall that cast the most beautiful colors on her face as she ate.

She had told me she loved me as we ate dessert. It was a delicate chocolate mousse that I fed her from across the small table. The sweet decadence inspired countless more chocolate kisses that night. I told her that the words 'I love you' weren't enough for me to express my feelings to her.

"I feel *everything* for you, Olivia," I'd told her. "With every ounce of my being, with all my heart and soul, I am full of the greatest affections, passions, and emotions that any man has ever felt for any woman… any time in the history of the world."

She stood up, putting her napkin in her chair, and held her hand out, palm up. I took it in mine and joined her next to the table. We kissed passionately, eventually releasing hands and innocently exploring one another's bodies with them. I backed her against the wall, so thankful we'd had a little privacy in that moment because I needed it as much as I needed her.

Realizing where we were–still in a restaurant, even though the waiters had agreed to leave us after we'd paid the tab–we slowed down, eventually leaning against one another breathing heavily, trying to figure out where we could go to be truly alone.

It didn't happen for us that night.

I'm losing hope. I'd thought I could make you see how I still feel about you through these letters. Everything. I feel everything.

Have I lost you? If so, I will always live with regret for what I did to you... but I hope I haven't made you into that bronze statue. Cold. Emotionless. I hope you can love again. I hope it's me that you love, but if not, I want you to have love, regardless.

Heart

BREAK

    Will and Ellen had planned to go on another date after their religion class on Wednesday night, and I'd told my brother I would drive him to the restaurant he'd chosen. After an exhausting day at work, a part of me wishes my mother could have driven them around, but another part of me wants to see how my brother is progressing in this relationship. It had only been a few weeks, but he was all in. He even took a couple of pink roses with him to class to give to her. It was his idea.

    As I wait for their class to end, I decide to read Livvy's latest work. There's a warm breeze flitting through the open windows, so I hold onto the letter with both hands, making sure it doesn't fly away. With one of the interior lamps broken in the car, it's not easy to make out her words.

> *I love you, Jon.*
>
> *While I was on Spring Break in Wyoming, I'd hoped every day you would find a way to visit me from Utah. Admittedly, I was high on Vicodin for a good part of my trip, but it didn't seem like a complete impossibility. Eight hours kept us apart... if we had both driven, it would have only been four.*
>
> *I should have found a way to make that happen. I never wanted to spend the week off from school away from you. It would be the second Spring Break without you.*

We were broken up during the first one. I had begged my parents to let me stay behind while the rest of my family went on their annual vacation, but they instead decided to stay home with me. They were worried about me, but they wanted to support my healing, and my painting.

This year, I made the first of many mistakes by allowing Finn to kiss me. It was brief, but it changed us... and it made our friendship more comfortable as we shared a secret with one another that no one else knew about.

I remember how she'd admitted to *actually* kissing him in an earlier letter. Had I known he'd succeeded at his attempt back then, I think I would have punched him a lot harder in the airport that day when we all got back to Manhattan.

As it turns out, I guess Spring Break is really what lead up to the <u>real</u> break. You had a taste of a functional family life, and Finn and I grew closer after that. It makes me wonder if you already knew back then that you were leaving me for the summer. Had you already made arrangements? And why in the world wouldn't you tell me sooner–as soon as you'd known?

Why did you make such a big decision without me? I'm beginning to see that you were having doubts long before I realized it. Maybe you really did want to break up. Maybe you just didn't want to be the one to do it... and then I made it so easy for you to walk away.

Or was it already going to be easy for you?

I knew early on that a little separation would be good for us. After all, the week apart in the spring–regardless of what happened with Finn–seemed to create more intimacy and trust in our relationship. When I got home, one glimpse of her reminded me of just how deeply I loved her. I felt more committed at the time.

But walking away from her was never in the plans; had it been, I know it would not have been easy. Just telling her about the temporary split I was planning was horrifying to me. I knew she wouldn't take it well. I didn't want her to be angry with me, but I'd hoped we would stay in touch over the summer, exchanging daily affirmations of love while she continued painting and getting back to the place she belonged. I'd envisioned the sweet reunion when I got home. I'd even made arrangements with Fred before I left to have the dorm to myself for a night before school started up again.

That would no longer be necessary.

We'd spent Spring Break apart. I broke your trust. You broke up with me. We are so broken right now.

We... aren't finished, are we?

A sudden pang emanates from my gut as I read her line. It's changed. Her confidence in us is shaken.

But what *are* we now? If we aren't finished, what are we?

Break

We aren't what we used to be. We would never be *that* again.

"Let me in," my brother says, trying the handle from outside the car. Before I can unlock the door, he reaches in through window and opens it himself, slumping into the seat next to me. I look at the building's door to see other kids his age streaming outside, and I see Ellen walking with another guy. "Can you go?"

"Aren't we waiting for–"

"No, we're not," he says, tossing the two flowers he'd brought with him out the window. "Just drive, okay?" he instructs me angrily.

197

"Home?" I ask.

"I don't want to go home yet."

I start the car and roll up the windows, giving him a few minutes to cool off. I decide to drive up to the worksite where I'd spent most of my summer days, always wanting to see it at night, where there's no ambient light to wash out the stars. I stop on the way to grab a couple of sodas and a bag of Will's favorite chips. He hasn't eaten... he was too nervous before his class tonight to even have a little snack, and his dinner plans have obviously been canceled.

I park the car near the large, etched rock, leaving the parking lights on. "Come on, let's go check out the moon." I hand him the bag of snacks and reach in the back seat to grab something for us to sit on. "Towels are very important things," I say to him as I toss one his way. He catches it with ease, even with one arm full, and I see a glimpse of a smile on his face in the dim light.

After we settle in on a hillside, he munches on his chips while I consume nearly my entire soda in one drink. I lie back, adjusting my glasses and looking at the sky above us.

"Can I ask you a question?" he asks me.

"Anything. You know that."

"Max wanted to know that since there is no known life on the planets in our solar system, who is there to turn on the lights at night."

I laugh a little. Ever since our trip to the zoo, Max has been obsessed with extraterrestrials... and he was asking very silly questions.

"What'd you tell him?"

"I corrected him and said that–while there may be no life like we know it on the other planets–there could still be some kind of life that we don't understand. I mean, what is the unknown, but things we don't yet know? Right?"

I'm impressed by my brother's line of thinking. "Right. Did you tell Max that?"

"Yeah."

"What was his reaction?"

"He couldn't grasp that concept."

"Didn't think so," I tell Will. "But how did you explain the light?"

"I told him that the planets don't emit light, but what we see is just what is reflected from the sun."

"Good answer." I smile at him proudly. He finishes his chips and takes a drink, then lies down on his towel a few feet away from me. "Know how to tell a planet from a star?"

"Yeah," he says, but doesn't answer.

"Yeah? Point out a planet," I challenge him.

"There are so many stars here," he says in awe. "It's weird to think the same stars are above us in New York. You'd never know that, from what we can see from the streets…"

"What is the unknown, but things we don't yet know?" I respond to him with his own statement.

"Exactly," he says. "It's beautiful. Oh, and there's Mars, to the left of the moon." He points at the planet that I'd already been focusing on. It's the most obvious one in the sky tonight with its close proximity to our satellite. "Stars twinkle," he finally answers. "Planets don't."

"Can you spot Jupiter?"

"I don't think it's visible tonight."

"Sure it is… it's in Gemini. Up there?" I point to the western sky at the brightest planet. "See it?"

"Oh, yeah," Will says, and I can hear him smiling.

"If you're still here next year when you turn sixteen and decide to get your license, you need to bring Max out and show him this sometime. In fact, you should get Mom to take you both," I suggest.

"Yeah… okay."

"Cool."

"Jon?"

"Yeah?"

"If there is life like we know it on other planets in another part of the universe, do you think they have one without girls on it?"

"Uhhh… if there is such a planet, I don't think I would want to go there," I tell him with a slight chuckle. "Why would you wonder that?"

"Girls suck."

199

"What'd Ellen do?" I ask him. "Why aren't you at Philmont's right now?"

"She thinks this idiot wrestler at her school who never paid attention to her before we started hanging out is *the one*."

"The one, huh?"

"Yeah. It's a dumb concept anyway," he says bitterly.

"I'm not sure I'd call it dumb. It's a romantic concept."

"Romance is dumb," he responds. "I really liked Ellen. She was cool… and I thought she was smart, too, but if she likes that guy, then… maybe I was wrong about her.

"But, like… she kissed me last weekend. *She* kissed *me*! A lot!"

"At the movies?" I ask, remembering back to the many dates I'd been on with Livvy that ended with us making out in an empty auditorium. I'd even mentioned a few of the dates to my brother when I'd come home from them, still high on *her*.

"Yeah. It was awesome," he laments. "Like *foreplay*," he adds.

"Whoa, whoa, whoa," I tell him. "Did you have sex with her?"

"No…"

"Then it wasn't foreplay," I whisper. "You were making out."

"Same difference," he says.

"Sure," I agree, not wanting to split hairs.

"How could she do that with me, and then be someone else's girlfriend a few days later? *Why* would she do that to me?"

"First of all, she's not as smart as you thought she was, because I have no doubt she could do no better than you. Secondly, Will… girls will break your heart. Ellen may be the first, but she won't be the last."

"It hurts," he says, and I can hear something catch in his throat. "Why would anyone subject themselves to this?"

"Oh, man," I say with reverence. "Because people can make you love in such extraordinary ways that the feelings they evoke in you can last for years… maybe even a lifetime. After wading through the pain, if the love was pure and good, that will be the thing you remember most."

"Why does it hurt like this, though? It's not fair! I'm so mad at her!"

"I know, Will, believe me, I know. It hurts because you allowed yourself to care for her... maybe it was the beginnings of love. You put down your guard. You became vulnerable. It's part of trusting another human being with your affections.

"I like to equate it to Newton's Third Law... do you know what that is?"

"No," he says after a quiet sniffle. I don't look over at him.

"*For every action, there is an equal and opposite reaction.* It may not sound like it relates to this, but think about it... if you're allowed to love someone so much... for the pendulum to swing so far in the direction of another person... if they let go, something has to fill that space that once carried that love. It can be pain... anger... hatred... just something that's in opposition to love.

"But it won't stay forever. Because what does a pendulum do?"

"It swings."

"Right. Love returns. Whether you let the pendulum swing as far next time, well... that's up to you. If you don't allow yourself to love someone with all your heart, it won't hurt so bad if it ends. But the good times won't be as fulfilling, either."

"Will you hold your pendulum back next time?" he asks me.

I'd loved Olivia as deeply as I could... and even after all the pain and anger, I want that again. Maybe I'm a masochist, I don't know.

"No," I answer. "For me, I've had a taste of the best of everything... and I don't want anything less for myself."

"Do you think you can find that with another girl? With someone other than Livvy?"

I think about his question for a minute before sitting up and taking off my glasses, allowing the lights in the distance to blur. I wipe my eyes and sigh.

"No, Will. I don't."

"Are you going to take her back?" he asks excitedly.

"I'm not sure what I'm going to do. I need a fresh start... but I only want that fresh start to be with her. I don't know how to make that happen."

"I hope you *do* take her back."

I smile, thinking of having her back in my life and back in my arms, my bed. I want those things more than anything.

"Hey," I say, changing the subject. "Before you met this girl, Ellen, didn't you say there was someone else you liked? Someone at your school?"

"Yeah. Her name's Laila. She's the one who wrote her number in my yearbook."

"That's a pretty name."

"She's a pretty girl," he says. "And she was the only person to get a better grade than I did in English. Plus, we were the last two standing in dodge ball."

"Why didn't you call her?" I ask him.

"I don't know," he answers. "I was scared I wouldn't know what to say..."

"Well, now you have a whole summer of experiences to talk about. Don't let this Ellen girl get you down for too long. So you weren't *the one* for her... so what? You know what she *did* do for you?"

"What?"

"She gave you confidence to approach a girl, to ask her out on a date, to go out on a few dates with her, to make out with her... so look at all that you have to bring into your next relationship. It may hurt now, but she's helped to prepare you for the next one... maybe the *right* one... although not *the* one because that's a dumb concept."

"Do you believe in that?" he asks me.

"I don't think I did when Livvy and I started dating... but somewhere along the line, yeah. I started to believe."

"So is she the one?"

"The girl I left behind at the beginning of summer isn't... but I haven't really met this woman she's becoming. Her letters tell me she's changed. She seems different to me.

"And I think, yeah, she has the potential to be the one. But we have a lot of ground to cover before we get there."

We both lie back once more, quietly observing the vastness of the world around us. I think about how great it is, and begin to think the concept may be silly after all, like Will says it is. What are the chances of *my one* being this person I met by chance when I was only a child in my small but diverse city? When there are so many other options on this planet, and likely beyond...

Is it dumb to believe?

"Jon? I'm gonna miss you."

"I'll miss you, too, Will. But I am so glad we've had this summer together. I wouldn't trade it for the world."

"Would you trade it for the universe?"

"Ummm," I hedge, teasing him. "Yeah, I think I would. Sorry, but I mean… it's the *universe*."

"I'd trade it for a planet," he counters.

"Which one?"

"…the one with *all* girls." He laughs after saying it.

"Yeah, I think you're going to be fine. By the time I leave, something tells me Ellen will be a tiny blip on your radar… just a speck… like that star right there." I sit up and push his shoulder. "And don't date girls who think cigarettes look cool. They don't, and they're not."

"Yeah, *that* was dumb."

"Yeah," I agree. "That was."

UNTHINKABLE

I can't get Livvy's letter off my mind tonight. It's been three hours since I read it, and I've thought of nothing else except the memory she reflected on today.

I take off my glasses to read it once more, starting with the word at the bottom.

Unthinkable.

Not hardly. Not even close.

I love you, Jon.

I trusted you. In a moment of passion and utter foolishness, I trusted you.

I still feel bad. I always will. I could blame Finn, but I know I have to take responsibility for my actions that day. I was brimming with jealousy. I'd felt very territorial. She was mine.

"I want to possess you." That's what I had told her that Sunday in my dorm room. *"Own you."* Like she was a thing. Like she was an item I could control and keep. She played along. She was all in. She wasn't thinking any more clearly than I was.

I have questioned my motivation since the day it happened… not every day, because I don't even like to remember that was me that took such a chance with our futures. It was by far the dumbest thing I'd ever done. It was the worst thing I'd ever asked her to do.

> I thought it was an act of love and commitment. You wanted to share something with me you'd shared with no one else. How romantic, right?
>
> I'm seventeen, Jon. I was still in high school... and I know every time we slept together there was risk involved, but it was nothing like that day we came home from our vacations.
>
> For one thing, why did you make me show you my pills? Why didn't I question you then? Did you not trust me, when I was willing to put everything on the line for you? You made me prove how responsible I had been... you made me prove I wasn't lying to you. I wouldn't lie to you, Jon. Not when it really mattered... and this time, well. It really mattered, and it could have changed everything in our lives.

I'm still so sorry about that. I never properly apologized to her. I had admitted to her it was incredibly stupid, but I don't think I ever explained just how remorseful I was.

If I had, I probably would be reading a slightly different version of this letter.

> What if I had gotten pregnant, Jon? At the time, when I chose to set aside the Plan B, I put my faith in God and in you... that whatever happened to me was a consequence of our actions, and it was something I was going to face, regardless. You were very certain, though, that I wasn't with child.
>
> Why did I trust you then? Where was my brain at all?

I'm glad God had my best interest at heart, because I am not sure you did, or do.

I don't blame her.

Would you have even stayed with me, had I been carrying your baby? I have so many doubts. I'm losing faith in you daily. It hurts me to even write it, but it's true. I can't fathom how you can just go on with your life like I was nothing... like we were nothing.

I thought you would love me through everything: through fights and mistakes and poor decisions. But you've turned your back on me and you walked away.

It's the second time you've left me... the second time you've abandoned me without really giving me a chance to fight for us. I thought these letters would convey everything I'm feeling. I thought they might break through your shield.

They have, Liv. You *have*.

Thank God I didn't get pregnant. Maybe you've learned something from your father... maybe you think it's acceptable to leave another life behind, but it's not, Jon. You make commitments, and you keep them. If you can't, you owe it to someone to tell them.

I know I owe her an explanation. I wish I hadn't let so many weeks pass. I wish I could be there to see her and talk to her now. I have every intention of making this right back at school.

I kissed Finn. I'm not even sure it was a conscious decision. How could it be when I loved you with everything I had? I gave you every ounce of me... I let you possess me. I put my life and my future in your hands.

Why?

We aren't finished.

I keep telling myself that.

Unthinkable

I feel bad about everything she's mentioned. How I didn't wear a condom. How I made her prove to me that she'd taken her birth control, even after she said she had. How my focus that day as I had sex with her was just me wanting to prove my dominance over her. How I have walked away from her twice. How I have been so selfishly silent this entire summer. How she compared me to my emotionless father, saying I abandoned her.

And she's right. I *can* be like my father in some ways. Driven. Intelligent. Curious. Serious. Ambitious. But there are negative traits of his that I could easily have inherited, or learned.

Abandonment... because for years, as a kid, I did feel that he had left us. That feeling was exacerbated by the acerbic tongue of my bitter mother, and it was valid on many levels. But I *never* would have abandoned my child. I can't stand that she thinks that of me. In that 2% chance that something would have happened, I would have stayed by her side through it all.

I wouldn't have abandoned either of them, no matter what. I won't be like my father in that way.

I can be stoic like him, though, I know this. It's how I've protected myself from further pain all summer, and I hate to say it, but the only way I can think about facing her at Columbia is to continue wearing this facade of strength and detachment. I don't want her to see how much she's hurt me. I don't want her to ever think she could do something like what she did again and get away with it. I don't want her to know how much and how deeply I have fallen for her. I have pride. There have to be consequences for her actions. There has to be an understanding that I wouldn't accept another lapse in her fidelity, even if it was an impulsive kiss with a close friend. Would I walk away a third time without warning? No. I would make sure she understood all my reasons for leaving, and for finally moving on.

But there can't be a third time. I don't think there would be.

I check my watch. Eleven-forty-five. It's nearly two in the morning in Manhattan. What are the chances she's still awake? Pretty good, if she's still painting... but I don't want to be a distraction to her. Maybe Jack was right all along. I *was* the distraction. I don't ever want to be what comes between her and her artwork again... between her and everything she knows about herself.

It would probably be easier to start the conversation while I'm still in Utah, though. I can keep my distance, emotionally, not having to see her... but that's not really what I want.

I want to know if I will still feel the connection. I need to know if the undeniable pull to be together still exists when we're in the presence of one another. I need tests. I need for every part of me to be a part of this decision. If I leave it to my brain, it's over. If I leave it to my heart, I am done for, and she will always have the ability to crush me with one tiny mistake. I want to touch her skin or feel her arms hold me close to her; to smell her hair or her natural perfume; to see her smile or tears; to hear each sigh or breath or word; to taste each kiss.

Tomorrow, I'll make sure I was able to get into the art class I'd chosen last week. It's Figure Drawing, since I've already taken the two introductory drawing courses, and I know Livvy will have to take at least Basic Drawing in the same building before she can get into Painting I... if they don't let her skip ahead, and they very well may. I've heard of them having portfolio reviews to allow for that, and I know her portfolio would blow everyone away.

But I've never heard of anyone bypassing Basic Drawing. It's fundamental. If they allowed people to test out of it, I surely would have.

That will put me in at least one building with her one day a week.

And I'm pretty sure I just leveled up on my stalker status.

Already I'm planning my life around her, and I'm not even one-hundred percent certain I'm ready to take her back... one semester together should be telling, though. We'll either be drawn together, or we'll discover other interests that take us in opposing directions. I hope it's the former. I'll at least be open-minded to the possibility, but this needs to be gradual. No rushing into things. Friends, then dating, then… whatever becomes of us.

I smile at the prospect, suddenly nervous and anxious to see her. What if all the hostility comes back when I see her standing in front of me? Then what?

Then maybe she *isn't* the one. I have to be open-minded about that, too.

THE END

"Max, bring me that marker, will ya?" I ask my brother with a box of books in my lap.

"Why do you have to go back?" he asks me, reluctantly handing me the Sharpie.

"I'm going back to school, silly. And so are you. We're going to be busy learning things, right?"

"Why can't you go to school here?"

"Because my school's in Manhattan, you know that." He watches me with his arms crossed as I label my belongings. I set them to the side. "Come here."

Max throws his arms around me, hugging me tightly. "I don't want you to go."

"I'm not leaving today, Max, so don't get all mushy on me yet," I say with a laugh, tickling his sides to force him to let go of me. "My flight's not until the day after tomorrow. So what do you want to do today?"

"You're not going to work?"

"Nope, my last day was yesterday. I just need to go pick up my paycheck today."

"Can I go with you?"

I shrug my shoulders. "Sure... why don't we get Will, too, and we'll just have a guy's day? Whatever you want to do."

"That sounds fun," he agrees.

"Go get dressed." Max leaves the room hurriedly as I put one more layer of tape on the box, hoping it will arrive in one piece after being manhandled by the airline. I put it against the wall next to my luggage by the door on my way out. "Will, wanna hang out with us today? Just the guys?"

"Sure! What are we doing?"

"Anything you guys want, if you can agree on something. Or else we'll just take turns going places."

"I want to learn how to ice skate," Will suggests. "They have hockey at school, and it'd be cool to play. I think Max is interested, too."

"Yeah? We could do that. I'm probably a little rusty, so don't look to me to teach you this lesson."

"Maybe I'll be able to do something better than you," he says.

"There's a first time for everything, right?" That earns me a punch in the arm. "Is that the best you've got?" I challenge him, daring me to hit me again. He does, but it's still weak. "Man, if you're going to play hockey, you'll need to learn how to hit a lot harder. And no, you can't practice on Max."

Will grins a little, grabbing the book he's been reading and going into the living room. This reminds me to go back to get my bag with a textbook and the letter I got from Livvy in this morning's mail. Our little brother joins us moments later, and we all head out to enjoy our day together.

Shane greets me at the the worksite with my check.

"I've put a letter of recommendation in with it… should you ever need it. Don't hesitate to use me as a reference. If you stayed here, I'd hire you for every job I've got."

"Thanks," I tell him.

"These your brothers?" he asks as we both walk toward the car.

"Yeah." I signal for them both to get out. "Will, Max… this was my boss, Shane."

"Nice to meet you, sir," Max says, which is much more polite than Will's simple, "Hey."

"Thanks to both of you for letting Jon spend so much time here. Thanks to him, we'll probably finish a week ahead of schedule." He smiles at Will and Max, then leans in. "I added a little bonus to your brother's check, so you make sure he takes you somewhere nice for lunch, you got it?"

"Yes, sir!" Max says.

"Thank you for the opportunity, Shane. You've been a great boss."

"If you find yourself back here, look me up… but go get that degree first."

"Yes, sir," I say with a chuckle, shaking his hand. "Best of luck to you."

"Thanks, kid. You, too." He pats my arm before heading back to the house. I wave at a few of my coworkers before corralling my brothers into the car.

"Where to, guys?" I ask them, taking a peek inside the envelope. In addition to my paycheck is five-hundred dollars cash. I glance out the window to see if Shane's still around, but he's already gone inside. *Wow.* I never expected that.

"Ice rink, ice rink!" Max is chanting from the back seat.

"Ice rink it is," I say, driving to a facility I'd seen near Audrey's house.

Once we're there, I help Max lace up his skates before putting mine on. Will has picked up a class schedule and tucked it inside his book. He heads to the ice, walking in skates with more confidence than he should probably have.

Max is equally excited, tugging on my arm while I secure our things into a locker. When we finally make it to the rink, he's cautious about stepping on the ice. "You're going to fall, Max, okay? That's just a fact."

"I don't want to," he says.

"I don't want to, either," I tell him, "but I'm going to fall, too. I don't believe that humans were meant to ice skate." After saying it, I look around for my other brother, and see him doing remarkably well on his own. "At least *this* human wasn't meant to."

I step onto the ice first, but Max is hesitant.

"I'm scared, Jon."

"Don't be, buddy. You're short, so you don't have far to fall… plus, they have bars you can hold on to around the rink, see?"

"Hold my hand?" he asks.

"Sure thing," I tell him, taking his small hand in mine and waiting for him to get enough courage to take his first step. "Just get a feel for it. You can just walk first." I pick up my feet and show him how it's not that different from walking normally. "Instead of heel-toe, you just pick up your foot and put it down in one motion. Just like you did on the carpet. You just want to be more sure of your step on the ice, because if you're not at the right angle, the skate will slip right out from under you."

"And then I'll fall."

"Yeah." I put him between me and the wall, encouraging him to hold on to the rail, too. Mom will kill me if he breaks a bone two weeks before school starts. We go very slowly around the rink, and when little girls start to pass us, Max starts to get a little more daring. He tries skating, still gripping tightly to my hand. At his slow pace, I just have to keep stomping in my skates. "You're doing great, buddy!" I tell him as his strides take him a little further.

"Good job, Max," Will says loudly as he passes us. He seems to be a natural at this. He stops abruptly and moves to the side of the rink. "Jon, let him try on his own."

"I don't know…" I don't think he's ready.

"Max, let go of Jon, okay? And then just come toward me. You can go slow."

Our younger brother nods as he releases me, and then lets go of the wall, too. Will cheers Max on as he glides cautiously toward him, taking tiny steps away, increasing their distance, but our youngest brother is laughing, liking the challenge.

"See, Max? You just have to try… it's not hard, is it?"

"No!" he says excitedly, stumbling a little but managing to stay upright.

"Jon, go skate," Will says. "I'll watch him."

"You sure?"

"Yeah."

"I'll do a lap," I tell them both, skating off slowly. Little kids still pass *me*, but I'm okay with that.

I remember wanting to go skating with Livvy. I was sure she'd been a million times, and I knew it was a cliché date idea, but I wanted us to cling together in the cold, supporting each other when one of us felt unsteady on our feet… kiss after we fell on the ice. It seemed like such a fun, free thing to do.

I pass my brothers a few times, trusting Max with Will more and more as I watch them together. When I decide to take a break, Will is holding Max's hand and pulling him with him. Our little brother can't stop smiling as the breeze whips through his messy hair.

I go to the locker, taking off the skates and putting my sneakers back on. I grab my backpack and head to the cafe area, ordering some ice water before settling into a booth in the corner.

I wonder if Livvy will continue to write me when I go back to Manhattan. I've become accustomed to her letters. If they were to stop, I know I'd miss them, and her.

I love you, Jon.

I loved you when you first kissed me. I loved you when you last kissed me.

I loved you when I kissed Finn.

Ugh. Seeing his name still irritates me, but I'm interested to see where she's going to take this letter.

My graduation day was supposed to be really special. It was a milestone, and not because I was leaving high school behind, but because it was another step toward independence. Imaginary barriers that once held me back simply because of my age or grade would no longer stop us from moving forward with our lives.

I had been looking forward to that day for a long time.

When I woke up that morning, I couldn't wait to see you. At first, I'd forgotten we'd even fought. But as soon as I moved in my bed, the throbbing pain in my head brought back all the bad memories from the night before. I started crying, waking up my mom. She'd slept with me that night to make sure I was okay.

The morning was fraught with confusion for me. Nothing really made sense. Why was I rushing to get ready? Why did I pick out the dress I was going to wear? What did I want for breakfast? Why couldn't I stop crying? Why wouldn't my brother settle down? Every decision seemed difficult. I was annoyed.

Had it been any other day, I would have crawled back into bed and stayed there. I'd even asked my dad if I had to go, but of course he said yes.

I see no reason why I should have listened, though. If ever I should have stood up to my father, it would have been that day.

It was a horrible day.

To begin with, I had a terrible bump and bruise on my head. It was my own fault, I know, but I still should have taken time to heal.

Then, we were fighting. I'm not sure what more I could have done to work things out. You weren't answering my calls or texts. Why did you do that, Jon? Why do you shut me out when we have bad fights? I can't stand it. All I want to do is work things out, and you always run away.

Why?

I don't think I can accept that anymore. We've been through too much for you to just walk away without trying. If that's the only way you can cope with arguments, well... I don't think it's fair or right. I'd even say I don't think it's mature.

She's right about all of it. I should have picked up the phone the first time she called. Ignoring her over and over again just created more tension, more distance, and look where it's gotten me. For someone who was constantly thinking she was the immature one, this is one of the worst things I could have done.

An *adult* faces these problems. An *adult* gives other people the chance to explain, to apologize, at least to talk.

What an ass I've been.

You didn't show up to my ceremony... when we should have been celebrating it together. It was a monumental disappointment, Jon. Remember how you felt when your mom missed yours? I never thought you'd do that to me.

How could I have done that to her? I remember the immense sadness. I hate that I made Livvy feel the same way.

To make matters worse, they called me by my birth name at graduation. And it wasn't just embarrassment. It disassociated me from my family. It reminded me that this wasn't where my life began. People laughed at me. They laughed as they watched me remember that I was once an orphan, and didn't always belong to this loving family.

I wanted to cry. I wanted to, and then I did.

For someone who was already in a state of confusion and sadness, this sort of pushed me over the edge. I lost it.

Please, try to put yourself in my shoes. If you were in my head that day, you would have been just as lost and as low as I was.

I'm not saying what I did was right. I'm not saying it was excusable. I'm not saying it was smart or warranted or forgivable. I'm not saying it was what I wanted. I never wanted to kiss him. There was never a conscious thought that led me to him. It was not premeditated. It was not done in a moment of passion. It was not anything you're making it out to be.

The only thing it was... was a mistake.

I wanted you. I wanted you to hold the icepack to my head. I wanted you to sleep next to me that night and make sure I was okay. I wanted you to stand backstage at my graduation and hold my hand, tell me that I looked beautiful even though a large, white bandage was sitting just beneath my cap. I wanted you to be there when they called me the name of a girl I haven't known in thirteen years. I wanted you to hold me and console me. I wanted to cry in your arms. I wanted you to kiss me.

I wanted you to kiss me and make it all better. That's all I wanted at all that day.

You.

Only you.

Always you.

Where were you?

I've felt bad all summer for what happened. I won't feel guilty anymore because I know there was no intent or motive. I know what happened was innocent. I am just sad you haven't given me the chance to make you see that.

I know where my heart is; where it's been for the past two years; where it's been every single day this summer. It's been with you, waiting for you, yearning for you, making plans with you...

Has it been a waste of time?

Is it time to let go?

I've learned so much about myself this summer. I'm strong-willed. I'm independent. I'm expressive. I'm unpredictable. I'm worthy of love.

If not yours... someone's.

I put the letter aside and put my head in my hands. It would serve me right for her to give up now. All this time, I've been blaming her. She's been the bad guy, the one who ruined everything... but I've done just as much damage. I know I have.

You're making me question everything. I felt like I knew where my life was headed, but maybe I'll be traveling that path alone.

We aren't finished.

Is there any point in thinking I can convince you of that now? Should I continue to try?

I guess the point now is... I'm not finished. I have a full life ahead of me, and I'm excited about it.

I wanted you to be there to share it with me. I can't stop you from walking away, though.

I won't try to anymore, either.

The End

I turn the letter over, face down, to hide those words. Is it over? For good? Has she given up on us?

The End, it said. This must be the last letter. She has to know I'll be back in Manhattan soon. I'm sure she knows when the move-in days are. She'll be going to school with me.

The End. Like the final scene of an epic love story. I can see it now, written in a flowing typeface. White text on a black background.

The End.

Fin.

Finn?

How prophetic.

After Max and Will had exhausted themselves on the ice rink, I took them the hamburger place that Audrey and I had gone to on our first date. We took pictures of each other with milkshake mustaches. We even had a woman at the next table get one of all of us. We laughed so much together that I forgot about the letter for a little while.

I took them to a movie after that, and while they laughed at the inanity of the film, I couldn't help but think that this was just the type of movie I would take Olivia to. I imagined she was sitting in the empty seat to my left. I couldn't sustain the fantasy, though, because I couldn't feel her touch. When we were at the theater together, not a second would go by that we weren't kissing or cuddling or being gently affectionate with one another. I yearned for her, and I felt broken-hearted, thinking of her letter.

The End.

On the way home from the movies, I told myself I'd call her when I got back to the house. My brothers had other ideas, though, and got out a Scrabble board and a deck of cards. Max fell asleep next to me on the couch after about an hour, but Will and I played games with my mother and aunt until two in the morning.

After I carried my youngest brother to bed and tucked him in, Will followed me to my room and talked to me until the sun came up. I was grateful for the company, and by the time we both went to bed, I was so tired that I drifted off in a deep and dreamless sleep.

It was exactly what I needed.

HEALING

Mom has the day off on my last full day in Utah. We spend the day together as a family, starting it off by taking some pictures before it gets too hot. At my mom's request, my brothers and I all wear nice shirts and ties. It's been weeks since I've dressed up like this, and as I secure the knot beneath my collar, I can't help but think of Livvy, and the many times I dressed up to take her out. I wore the same tie to her graduation. I still remember tearing it off the second I got home, feeling unable to breathe. Of course it had nothing to do with the neckwear.

The posed pictures seem silly and foreign. While I'm proud of my mom and how much she's accomplished in the past few months, it's not easy to forget the years of neglect we all suffered through because of her actions. I still smile, though, hoping that framed photos of us around the house will remind her why she's doing this, and keep her from going back to the alcohol.

Will isn't quite as accommodating. More than once, I've heard him mumble how stupid the photo shoot is. I am ashamed to say I agree, so I don't. I think we are both old enough to realize this is only a start; that there is a long road ahead of us that threatens to keep us apart.

"Mom, when can we go back to New York?" he asks at one point.

"I thought you liked it here," she says to him. "I thought you liked the school, and your friends."

"They're great, but I don't like Jon being so far away."

"I know," she says, putting her arm around his shoulders. He shrugs away, and she looks at me, frustrated. "One day at a time, though, alright, Will? That's how we live today."

"Well, I want to go back."

"I understand that," she says. Max takes her hand in his and walks toward a small pond in the park.

"Go easy on her, Will, okay?" I plead softly, following them slowly.

"Why?" he asks.

"I know she seems fine and normal now, but she's fighting a lot of battles you can't see. She needs time to get into new habits and make new friends."

"If she makes too many friends here, Jon, we'll never get to go back home."

"Will, I have told you I will help you come back after you graduate. Keep your grades up, get some scholarships, and we'll make it work."

"What if I don't want to graduate here?"

"I can't take you back now," I explain, stopping beneath a tree for shade. "You know this. I have to concentrate on school, and I can't give you two the attention you need. Mom can now. Aunt Patty can."

"What if she relapses?"

"It's a possibility," I tell him plainly. "I'll try to call her daily to make sure she's going to her meetings and living up to her responsibilities as a mom. And if you start to see changes–any changes at all–you have to call me. You have to let me know."

"Will you come back then?"

"I can't make any promises, Will, but I'm going to make sure you and Max are taken care of… that you have a safe place to live, food on the table… and each other. Our aunt has committed to helping out. She's told me you two are her top priority. She wants you to have a normal life, just like I do. No one wants things to go back to the way they were.

"I won't let them."

My brother nods his head and takes the knot out of his tie, letting it hang loosely. He doesn't look at all satisfied, simply resigned. I put my hand across his shoulder and lead him toward the rest of our family.

As we walk quietly, I imagine having a conversation with my mom if she were to relapse. I could see me yelling at her. I could see me having no patience and no empathy for her illness. I won't stand by to watch her hurt my brothers anymore.

But I truly feel like they're in good hands for once. And I have to believe she's seen enough wonderful things about Will and Max that she will want to be clearheaded to watch them grow into young men.

"Don't give her a lot of trouble. When you're feeling angry, please don't lash out at her. Walk away and take some deep breaths, but come back and talk to her. Be constructive. Set a good example for Max. What he doesn't remember, he doesn't need to know. Okay?"

"I mostly just don't want to talk to her at all," he admits.

"I understand. It will be hard to forgive her. It could take years. You may even want to go to an Alateen meeting or two… they actually have sessions once a week at the community center that's two blocks away. It's free."

"That's embarrassing…"

"Will, it's not when you realize everyone in the room with you has had similar experiences. Just think about it."

"Alright," he says reluctantly.

"Thank you. Just try to give her one more chance. We've given her so many, but… maybe it's just this one more chance that she needs."

Will rolls his eyes.

"Promise you'll call me when you're angry and frustrated. Just promise me that."

"'kay," he says as one corner of his lip raises.

"Okay. And call me when you need another book recommendation… or if you have one for me." I release him and shove him away lightly.

"I will."

Mom insists on taking us shopping before dinner. My brothers need some new school clothes, and she keeps asking me to pick things out for her to buy.

"Mom, I have everything I need," I keep telling her.

"Let me take care of something for you, Jonny," she begs. "Let me do one thing… I want to help you. I owe you so much," she says, getting teary-eyed as she talks.

"Mom," I say as we stand outside of the dressing room my brothers are sharing, "all I want is for you to be a good mother to Will and Max. You don't owe me anything."

225

"Do you need some new shoes?"

"No. I don't."

"A suit? What do you wear to work? Do they make you wear a tie?"

"No, Mom. I don't work directly with clients, so I can usually get by with some nice jeans and a button-down shirt."

"Do you need some new shirts?"

"No. I'm set."

"Books?"

"Paid for."

"Supplies?"

"They're all in storage. I'll be getting them out this week."

"There has to be something…"

"Send me a picture of all of us. I would love to have that hanging in my dorm."

She smiles. "I'll do that for you. And maybe put it in a nice frame."

"Whatever you choose," I agree.

"I think I'll go look for one now. Can you watch your brothers?"

"Sure." She looks so happy walking down the aisle of the department store. "What are you guys doing in there?" I ask over the door. They both start laughing. "Open up."

When they do, Max is dressed in the shirt we'd picked out for Will, and the long sleeves hang next to his shins. Will, in turn, has on the superhero t-shirt we'd selected for Max.

"You're gonna rip that, you idiot," I tell him, laughing at his bare midriff. "You need to do some serious sit-ups, too." I poke his belly, and he swats my hand away.

"Want a picture of this?" Max asks, grinning from ear-to-ear.

"Actually," I say, getting out my phone, "I do."

After eating dinner at home–a hardy meal of steak and baked potatoes and grilled asparagus and salad–a somber mood settles over the house. I go to my room to do a little more packing.

"Can I come in?" my mother asks from the door.

"Sure, yeah." I glance up to see her carrying a gift bag. "What's that, Mom?"

"I found something else you might want today. Don't argue. Just open it."

I do as she says, pulling out a square wooden box from the paper. It's sanded and stained, but it looks rustic and worn.

"Is there something inside?"

"As a matter of fact, there is."

I open it slowly and see another letter from Livvy. I hadn't expected to get another. I look up at my mom.

"Do you think they'll all fit in there? All her letters?" she asks.

"Mom," I say softly. "This isn't necessary. I don't even know what's going to happen with her."

"But I have seen how you've cherished her messages, Jonny. You at least need something to carry them in. If you keep the box closed for the rest of your life, well, that's your choice to make. But someday you may want to remember her… or remember what it was like to be loved by her."

I nod and hug her. "Thanks, Mom. I'll use it."

"You're welcome," she says, then kisses my cheek. "I'll leave you to your letter."

I love you, Jon.

We aren't finished.

I believed it when you told me that the night we fought. I have heard that phrase, in your voice, echoing since the moment you said it.

"Don't try to go, Livvy. We aren't finished."

Do you even remember saying that to me?

In that context, I do. I hadn't realized she was quoting me at the end of every letter. I was trying to get her to stay… to talk to me about my plans. She was so angry with me. I don't ever think I've seen her that mad. I don't ever want to see that again.

Her brows were furrowed in confusion and frustration. The wind had blown her hair, and it hung over her eyes. I'd wanted to move the strands so I could see her more clearly, but I knew she would slap my hand away. Her face was beet red as tears began to form in the corners of her eyes. I'd hurt her so badly.

She was so caught off-guard. I never should have sprung that on her in the way I did.

> *I wonder. Did I give you permission to just leave me because I drove away that night? Is that why you did this?*

It's absolutely *not* why I did it. I made the choice to leave her. It wasn't out of spite, or revenge. I was trying to protect myself, my pride.

> *I can't help but regret not listening to you. Had I stayed to talk, I wouldn't have wrecked my car and hit my head. I wouldn't have had a concussion. We probably wouldn't have been fighting the next day. You would have been there to console me.*
>
> *Everything snowballed because I left you that night. You know the consequences of my actions.*
>
> *Honestly, Jon, I don't think I want to know what you've done since you left me. I'm not sure I can bear the truth... or the consequences of your actions. How much will they hurt me? As much as mine hurt you? More? I can't stand to even think about what you've been doing without me.*

I'm proud of how I handled myself this summer. I was faithful to her– faithful to a girl I'm not even dating anymore. As much as I wanted to walk away–to really, truly, permanently walk away from her–my heart had other plans. All along, and still. It longs to be back with Olivia Holland.

She would be happy to hear that it didn't stray. My mind may have wandered. My anger may have tried to push her away. But the thing that matters… my heart would never let her go.

Maybe it's better this way… not talking… not knowing.

I've hurt enough. I'm beyond the pain.

We weren't finished then. You said so yourself.

Are we now? I don't think I need to hear you say it.

I don't think I ever could. Not to her face, anyway. I don't think I want that.

We have to work through this, somehow. I've made it so much worse… and this won't be easy. It's no longer about me forgiving her. I think I have.

Now, I have to wonder, will she ever forgive me?

Healing

At the airport the next morning, I stand on the curb with my luggage on a cart and watch the sun rise over the mountain in the distance. I'll miss the Utah skies almost as much as I'll miss my family.

I'd awoken my brothers early to tell them goodbye. Will was half-asleep, but Max was awake, and cried a little bit as he hugged me. He was still groggy, though, and I couldn't really understand what he was whimpering in my ear. I'd heard "I love you," and that's all that I really wanted to hear. I promised him I'd call him when I landed and I gave him another big hug after I'd put him back in his bed.

"Do you have all your things?" Mom asks, patting the top of the box next to her.

"I think so," I tell her. "Thank you for putting me up all summer."

"Anytime, Jonny," she says. "You are welcome anytime… but I hope we can eventually come back to the city where you are. I know that's your home."

229

"I'll welcome you back with open arms," I assure her. "I look forward to the day when you all can come home, but take your time, Mom. Just get better. *Stay* better."

"I'll do my very best."

"I'm proud of you, Mom," I whisper, holding her close to me. I can feel her begin to cry against me. "Don't cry, please. I'll see you soon. And I'll be fine."

"Will you?" she asks.

"Of course," I say with a laugh, pulling away and looking at her curiously. "Why wouldn't I?"

"You think you're so tough and grown up, don't you?" She pinches my arm loosely, but then holds my hand in hers.

"I can take care of myself," I tell her smugly, but playfully.

"I know you can. You always have."

For a few moments, we both look back out to the sunrise and breathe in the fresh air.

"Jonny?"

"Yeah, Mom?"

"I never thought I'd be giving this advice to my son, but... follow your heart."

I'm a little caught off-guard, and I scoff at her words, feeling bad seconds later as I realize the sincerity in her sentiment. "But look what that did for you," I tell her in an effort to explain my reaction.

"No," she says, grabbing me by the shoulders and speaking passionately. "You listen to me. One day on this earth with you is worth all the moments of heartache I have suffered because of that relationship. In everyone else's eyes, it was a failure, but you came from that... and there is not an ounce of failure in your body. You are my greatest success, Jonny. You remember that. Good things always happen when you follow your heart."

"Mom–" I nod my head, having never heard her speak like that or say such things. My eyes well up with tears. "Thank you," I tell her, hugging her with all my strength. "That's the kind of advice I need to hear from my mother."

"I love you, Jonny," she says. She's crying uncontrollably now, freely. "You are the best thing that's ever happened to me," she struggles to say.

"Mom," I whisper, still holding her, unable to stave off the urge to cry. "Thank you. I love you, too." I tuck my head into her shoulder, not wanting everyone else entering the airport to see me… but I don't want to stop crying yet. I don't want to leave this moment. I've never had a moment like this with my mother.

"If you learn nothing else from me, do that." She pushes me away just enough so she can kiss my cheek. "Follow your heart. Promise me."

"I will."

REUNION

"So they won the bid?" Frederick asks as we both settle into the dorm room. We'd arrived only moments apart, and decided to relax for a minute before continuing the arduous task of unpacking.

"They did," I tell him. "The firm left a message while I was on the plane home. They want me to call them first thing tomorrow to let them know my school schedule. It sounds like they want me to be pretty involved in this project."

"That's incredible!" my roommate says.

"They said those bench structures I'd designed were one of the things that helped sell it."

"The natural ones?" he asked. He'd been at the desk next to me when I had the idea.

"Yeah." I smile, proud of my contribution. I can't wait to get back to the office now.

"Well, it looks like you won't need help with job placement once you graduate."

I shrug my shoulders. "I guess anything could happen between now and then. That's a long way off."

"That'll look killer on a resume, though. This bid process has been pretty high-profile, from what I hear. My mom tracked its progress, since she knew you worked on it."

"Your mom's awesome," I tell him with a laugh.

"Speaking of that…" He gets up to get something out of his duffel bag. "Mom made them just for you." I open the tin, seeing a mound of peanut butter cookies. When Frederick brought them back from a weekend visit last year, I told him they were the best cookies I'd ever had.

"Oh, man, no way." I offer one to him before taking one for myself. "When you call her next, let me thank her."

"Sure thing." He starts to open boxes, starting with a large, flat one. I know what it is. "Can we hang it?" he asks after revealing the Richard Meyer drawing.

"Yeah. Same place?" I ask, getting up to grab my small tool kit for a hammer and a nail. We center it on the wall between our desks, so we can both look at it and be inspired by the brilliance of it.

"How are things?" Fred asks.

"Same as last time," I explain. "She kept sending letters."

"You never wrote her back?" I shake my head. "You're through?"

I don't really know how to answer him. "We're... I don't know. I'm sure she's rightfully angry with me now."

"Are you mad at her?"

"No," I admit. "I get it. I still wish she'd never kissed him, but I believe with all my heart there were no feelings shared between them. I'd like to hear it from *him*," I tell him, "but I know Livvy doesn't like him like that.

"The last few letters seemed like she was losing hope... which, in a way, I kind of want to start at zero with her. I think we both need to go back to being friends and learning about each other. Our feelings were intense when we were together–always. I want to know if they were real. I want to know if we'd still choose one another after everything that's happened."

"I can understand that. So what are you going to do now that you're home?"

"I guess I hope to run into her on campus someday. I want it to be casual and light. I know long conversations will have to follow, but I don't want getting back together to be a chore. It shouldn't be an assemblage of altercations. We should want to be together, not feel like we *have* to be." I haven't really been able to figure out how I wanted things to go in such a succinct thought, but that seems pretty perfect. "I guess she'll be moving into her dorm next week. Then classes will start a week later, and we'll just see where things go from there."

"You're gonna be so busy with school and work now... maybe this is a good thing, putting the relationship on the back burner for a bit."

"Maybe so," I agree. I hadn't even had time to think about that yet since landing. How would I fit her in, with everything else? We'd have to meet up on campus between classes. Have lunch together. There probably wouldn't be more date nights than what we're used to. I know it's not what she'd always wanted for us, but it may be necessary.

As I put my clothes away in the single dresser we're allotted, I think about that conversation. If she couldn't accept it, then maybe I'm not what she's looking for. I can't put my dreams on hold for her. She would have to understand that.

After all my socks are organized in the top drawer, I shut it and glance up in the mirror. If I close my eyes, I can still see her face looking back at me. I'm still ashamed about how things happened that day in my dorm, but I still can't regret any moment I was with her.

"Can I come in?" a woman says from the door. It's Fred's girlfriend.

"You remember Jon?" he asks her.

"Good to see you," I tell her, smiling, just as my phone vibrates in my pocket. She reaches to me to shake her hand, and eventually hugs me awkwardly. "Are you excited to start at Columbia?"

"I can't wait," she says. "But I'm secretly hoping you'll fall madly in love with my roommate so we can switch dorm rooms," she teases.

"What's she like?" I ask, playing along.

"I haven't met her yet in person, but we did a few video calls over the summer. She seems pretty meek. She never had an opinion about anything."

"I think that would drive Jon nuts," Fred says.

"You like a girl with an opinion?"

"I like a girl with a little spirit," I say. "And I like her to know her own wants, and be able to tell me. I don't want to dominate a relationship. It should be a partnership." Just like Livvy's letter described our relationship. We're partners. Or *were*.

"Well, hopefully we'll both grow to love her because I intend to spend a lot of time over here, and she may get lonely."

"Oh, really?" I ask, directing the question to my roommate.

"We *are* looking forward to being together here," he says sheepishly.

"Why didn't you just get a co-ed room then? I would have been okay with that."

"Our parents wouldn't go for that. No living together before marriage."

"Your parents, huh?" Even if my parents had been overly loving and attentive all my life, I still don't think I'd consider their opinions of how to live my life at nineteen. "You're adults," I whisper to them both.

"It's different, Jon," Fred says. "We've talked about this."

"Right, right. Wait," I say, suddenly feeling like the third wheel, "is that why you're here?"

"My roommate could show up any minute," she says, "and that would be an awkward way to meet."

I look at my watch. "I could go for a run," I tell them both.

"Maybe an hour?"

"I may die of heatstroke, but yeah, okay. An hour."

"Knock before you come in."

Annoyed, I nod and go into the bathroom to change into some running shorts. I don't even bother putting a shirt on. It's way too hot outside for that.

"Jesus," Fred says when I come back out into the room. "Look away," he tells his girlfriend with a laugh, but she stares at my chest, her eyes widened. "Manual labor did that?"

"It did," I tell him with a sly smile.

"I've got work to do," he says quietly as I set my glasses aside and grab my key, phone and a few dollars before leaving them alone. Once I make it the courtyard, I check the time on the display.

Olivia: 1 voicemail

I guess she's figured out that I'm back. She never tried to call after the first few days I was in Utah. I listen to the message. "It's Livvy." Oh, God, her voice. It's shaky and cautious. "I'm at the loft. I'll be here until ele–" The message is cut off. I listen to it once more to make sure, and to hear her again.

I know exactly where I'll be running today. I shove my things into my pocket, making one stop along the way at a local market to get two large bottles of water. I drink one of them in its entirety before continuing.

The route through Central Park is a smart one, my body needing the shade of the trees. It is insufferably hot here today, and I don't think I've sweat this bad in all of my life. It burns my eyes, and wish I'd brought a towel with me. I laugh, thinking about my brother and the *Hitchhiker's Guide*. Douglas Adams was so right.

If not a towel, though, a shirt would have been wise. I'd use it to blot my forehead and block my skin from the sun. I can feel the burn setting in as I run.

Seeing the Guggenheim beyond the trees is encouraging. The loft is on the next block south. She's right there. I keep running toward her, my pace quickening even though I can feel the energy draining with each step and each drop of sweat.

I stop running when I see her building directly across the street. Leaning against a tree, I drink my second bottle of water and look up to the top floor. Squinting, I notice one of the windows is cracked open. If she looked down, she'd be able to see me. I wonder if she'd even recognize me.

I know one way she would. I find a trashcan and throw the bottle away before returning to the tree. I turn around, putting my hands on the thick trunk and stretching my legs. She would know my tattoo. After giving equal time to each leg, and plenty of time for her to see me if she looked outside, I turn back around and look back up at her apartment.

I rest for a few more minutes, but never catch a glimpse of her. I have no idea what I would have done if I had, though. Lord knows what she would do if she saw me anyway, looking like this. I imagine I don't smell very great, either.

My phone vibrates in my pocket again. Fred is telling me I can come back.

Only a half hour? Okay.

I run back the way I came, stopping at a drug store to get a few more bottles of water. We haven't even been to the store yet, so there's nothing at the dorm to quench my thirst. I expect people to back off after seeing me, but they don't. Men look away, sure, but women stare.

Hmmm… that's new.

Most of the windows in my dorm building are opened, as are the doors when I get back.

"No electricity," the RA says on the steps.

"Huh?" I'm very much in need of some air conditioning.

"We're having rolling blackouts," he says. "Welcome back, right?" he says with a shrug.

"No joke. How long do they last?"

"Usually just a couple of hours. But it won't stop the cookout," he says. "We're going to start things early, in just a few minutes. Lots of cold drinks. Looks like you could use one."

"And a shower," I agree with him.

"It'll be pointless," he says. I'm sure he's right. I'd lived through plenty of summers in my mother's apartment where the AC unit stopped working and we couldn't afford to get it fixed. I usually retreated to the library until it closed, but there were many nights where it was so uncomfortable we simply couldn't sleep.

I go to the second floor and shower anyway, even though the windowless bathroom is already sweltering. I can see why Fred and his girlfriend had cut their activities short–or maybe her dorm had electricity and she decided getting caught was still a better option than our single room, two-bed *sauna*.

I'm still sweating when I get out, even though it was a cold shower. I find another pair of shorts and a sleeveless tank. I can't imagine wearing anything more than that, and I don't care what the rest of my classmates think. I bet I won't be the only one dressed in the equivalent of underwear.

And I'm not. When I get outside, girls are in bikini tops and guys are in swim trunks, lounging on the ground or canvas folding chairs. Campus organizers are quickly setting up drink and food stations while students limit their activity in the heat. Most of the coveted shaded areas are taken, but I see Shu, one of my original roommates, beneath a tree. He waves me over.

Standing up, we exchange a casual handshake before he invites me to sit amongst his group. He's got a cooler, and reaches inside to get me some water.

"Thanks, man," I say. "This is insane."

"Yeah," he agrees. "They say there's power in Carman Hall, but that's it. Since it's a first-year only building, no one's moved in yet, so they're allowing people in the lobby. Nowhere else. There's talk they may let some people sleep there if the power doesn't come back on."

"Stampede!" I exclaim, imagining how all of the students around me would act in that situation. Shu and his friends laugh. He introduces me to them. I recognize a few from classes last year.

Fred joins us after a few minutes.

"See what living in sin gets you?" I tease him. "*Hell.* You've brought *hell* upon us all."

As the sun begins to set, they start serving food. Having only eaten a cookie all afternoon, I'm famished, and fill my plate to reflect that. We all eat together, discussing last year and plans for this year. It's nice, meeting new people and catching up with old friends. At some point, one of Shu's friends brings some beer, and people start secretly filling red cups with it. I take one, surprised that it actually tastes decent. I'm still so thirsty, though, I'd probably drink anything.

Over the next few hours, the beer starts to taste better and better. Four cups later, I'm incredibly relaxed and could probably sleep through the night even without power or the AC unit. I could probably sleep right *here*.

"So what happened at the end of last year?" Shu asks, the alcohol making everyone less inhibited with questions.

"What do you mean?" I ask for clarification, even though I don't need it.

"With Livvy. And that guy."

"You heard about that?" I say sarcastically. Everyone is listening intently. I take it that–even though I've only met some of these people for the first time tonight–they all somehow know I used to date Livvy Holland.

"*Kissing Cousins.* It was news for days," a girl says.

"He's her cousin's cousin by marriage," I state evenly, then take a deep breath. "It didn't matter who he was, though. She kissed another guy, and I left."

"You were still dating, though?" Shu asks.

"Yeah, we were." I feel the pain and resentment again. I know these feelings are just amplified by the alcohol in my system, and I have no doubt it's made worse by dehydration. While I know this, logically, I can't stop myself from feeling things again.

"Well, still," Billy, Shu's new roommate says, "you got to sleep with Livvy Holland."

I glance at Fred uneasily. This isn't something I want to talk about, and I'm tempted to walk away. He shrugs, and I sense he's telling me to do the same. Shrug it off. He puts his arm around his girlfriend, who I hadn't even noticed joined us at some point.

"Yeah," I say simply, quietly, my response clipped, my eyes glaring at the guy who asked the prying question.

"What was *that* like?" he prods further.

"Shhh!" Fred says sitting up straight. I look back over at him, grateful that he is stopping the conversation. "She's behind you."

All eyes on me, I turn slowly to see if she's really there. Before I can even see her, others in my group confirm what my roommate already said.

"It's her!"

"She's hotter in person."

When my eyes finally meet hers, I have to look away quickly. She's hotter than she was in my memory. Granted, she, too, is wearing shorts and a tank. Her shorts are *short*, and her top is *tight*.

Get it together, Jon.

My group is silent as I take a few breaths, deciding what to do. This isn't the time or place for a conversation with her. I don't feel like myself, and I haven't prepared enough for this moment.

I stand quickly, avoiding eye contact with anyone around me, and walk toward her. "What are you doing here?" I ask her urgently, quietly.

"I have this for you," she says, holding a letter out for me. I'm smiling on the inside, but try to maintain my composure as I take it from her. Something inside is weighting it as I tap it in my palm, trying to figure out what it is.

"Thanks." I drop my hands and turn slightly.

"Jon." Her hands hold on to the hem of my shirt. "We need to talk."

When I look again, I notice the necklace that she had worn nearly every moment we'd been together since I gave it to her is no longer there.

That's what's in the envelope. It feels like my lungs collapse.

I remove her hand and let go of it.

I swallow, wanting to avoid a scene in front of my friends and classmates. "Go home, Liv."

"Will you read it?" she asks. I don't want to open it at all. I can't be sure it's the necklace until I see it. So, no, I don't want to open it. I shrug my shoulders. "Have you read any of them?"

Saying 'yes' will lead into more of a conversation. *Why'd you give up on us, Livvy? I thought you wanted me. You spent all summer telling me that, and for what? For you to publicly break up with me? In front of a crowd, again?* It takes me every ounce of energy to remain unaffected. "I had a busy summer."

"Oh," she breathes. I can see the pain that causes her.

"Go home, Liv," I tell her again, feeling my blood pressure rise as my heart pounds in my chest. "Freshman move-in day isn't for another few days."

"Right," she says, looking even more hurt. I can't stand seeing her like that.

"Where'd you park?" I have to get away from the curious eyes of the other people around me. I don't want to see Livvy's pain, and I don't want anyone else to see mine. I guide her back to the direction I assume she came from. She starts to pull away, angling her walk until I notice her car at the curb.

"I thought we could talk. I thought you could start to forgive me." The look in her eyes crushes me. She's starting to cry. I feel weak.

"Here." I hold her close to me, rubbing her neck just below her hairline. She looks cute in a ponytail. She hardly ever wears her hair like that, but I can't blame her, with this heat. And her hair smells like paint. She must have been painting at the loft. I breathe it in slowly, relishing in the scent.

Her shoulders move as she lets her emotions out in waves. She steps even closer to me, a posture that's too familiar and intimate and I'm sure she can tell I'm turned on. She can't think it'll be this easy.

"It can't be like it was, Liv. I've changed," I tell her quickly as I step back, putting a little space between us. "Go home," I plead in a whisper. If she doesn't go home soon, I'll change my mind. I'll go against everything I'd planned. I'll tell Fred to find another place to stay and take her back to my room. I'll make it easy.

But does she even want that anymore? She's given me back her necklace.

She looks up at me, licking her lips ever so slightly, as if preparing for a kiss.

I let go of her.

"I–" I put my finger over her lips. I don't want to hear anything more. She has to leave. She has to get out–of my arms, my personal space, my field of vision, my neighborhood–before I cave and take everything I want from her.

"Go home, Livvy." This time, I say it with more authority. *Please, just go, baby.*

"Please read them," she pleads, glancing at the letter I'm gripping tightly in my hand as she gets into her car. I hold the door for her. "Read them all."

I have. I have read, lived, and felt every last word, Liv. "I'll try." I shut the door, happy to have something dividing us. She rolls her window down, fighting the barriers I keep hoping for; needing.

"Do you promise?" she asks.

She wants another promise from me. I lean toward her car, needing the support, and put my hand on the door where the window had been. She immediately puts hers on top of mine.

My eyes begin to water, thinking of all the promises–kept ones, broken ones. I look down before she can see my emotions and breathe a few times for composure. I need to walk away before I completely break down.

"I guess I'll see you around." I take my hand from hers–the same hand that yearns to hold hers like it did that night in Mykonos. I feel a lump in my throat and turn my back to her.

"No," she says, stopping me. "I'll be at Yale."

Yale? Don't go. You were supposed to be here with me. I have it planned, Liv. We were going to work this all out. Somehow, over time, with casual interactions and dates and late nights drawing and painting. If you go to Yale, I'll never see you. I'll never get to find out if this is how it's supposed to be.

So then is it *not* supposed to be like this? I have so many questions for her, but can't formulate a single one.

"Goodbye, Jon," she says.

"Yeah," I say, releasing all the air from my lungs. "Bye, Livvy." I stare after her, watching until her car is out of sight.

The humidity feels like it's trying to strangle me. The muscles in my throat cut off my air. *I can't believe she's leaving me.* I have nowhere to go to find solace. When I turn around, the outdoor party continues with music and dancing and food and drinks, and I want no part of it.

I go directly into the dorm and up to the second floor to our room. It's dark and quiet and I don't care if it's hot. I need to be alone. I open the windows all the way, and feel a hot breeze that brings a little relief. After taking off my shirt, I lie on top of my comforter and take my phone out of my pocket. It's dead. I wasn't going to call her, but I was wanting the display to illuminate her letter. What would this one say? I'm almost certain it's the last one.

Maybe I can read by the window, and the moon can provide enough light to see what she's written. I get up and open the envelope, not remembering something was inside until it falls onto my foot and the floor with a soft clink. I don't need to be able to see it. I bend over to pick it up, and feel it between my fingers.

Choisie. I can feel the engraving.

No, baby. Don't do this.

I put the letter on the desk and lie back down, letting the tears fall. I retrace the steps of the night, thinking over the things I said, what she'd spoken to me. How I held her. How she wanted to be closer. How she was wearing the ring I'd given to her.

Wait, *was she? She was!* I remember feeling the cool metal against my knuckle when my hand was on her car. I'd taken the sight of it for granted. I'd seen it so many times it had become an extension of her. But I know she was wearing it.

I don't understand why the necklace is back in my possession, and I guess I won't know until I read that final letter, but I'm confident the *goodbye* she spoke won't be the last one.

How is this going to work?

I take measured breaths to calm myself, trying to figure out my next move. There will be no chance meetings in the hallway. No excuses to linger late in the art building in hopes of seeing her. No offers to help with her Contemporary Civilization class. No common parties. No gallery shows that I know she'll be attending.

There's no longer an opportunity for that casual, accidental friendship I was wanting. I didn't want to immediately return to the absolute commitment of *everything*. I didn't want her to know that I was purposeful in my desires to see her. Because–let's face it–I want her back.

And it's okay for me to want her back.

If I want to *get* her back, I will have to formally face her. It will have to be contemplated. It will have to be planned. It will have to be premeditated. She will know I still want to work things out.

And that, too, is okay. I *should* be honest with her. I should stop my brain from interfering and creating these false environments for me to live within the confines of.

So what if I want Olivia Holland back? I smile, then say it aloud. "I want Olivia Holland back. I want Olivia Holland back!" Maybe it's the heat, but I'm feeling deliriously ecstatic. I feel settled. I feel like things are falling into place, even though it's not the place my brain thought it would be. We can work this out. And we will. And it *will* be easy. I have to do one little thing; follow one piece of advice my mother had given me.

I just have to follow my heart. It's the only choice I have to make, and it's the easiest one I've ever made.

If I follow my heart, good things will happen.

MORE BOOKS BY LORI L. OTTO

Lost and Found
> Emi Lost & Found series : Book One

Time Stands Still
> Emi Lost & Found series : Book Two

Never Look Back
> Emi Lost & Found series : Book Three

Not Today, But Someday
> the prequel to the Emi Lost & Found series

Number 7
> the prequel to Steven War & Peace

Contessa
> Choisie : Book One

Olivia
> Choisie : Book Two

Dear Jon
> Choisie : Book Three

Livvy
> Choisie : Book Four

Check loriotto.com for release dates and extras!

SPECIAL THANKS TO

Nikki Haw, for being there when this idea to write from Jon's point of view was born. Thank you for always brainstorming with me and for knowing my characters just as well as I do.

Daniela Conde, for being such a positive and creative person. Thank you so much for your support, and for all the graphics you've done for me!

Street Team Emi, for helping to spread the word about Emi and Livvy.

Angela Meyer, Christi Allen Curtis, and Katrina Boone for being very early readers of this book. Sorry you had to suffer through so many typos!

So many blogs for giving my books a little boost! There are too many of you to thank, but I know you all know how grateful I am.

ABOUT THE AUTHOR

Inspired by popular fiction and encouraged by close friends, Lori L. Otto returned to writing in the winter of 2008. After a sixteen-year hiatus, she rediscovered her passion for fiction and began writing what would soon become her first series: Emi Lost & Found. Although the books of Nate, Emi and Jack have concluded, other characters from the books continued their own journeys, demanding their stories be told.

Lori is currently working on two spin-off series. Dear Jon, the third in the Choisie series, is Lori's seventh novel.

Website: http://www.loriotto.com
Twitter: http://www.twitter.com/lori_otto
Facebook: http://www.facebook.com/LoriLOtto
Goodreads: http://www.goodreads.com/lori_otto

Made in the USA
San Bernardino, CA
23 August 2014